Love and War at Stag Farm

# Love and War at Stag Farm

the story of *Hirschengut*
an Austrian mountain farm 1938-1948

## CHRISTINE SAARI

Rocky
Shore
Books
Marquette MI

ISBN 978-0-98223319-5-8

Design: Doug Hagley
Printed in U.S.A. by McNaughton & Gunn, Saline, Michigan

**Rocky
Shore
Books**
Marquette MI

*In memory of my father who found Hirschengut*
*and my mother who preserved it through hard times*

# ACKNOWLEDGMENTS

*Thanks go to . . .*

My parents, who wrote and saved letters and kept journals.

My mother who was a vivid storyteller.

My husband, Jon, who shares my fascination with the time and place of this story and lent encouragement all along.

Jon Saari, Judith Minty, Esther Barrington, Paul Lehmberg, Linda Stenlund, Matias Saari, Christine Garceau, Annelies Grady who read drafts and offered critiques and advice, and Doug Hagley for design and persistence.

My "writing sisters," who made me feel this story was worth telling.

The Joy Center, which provides a forum for sharing works in progress.

# PREFACE

My parents' story has haunted me all my life. I have spent years deciphering their journal and reading, transcribing and translating their correspondence. All written quotes in this book come directly from these sources, and these documents, as well as my mother's memories, provided the details for the telling of this story. All characters are based on real people. I did have to invent specific scenes and dialogue.

The culture of Austrian mountain farmers has deeply influenced me and my childhood. Klari is still my good friend. Despite my emigration, the farm has remained in the hands of our family and provides a refuge to this day. It is also the repository for my visual artwork (Family Album) and the family archive.

Initially, I thought of this story as a novel, but I now realize it is more aptly described as creative nonfiction.

*Marquette, Michigan*
*December 2011*

Both Anna and Michael knew at their first meeting they were meant to spend their lives together. As they gazed at the golden icons in the Orthodox church on a hill high above the Finnish city of Helsinki, they felt fate had brought them both to this place. They understood how very different they were. Michael came from the Bavarian South, Anna from the North on the Baltic Sea. Michael was brooding, melancholy, and insecure. Anna was adventurous and full of joyful energy. They both came from bourgeois households, but their childhoods had had little in common.

Michael had grown up in a four-storey corner house in the market square of Wasserburg am Inn. He loved the medieval town, but never cared for his family's elegant 19th-century *Biedermeier* furniture. He had always preferred the practical simplicity of farmhouses in the surrounding countryside. His mother had died at his and his twin sister's birth and he had been raised by his grandmother and her two sisters until he was five. By then his father had remarried and there was a half-brother, Lutz. Michael never felt fully part of this newly constituted family. Agnes, his father's new wife, young, beautiful and jealous, fit the image of a fairy-tale stepmother. The household was frugal and Agnes was stingy when it came to her husband's children. If Michael and his sister wanted to eat apples, they had to steal them from the cellar.

Anna was raised in a well-to-do Pomeranian merchant house-hold, with maids and fine china, glassware and engraved silver. There were sleigh rides to surrounding estates in winter, festivities with *Baumkuchen*, the fanciful pyramid cakes, and champagne at New Year's and summer picnic excursions to nearby lakes and forests. Laundresses washed the damask table clothes, embroidered bedding, handwoven linen towels. The making of liver paté and the plucking of downs for feather beds during the fall slaughter of geese required extra help. So did the sausage production when a pig was killed for the holidays. Anna's mother, the second wife of Max Dahle, oversaw the household, made sure fresh flowers graced each room and sewed delicate lace clothes for her daughters' dolls.

When they met, Anna and Michael were students in Königsberg, near the edge of the Russian empire. Anna, at twenty-five, neared the end of her studies in literature, history and philosophy. Michael was a student of law, a field he had pursued to satisfy his parents, instead of fulfilling his own dream of studying agriculture. Five years younger than Anna, he was just beginning to discover himself and he knew intuitively on this, his twentieth birthday, that Anna would help him become who he was meant to be.

As the two sat quietly in the glow of the mysterious icons they did not know how long their courtship would last, that they would spend seven years writing letters and meeting only for special occasions. They did not know then that Hitler would rise to power in a few years, turn the world upside-down and cause them to change the course of their lives. But they understood the synchronicity of their souls and experienced an inexplicable union of their beings.

*Part I*

# ARRIVAL
## December 10, 1938

Michael stood at the little train station in the valley, in a brisk December wind, waiting for Anna. After their separation of many months his heart overflowed with love and anticipation. But he wondered, again, whether they would be able to live in peace — after so much familial strife — here, in this place he had found. Would they learn to tame their stubbornness and give in when they fought about nothing? Would they be successful farmers, despite their city backgrounds? Would they find the golden mean they envisioned, the balance between physical work and the life of the mind? Would they finally be happy here?

The little narrow-gauge steam engine chugged into the Haunoldmühle station and Anna stepped down, into Michael's arms. It had been so long since he had held her and he wished he could prolong this moment. But suddenly his heart almost stood still. "Where is the child?" he asked anxiously, for Anna seemed too thin to be seven months pregnant. "Don't worry," Anna laughed, opened her wool coat and put his hand on her tight stomach, so he could feel the life inside, the new life they had created, their long-awaited child! The child they would raise on their own land, here in the foothills of the Alps, here in *Oberdonau*,[1] as the Upper Austrian hill country was named after Hitler had made Austria part of the German Reich.

"I can't wear them," Anna said immediately when Michael presented the new green hiking boots he had bought for her, so she could walk into their new life in new shoes. "They'd get too dirty." As though the dirt could not be washed off, he thought, hurt. He expected their new life would not always be squeaky clean. He simply could not understand how Anna could reject a gesture that meant so much to him.

The hour-long hike up to the farm helped him walk off his anger and disappointment. After crossing the wooden bridge over the clear emerald-green Steyr river, they walked on narrow foot paths, gradually climbing higher. Only the steep hill behind the Ebner farm slowed Anna's pace. "After we cross the woods on top, we will see our farm," he said to cheer her on. Soon they emerged from the forest, stood arm in arm, and looked. In the distance, on a plateau, they saw the red roof of the farmhouse, nestled amidst tall pear trees silhouetted against a clear sky. To their left a sunny hillside dotted with farmsteads rose steeply from a small side valley below. Straight ahead they saw the hump of the wooded Kruckenbrettl hill and behind theirs and their neighbors' farm rose the hillside of the Rieserberg. "We must go up to the top of that hill soon. From there you can see deep into the snow-topped Alps," Michael told Anna. Although this was the most barren time of year and no snow softened the outlines of the land, the landscape was beautiful. "This will be a good place to raise our child," Anna finally said, smiling.

Soon they had reached the house, approaching the backside, the wooden barn area facing the valley. They took in the wide-open view and then Michael brought Anna to the front, to the stucco living quarters. The front of the house looked fortress-like with its wide, many-windowed facade facing the neighbors' farm and the Rieserberg. The size of the house stunned Anna, although she should not have been surprised. After all, the living quarters, the stable and the pigsty, the woodshed and the hayloft, the barn and the wagon shed, everything that was part of a farm, was housed in one large square structure, under one roof, with a courtyard in the middle. This farmhouse architecture, common in this region of Upper Austria, was called *Vierkanthof* — four cornered farm — Anna had learned, and she could now see that this was a perfect term for such a structure. Michael had named it *Hirschengut*, which meant "Stag Farm."

"*Hirschengut*," Anna said, "what a beautiful name!" The locals called the two farms the upper and the lower Hiasn farms, Michael had told her, the neighbor's being the *Oberhias*, and theirs the *Unterhias*. The name *Hias* probably referred to a former owner named Matthias. But Michael said he preferred the similarly sounding *Hirsch*, meaning stag and coined the new name: *Hirschengut*. He had designed their stationery with a mighty stag jumping over three hills and their initials underneath. In feudal times these farms' responsibility had been to organize deer hunts for the counts further up the valley. Thus it seemed not inappropriate to Michael to rename the place. At the same time he was wondering what the locals might think about the more lofty name Stag Farm. "*Hirschengut* is a good name," Michael finally said. "After all, it is our place. We can call it what we want. Let's go inside."

Anna liked the wooden door with its unusual hexagonal patterns. Michael would have liked to carry her across the threshold, but after the shoe incident he stopped himself. So they stepped into the dark entry hall, hand in hand, and Michael led Anna into the kitchen. The kitchen with its two windows facing the courtyard looked gloomy this time of year. The furniture had not yet arrived and only a built-in bench and a small table sat in the corner; the large tiled cook stove, radiating heat, dominated the center of the sizable room. Michael pointed out the cold-water faucet near the door. "Most farms only have a well in the courtyard," Michael explained. "And we have an inside toilet, not just an outhouse in back of the court, even though we have to pour the water from a bucket." All this might look primitive to Anna, he thought, despite all the time and effort he had spent to make this place livable. Still, now, as he looked at it all with Anna's eyes, he realized how bare it must appear to her. "It will look more like a home, once the furniture arrives," he said, putting his arms around her. And Anna swallowed and said nothing.

Happily the crate with bedding had already arrived. "Let's make the bed together," Michael said when he showed her the bright room on the south side where they would sleep. But Anna insisted on making the bed herself. She sorted through the linens, until she found just what she wanted to put on their first bed. "Strunckmann and Meister," she said admiringly. "The most exclusive firm! My mother chose the best there is." Then she set upon carefully straightening and tucking in the sheets, pulling on the pillow cases, buttoning the embroidered under-sheets unto the yellow and green silken down quilts she had selected in Berlin. When she was done, everything was perfect and straight, and at that moment, Michael was glad he had not attempted to make the bed before her arrival, as he had initially intended.

Later, when they lay together in bed, Michael regretted Anna had not at least let him help put on the sheets, even though his bed-making skills might not have met her standards. He had so looked forward to making their bed before they slept at their farm for the first time. *This fancy quilt will keep us warm in our icy bedroom*, Michael thought, *although I wish we had more rustic bedding, maybe red-and-white checkered cotton covers. If only we will be able to overcome our differences in taste. If nothing else, necessity will make Anna more flexible. Hopefully she can adapt to simpler ways. At least she is here.* He sighed, put his large warm hand on her rounded belly and felt happy. *Now our new life can truly begin! The main thing is, Anna is finally here,* he thought again. Overall, despite the squabble about the shoes and the trouble with the bed-making, it had been a good day, he concluded. He needed to sleep now so he could get up at five in the morning to milk and feed the cows. Slowly he drifted off, filled with faith in the future and a slight undercurrent of apprehension.

Anna lay wide awake. She felt Michael's hand on her belly and shared his gratitude for this child they had wanted for over four years, ever since they had decided to change their lives and become farmers. She too was grateful for this place, their own farm, where she could give birth to their baby. But, weary from this long day of train rides and new impressions, she felt too tired to talk and pretended to be asleep.

In her mind Anna relived their reunion: her excitement when she saw Michael standing at the tracks and felt his arms around her again, Michael presenting the new boots and her objection to dirtying them. *Why did I have to spoil his joy? Why did I have to make the bed myself? Why did I have to be so petty, such a perfectionist?* she wondered. *I wish I could tell him how sorry I am.* But Michael was already snoring.

Anna remembered how they had stood in back of the house, looking down into the valley. They could see a glimpse of the onion-towered village church in the distance, the river below, the hillsides beyond. She had to admit Michael had found a beautiful place. It was a bit far from the train and the village, even further from the closest town, but at least there were two neighboring farms close by, and she was confident their friends and relatives would find their way up here, in good time.

The house was quite majestic, she thought, but how dark and barren it was! The *Stube*, the main room, with its tall, tiled stove and three windows facing south was more cheerful. *Everything will be more homey once the furniture is here*, Anna hoped. *I will put flower pots on the deep windowsills, and curtains and pictures will soften the starkness! This place definitely needs the touch of a woman!* The nursery upstairs was nice, Anna thought, happily. Fortunately there was a little wood stove to take away the chill. The walls in the unheated bedroom glittered with ice crystals! *How will my mother cope with this cold, with the kerosene lamps and the lack of a nearby store when she comes to help with the baby? After all, she is seventy-one-years old. How fortunate I bought cooking utensils and kitchen equipment in Berlin before I came here*, Anna thought. Michael had niggled over every sieve and spoon, but she was relieved she would not have to go to the city or scrounge for needed supplies here, where she did not know her way.

And what a relief to be here, in the countryside, away from the urban existence and the politics of Berlin! She knew living on an isolated farm would protect her. She had a hard time keeping her mouth shut and a tendency to get involved too deeply. So she was grateful that they, for themselves at least, had escaped the political turmoil, since she felt there was nothing they could do to change things. She thought with horror of her recent stay in Berlin. She'd been there only a month ago, she realized, to shop and see her friend Friedel. They had spent an evening together, drinking wine and talking, oblivious to what was happening in the streets. Anna was horrified by what she witnessed on her way to her hotel: synagogues going up in flames, stores of Jewish businessmen being ransacked. What she considered an isolated incident then had turned out to have been a nationwide pogrom, a full-blown terror attack against Jews. Huge piles of glass had littered the streets all over the nation, even in Vienna's shopping streets. All that shattered glass gave that November night its name: *"Kristallnacht,*[2] the Night of Broken Glass." Yes, it was good to be here, far away from all that, even though things would not be easy here either.

Even cooking would be difficult, without the benefit of a harvest, Anna was sure. *Potatoes, poor man's food in Pomerania, will have to be bought and Michael considers them luxury. Onions, carrots and cabbage will have to tide us over until we can grow our own garden. But surely everything will be better next year, after our own harvest. For now I'll have to be creative with what we have. I am glad I learned how to cook Bavarian dumplings and flour dishes that are cheap to produce and filling.*

Anna was grateful she was so strong and vibrant during her pregnancy. *My main focus will now be on the birth of this child. In less than two months we will be a family of three*, she thought, nodding off.

## FIRST CHRISTMAS
### *December 24, 1938*

Anna sat on the low milking stool, in the dim light spilled by the kerosene lamp, leaning against the big curved belly of the cow. She breathed in the warm moist air in the stable, heavy with animal smell. *It gives me such happiness to milk a cow*, she thought, and felt like many years earlier, when she had squeezed a cow's teats for the first time during a student summer camp, long before she had met Michael and considered taking up farming. Milking gave Anna a sense of deep belonging, a feeling of connectedness to everything alive, a knowledge that she was part of the essence of life.

Of course getting up at five in the morning, or shoveling cow manure in the evening, tired from a full day's work, could numb this joy. Today, for instance, she wished she'd be done early. It was Christmas Eve and already dark and who knew when they'd finally get to rest and celebrate their first Christmas on the farm. She still had to make supper and had nothing distinctive to offer, she thought, as she remembered the rich display of shrimp and fish and pickled delicacies they had eaten on this night in Pomerania.

It occurred to Anna she still had to heat big pots of water on the stove so they could take a bath. On this special evening they would at least be clean and not reek of pungent cow dung.

They would have a very simple celebration, if any at all. Anna could not help but think of the enormous Christmas trees of her childhood, hung with silver balls and bells and birds, of the festive house the maids had cleaned for days, of her mother dressed elegantly for the occasion, of heaps of packages under the tree. At least Michael had gone and cut a little spruce in their woods. "It's a bit crooked," he had said. "I did not have the heart to cut a good one." They had dipped their own candles a few days earlier and Michael had brought along wooden ornaments of angels and little boys on sleds or horses, some of which he had made himself as a child. *At least we'll have a tree, even if it's humble*, Anna sighed.

Anna would give Michael a book she had bought in Berlin, a volume about the massive Bavarian baroque monastery of Ottobeuren, where they had been so happy four years earlier when they decided to make a life together. She was glad she had thought of this gift for Michael ahead of time. *I wonder whether Michael will have a gift for me*, she mused. *He has been so preoccupied and overwhelmed with work. The greatest gift he could give me would be a bit of joy to break up the gloom in which we are living these days.* All she wished for on this Christmas Eve was an hour of unadulterated peace and contentment, an hour of unspoiled happiness like they had experienced in the past. She longed for his boyish smile, for his loving attention, for his intensity when they made love. All that seemed to have vanished. *Will we ever be happy like that again, now that we have our own place, now that our child will soon be born?* Anna wondered.

Refreshed from his bath, Michael bustled around in the *Stube*, while Anna was waiting in the kitchen. They had finally finished their chores and bathed and he could now think of their little Christmas celebration. It was later than he had wished, but not too late. He had made a stand for the tree and started to clip the metal candleholders onto the branches. He regretted the furniture still had not come. He had to set the tree on a rickety table the tenants had left behind, and Anna had unpacked an embroidered table cloth from one of the crates filled with treasures sent by her mother. He wondered how much this might remind her of earlier more glamorous Christmases. He loved their stripped-down, bare bones existence, but would Anna feel deprived? She now sometimes wavered between her exuberance, which had always buoyed him, and sadness, especially after their all too-frequent fights. He pushed the thought aside. *Tonight I want to hold on to hope!*

Michael was setting up the little molded red wax figurines he had made and brought for this occasion. He had poured them in Wasserburg, from old hand-carved oak molds his father had collected all over the Bavarian countryside. Michael had experimented for some time until he got the knack. The wax had to be just the right temperature, not too hot and not too cold. He had spent many an evening creating these delicate objects, which in earlier times were used as votive gifts and brought to church. People would bring them, a visual representation of a prayer, or as thanks for a granted wish. *This basic desire for health and children has not changed over the centuries*, Michael mused. *We are lucky. Anna got pregnant without bringing a wax baby in swaddling clothes to church. But maybe we should present a flaming waxen heart and ask for our injured love to be healed.*

He set out the fruit of his labor. *I hope this will be a happy surprise for Anna!* He smiled. There was a cow, a horse, a stag, a little cradle, a woman spinning, a couple and a set of quadruplets, hearts and fish. He had put green fir branches into a beautiful copper vessel he had abducted from the Wasserburg attic and set it in the empty corner where the desk would go later. They could barely wait for the furniture to come. They had ordered all the necessary farmhouse furnishings from a Bavarian carpenter who made simple beautiful items, everything from tables and chairs to beds and wardrobes, chests of drawers, kitchen cabinets and a couch — everything including picture frames and curtain rods, made out of tamarack wood. *These household goods will last us a lifetime,* Michael thought, as he lit the candles. Then he rang the brass bell and opened the door for Anna, who came in wide-eyed and looked as though she was ready to cry. "I am not sad, Michael, I am happy," Anna said, to reassure him. "This is our first Christmas here, and you have made it so special." They held each other tightly, as in old times.

Konrad Klausriegler, the *Oberhias*, owner of the farm next to Michael's and Anna's, sat on the bench in his *Stube*, leaning his arms on the large square table. On the normally bare wooden surface lay a clean cloth, for this was the holiest of nights. The *Oberhias* wore a freshly washed checkered shirt. His mustache carefully twisted, he felt handsome in his new grey wool sweater with green edging and stag-horn buttons. His wife had knit it for him for Christmas from wool his mother had spun on long winter nights. He knew this would be his Christmas gift and he was glad, for now he could retire his old shabby sweater to use for work. *There is still plenty of life left in that one,* he thought.

The women folk, his wife Klara and his two daughters, Maridl and Resl, had left to walk down the mountain to midnight mass in the village church. *It must be nearly midnight,* he thought, and made sure the Christmas candle was burning bright and clean. Tending the candle was his task; that's why he had stayed back, to watch the candle from six in the evening to six in the morning. It was the only night he ever stayed up, at least these days.

The *Stube* was gleaming clean. Klara had scrubbed the wide floorboards and even polished the windows. The little tree sat in the corner and the house was still filled with the fragrance of incense. That too was Konrad's task on this night, as well as on New Year's Eve and Epiphany, to bless the house with incense, driving out any evil spirits that might float around. He had gone through every room in the house, the stables and the barns, the courtyard and the pigsty, swinging the incense burner so the fragrant smoke might reach every nook and cranny, including the outhouse. He had given a piece of their dense rye bread to each of the cows — their Christmas treat — and he could hear them settle down now in the nearby stable. His mother was already asleep in the tiny room next to the kitchen. It was too hard for her to walk to the village these days, especially on such a cold winter night.

The *Oberhias* felt content and satisfied, as he sat in the dimness of the candle light. This was the way Holy Night had been as long as he could remember. Only in earlier times, his father had been the guardian of the candle. Now he was dead and a while back Konrad, the only son and heir, had become the owner of the *Oberhias* farm. This was a good year, he thought, without any major calamities and with a decent harvest. Another year of hard work, of funerals and weddings, of changing seasons. Not much had changed, except that they had new neighbors and that Austria was now part of the Great German Empire. Maybe that meant a big change. But he had already lived though one such major upheaval, when the monarchy collapsed at the end of World War I, only twenty years earlier. And now another war was in the air. But up here, in these hills, life would go on, the cows would be milked, the fields tilled, grain sown, meadows mowed, no matter who the rulers were at the time.

Soon his wife and daughters would return from church. *Our life here is good,* he thought, gratefully. *I would not wish for anything to be different, except for one thing. It would be nice to have another child, a son, who could inherit the farm one day and become the next Oberhias. Klara is a bit pale these days. Maybe . . .*

## NEW YEAR'S EVE
### *December 31, 1938*

Anna and Michael had never liked noisy celebrations when one year turned into the next. They preferred reflecting on the year past and the year to come, writing down their thoughts. "What a momentous year this has been," Michael said, pulling out their leather-bound journal. This seemed a good time to start writing about their new lives: "We got married, we bought a farm, and we are about to become parents. All we have striven for over the past four years has become reality."

"Yes," said Anna, "but our child will be a child of war."

Michael frowned.

"War is almost inevitable, I can see it coming," Anna said, thinking back over the years in Berlin where she had worked for the *Berliner Tageblatt,* the leading daily newspaper, and had followed Hitler's rise to power. "I realized what a demagogue Hitler was, when I heard him speak for the first time!" she said, shuddering. She remembered her visceral response to his voice alone, how she had felt her hair stand up. "I just cannot understand how women can be attracted to this man and swoon when they see him. And *Mein*

*Kampf* [3]! I was so horrified when I read it!" Still, she had belittled much of what she had read then. It seemed utterly impossible that Hitler's ideas about race and his ideology of German expansion could ever become reality, that his visions could be carried out. She simply did not take it seriously enough at first. Later she had noticed how the lives of Jews had become more and more restricted, how those who could, had left and how the others lived in fear.

"Remember, when we were in Vienna for our honeymoon in April and I bought that bracelet?" Jews were selling jewelry in the street, and Anna could not decide whether she should buy something or not, whether it would be helpful for the sellers, or whether a purchase meant support of Hitler's policies. In the end, she had bought a Bohemian garnet wristband, hoping to do the right thing. "I just can't wear it," Anna said now, distressed. "I am glad I did not buy anything at those household sales when I was in Berlin." On her shopping trip to Berlin, in November, she had come upon auctions held by Jews trying to leave Germany. She could have gotten what she needed for a quarter of what she spent in the stores.

"You could have saved us a lot of money," Michael countered, but Anna objected.

"I just could not get myself to exploit those poor people, even though they needed the money." And Kristallnacht! Thinking of it still gave her shivers. Anna had recently received a letter from Friedel: "Esther Blaufarb killed herself after that night," Friedel had written. "And she was not alone." Anna would forever treasure the crystal goblet Esther had given her as a farewell present when she left Berlin.

*Despite it all*, Anna thought, *the frightful turn of events in Germany has been good for us.* They had been instrumental for the changes they had made in their own lives. The political circumstances had made it impossible to work as a lawyer without joining the Nazi

Party. At New Years 1934 Michael had come to Berlin to tell her of his intentions to fulfill his dream to farm, to become a *Bauer*.

Sometimes Anna was still surprised what an unexpected turn her life had taken. Nothing had prepared her to be a farmer, but when Michael had decided that's what he wanted to do, she found it easy to join him. Anna too needed to change her life: the rise of Fascism had made it impossible for her to work as a dissident journalist. The party had begun to interfere in internal matters at the paper. Anna had been reprimanded for writing a review of a book authored by a Jew. Early on, one of their writers had been fired because of his Jewish background. Anna knew then it would only be a matter of time that their paper would be closed or be made a mouthpiece of the Nazis. She knew she'd eventually have to leave, but she never saw herself as a farmer.

Anna remembered how quickly they had set about dismantling their old lives. Michael had apprenticed on a Schleswig Holstein farm, in the North German flatland. His parents had fervently objected to his taking up farming and to his relationship with Anna, a Prussian! Thus he had chosen to intern in a place as far away from his Bavarian home as possible.

It still took almost four years until they reunited in Bavaria, and married. "Remember our wedding day?" Anna asked and her face lit up. "What a glorious spring day! We walked through the wildflower meadows all the way from Wasserburg to the little church of Pfaffing. There were just the two of us and your father and brother as witnesses. Your mother had not come. On the walls of the church floated little angels on clouds. They looked like babies."

They had been so glad when Anna became pregnant right away, even though it meant that they would need a place of their own more than ever. Mumm, Anna's mother, had given all her savings to help them and after much struggle Michael's parents had finally also contributed money for buying a farm. Michael had crisscrossed Austria on a borrowed motorcycle in search of a suitable place.

"I was so relieved when you found *Hirschengut*," Anna remembered. Now their vision could become reality. They would live on the land, in charge of their own universe. "War or not," Anna finally said, "it's taken us a long time to come to this point."

"Yes," said Michael. "Much has happened that brought us here." He opened the book. A whole book of blank pages. What would the future hold? *What stories will fill these pages?* he wondered. *I'd better start at the beginning.* He sat for a long time thinking about it all. Then he wrote: "Four years ago, on New Year's Eve 1934, I traveled to Berlin to see Anna . . ."


EPIPHANY
*January 6, 1939*


Anna was surprised to hear a knock on the front door. *It's open,* she thought. She went to look and found three boys standing there, singing in high clear voices. They were dressed in altar boy robes and wore handmade paper crowns. After their choral presentation they chalked on the door lintel: 19 + K + M + B + 39. "What does it mean?" Anna asked. The boys seemed puzzled. Everyone knows, their expressions seemed to say. "The three kings!" they said in unison and held out their basket. "We are collecting for the Mission." Anna went to get money. How much does one give? she wondered. *Do I have to do anything else? Invite them in?* The boys thanked her profusely for her donation and turned around to go to the neighbors'. *I must have given them more than necessary,* Anna thought. *Michael will not be pleased.*

Later, Anna went to the neighbors' to ask. As a Lutheran she was unfamiliar with such local Catholic practices. "The numbers are for the current year, 1939, and the letters are the initials of the three kings: Kaspar, Melchior and Balthasar," Klara explained. "They are to protect the house throughout the year. Three King's Day is the last holiday of the Christmas season, the last day to bless the house with incense." Anna took in the fragrance. It reminded her of Christmas and New Year's Eve.

Michael was reminded of *Frohnleichnam*, the *Corpus Christi* processions in Wasserburg, when Anna told him about the kings. "I am surprised I miss what I thought I rejected," he said. Generally he disliked everything Catholic, but he had discovered that he found some of the rituals nourishing and beautiful. He told Anna about the *Corpus Christi* celebrations in honor of the Eucharist: "In front of the archways birch trees are put up. The town has been scrubbed and cleaned. From the windows hang red banners and a long procession winds its way through the streets. The priest walks under a canopy, carrying the monstrance and choir boys ring bells. Four altars are set up, altars decorated with flowers and pictures, and the parishioners sing and pray. There are flags with painted saints, tassels and golden borders, trumpets and incense. What a spectacle! I am sure they have similar processions here."

Both Michael and Anna felt most attracted to the great Catholic churches and monasteries, especially the huge baroque structures, often set on top of hills. In the summer of 1934, they had had their first important reunion since they had met three years earlier. The exuberance of these structures, their abundant form and color mirrored how their souls then burst with joy. They were both immensely moved by these monumental buildings, how they were embedded in the landscape and how joyfully they reached heavenward. To Michael this architecture was the perfect expression of man's devotion to God.

And they were both entranced by a Madonna by Hans Leinberger, a small medieval stone carving mounted on a Berlin museum wall. They had first seen it together at Christmas 1931. This Madonna had moved them both beyond words and created a strong bond between them. For them, however, this sculpture was hardly an expression of Mary's saintliness. On the contrary, she seemed the embodiment of a very human experience, motherhood. She was the essence of a full-bodied young Bavarian woman who hugged her child with great gentleness and fervor. They loved how the child reached its arms around the mother's neck, how its butt, held tightly by the mother's hands, faced the viewer. They both owned the same photograph of "their" Madonna, which they would send back and forth to each other, so each would have the image which the other had touched only recently. She was a visible bridge between them and their vision of a child they might once have. Now Michael had framed the Madonna and put her up in the corner above the table in their *Stube*, way up near the low ceiling, where the local farmers put the pictures of their saints.

For Anna these Southern expressions of the Catholic faith, both in custom and art, were very different from the more cerebral kind of Catholicism she had been attracted to as a student and the philosophical Jesuit lectures she had listened to then. Or from the starkness of the white unadorned Lutheran churches and the great Gothic brick cathedrals of the North she had grown up with and also loved.

Anna happily talked about all this with Michael. She was reminded of their courtship years when all this mattered so much to them. "I like the earthy quality of the Catholicism here, of the rites that seem very pagan and in harmony with the lives of the people," Anna said to Michael, as the Madonna smiled down on them.

# THE BIRTH
### February 14, 1939

Anna could hardly believe she was holding her baby. *My very own child,* she thought, *the greatest gift I could give to Michael, the person I love most in this world!* How quickly it had all happened. Only the evening before her pains had started and had gotten fierce during the night. By seven in the morning she and Michael had decided it was time to make their way to the hospital. It would have been easier to have a midwife, like the *Nachbarin,* but the doctor had predicted a difficult birth, since Anna was built so delicately, and they did not want to endanger either mother or child. Thus they had opted to give birth in a hospital rather than at home, as was common in this rural area.

Walking down to the train over snowy, slippery paths frightened Anna, and yet, it calmed her at the same time. But then, during the four-hour ride — they had to change trains once — it seemed the baby would come right there and then. Thank God the doctor had given her suppositories to slow the birth, just in case. Michael had been terrified and had raced through the train screaming, "Is there a doctor anywhere? Is there a doctor?" Anna knew he could not shake the thought of his own mother dying shortly after his and his twin sister's birth. But, alas, there was no doctor. Luckily they had made it to the hospital by noon and now, three hours later, it was over and she held her little daughter.

Looking into the blue eyes of her newly born child, Erdmuthe, Anna lay in her hospital bed, exhausted and happy without measure. *What a miracle! An entirely new being Michael and I have created!*

The baby had Michael's upturned nose, a big bush of spiky brown hair, and all fingers and toes were intact. Holding her was worth every bit of pain to bring her into this world, Anna thought, deeply grateful and filled with wonder.

How long they had wanted to have this child! They had waited for four long years. Anna thought of their student days eight years ago, when they had met in the far north. Even though they had seen little of each other for the first few years — they were then students in different universities — they had held on to the idea that they were meant for each other.

Then, for the past four years, they had moved steadily towards the goal of living together. From meeting to meeting their love had deepened, all that time wishing for a child and waiting reluctantly until they would have a home of their own to raise it. Finally, after Hitler had invaded Austria and the barrier to transfer money had been lifted, they could go about finding and buying their farm in the Austrian Alps, where farms were cheaper and where they were far enough from Michael's parents. *The first few months have been hard, but now our child is here, finally here,* Anna thought and lay back on her pillow. *For now I am not going to think about what lies ahead. I am going to bathe in this happiness!* Anna decided she was going to let this feeling of joy and accomplishment wash over her. *This child is the fulfillment of so much love and longing, and I am going to enjoy being a mother, no matter what.*

As Michael climbed up to the farm alone that evening he tried to clear his head. *Thank god the birth is over; Anna is well and the baby is healthy.* He was relieved and full of gratitude. Only now he realized how much his mother's death had overshadowed the time before the birth of his child. Now the undercurrent of fear he had lived with for so many months had lifted, although he still worried how they would manage the additional task of raising a child. Their energy was already stretched to the limit! *At least Mumm will soon be here to help. Well, first things first,* he thought when he reached the house. *Light the lamp, make the fire, feed the cows!* He realized such concrete tasks helped keep his brooding in check.

After all the chores were done, despite his fatigue, he sat down to write into their journal. which he had begun at New Year's. There was so much to tell to his daughter: how important her impending birth had been to push him, and especially his resisting parents, to buy this farm. He wanted to tell her how he and Anna had met; how his life had only truly begun with that encounter; what a life force Anna had been for him; how she had helped him discover who he was and what he wanted to do with his life.

What a strange couple they were. His uncle Karl had said the reason they were together at all was Anna's "heroic love" for him, and maybe it was true that living with his stubborn nature required a degree of heroism. He knew he also had to write about their struggles, and he wondered what his daughter would think of all that one day. He envisioned things would get better by then. At any rate, he thought, she should know these things later, when she was old enough.

He knew next to nothing about his own mother and that had always pained him. *I will make sure she'll know more about her parents' and her origins than I do. I want my daughter to know as much as possible about her ancestors.* Now that she was here, he could fill in her *Ahnenpass*[4], her ancestral pass. True, it was a Nazi document intended to establish the holder's Aryan bloodline. But that was not why he was bothering with this task. He wanted to trace for his daughter who her ancestors were and where they had come from, although he had no idea whether she'd appreciate knowing that someday.

Thinking about the generations he would list in the ancestral record, it suddenly struck him that now he was not in first place anymore, but had moved up one spot. *How one's perspective changes, once one has a child,* he thought. *Now those who came before take on greater importance. But in the end, no matter how many generations one tries to remember, eventually they will all vanish and be forgotten. What a morbid thought!* He smiled. *After all, she has only just been born. No, I will not give in to melancholy!*

He knew it would take time to tell Erdmuthe all he wanted her to know. This would only be a beginning. Today he would tell her what was foremost in his mind, how important it was for him to give her a place where she could belong. "Although I have traveled to many places," he wrote:

> I want to sing a song of praise for home, for the place where one belongs and grows up. A song of praise for the path one walks often, for the trees one sees every day. How deeply I wish that you will never have to question the years of your childhood, that you will not need to fight for them. That they may be without strife, that you may solely be happy in them. How much do I wish that and that I will be able to help make that happen.

It occurred to him that everything he wished for his daughter he had lacked himself. He had always felt out of place in his own family, as though he had come from a different star, and increasingly so as he got older. He had never been able to take things for granted. He hoped Erdmuthe would be happy on this farm and feel fully at home in this place and in herself. What more could he wish for her?

Tomorrow he would design Erdmuthe's birth announcement. He could already see it in his mind: the jumping *Hirschengut* stag with his and Anna's initials on the left, a cradle with a rose floating over it on the right. Our daughter ERDMUTHE was happily born on February 14th, 1939 it would say underneath. "Erdmuthe," he said aloud, smiling. The name was bit lofty for such a tiny creature, but its meaning, "earth mother," was fitting if one took her parents' return to the land into consideration.

It was time to crawl into his cold bed. *I miss Anna,* he thought, *her warmth and her presence. Why is it that we have such longing for each other when we are apart, and such trouble living together? Well, tomorrow is another day. Much work is waiting.*

## FIRST WEDDING ANNIVERSARY
### *April 2, 1939*

After the work was done in the stable, Anna walked out into the early morning sun to gather wild primroses. The yellow blossoms carpeted the meadows around the house. Anna brought a large bunch of the *Himmelschlüssel* — keys to heaven, as primroses were called here — inside, breathed in the subtle fragrance of the delicate blossoms, placed the flowers into a bright blue vase and set them on the kitchen table. Anna was disgruntled. It was Sunday and their wedding day, but Michael had decided they needed to spread manure!

Anna was glad she could not help. She had pulled her tendon the day before and had to take a break from lifting the heavy manure off the wagon. She had put tar cream on her wrist and wrapped it tightly, but that did not seem to minimize the pain. It would take time to heal and she knew Michael would get impatient if she could not do any heavy work.

Michael came in, leaving a trail of manure on the kitchen floor. Anna cringed, but stopped herself from getting the rag and cleaning up after him. She did not want to upset him on this day. But Michael had noticed. "I can't take off my shoes every time I come in here," he said, annoyed. "Sure," Anna countered. "But I'm the one who has to scrub the floor." Anna knew Michael found her need for cleanliness excessive. "Can't you let the floor go, when we have so much work to do outside?" he asked, losing his patience." "No," said Anna, raising her voice. "I have my standards. We don't need to live in a pigsty just because we live on a farm." Then she remembered. "Ach, Michael, let's not quarrel," Anna pleaded. "It's our first anniversary. How much longer it seems," she reminisced.

"It *is* longer," said Michael. For him their life as husband and wife had begun at New Year's 1934, when they had become lovers. "It's over four years since we began this path," he said. He noticed the vase of flowers, smiled and reached for Anna's hand. "Everything was so easy then," Michael said, thinking back to those rapturous days when they had first made love, those intense times when he had decided he would fulfill his dream and Anna was willing to follow him to the end of the earth. "Maybe we can celebrate later," he added, as he went back out.

*Actually,* thought Michael, as he loaded the manure unto the wagon, *it's been even longer than four years.* He thought of the summer of 1931, when he and Anna first met, under the glow of the holy icons in Helsinki, of the glorious days three years later, when they were both overwhelmed by the confluence of color, form and space of the mighty Bavarian baroque monasteries. *Everything was so simple and natural then. And now that we have achieved everything we strove for, now that we own our own farm and are the parents of a lovely daughter, we are not happy. We were so idealistic then, so full of hope, and dreams,* Michael thought. *We had no idea that work would overwhelm us and we would not be able to rest, even on days like this.*

To brighten her day, Anna pulled out the box of congratulatory cards and letters they had received a year ago. *Amazing, how fast one can forget,* she thought. She had forgotten how surprised everyone had been about their announcement. She had forgotten some of Michael's relatives had signed their greeting cards "Heil Hitler"! She had forgotten the card from Michael's friend, celebrating the annexation of Austria a few weeks before their wedding. "One People, one Nation, one Führer" was printed underneath the picture of two soldiers, one German, one Austrian, jointly holding a swastika flag. And that was sent as congratulations for their wedding! It was nauseating! They were both so consumed by the troubles of their relationship, Anna realized, they often forgot in what scary times they lived.

The State's gift for their wedding had been Hitler's *Mein Kampf,* this book of hatred, a gift for their celebration of love. How ludicrous! Anna and Michael knew enough about this book not to want to read it. Anna had only been twenty when the second volume of *Mein Kampf* was published. She remembered that no one she knew, even her colleagues at the paper where she later worked, took the author's ramblings seriously. His racist ideas seemed simply too absurd to be taken at face value. What a lunatic! Such hogwash!

Now the book sat on their shelf, which also housed the giants of German literature: Goethe and Schiller, Herder and Hölderlin, philosophers like Kant and Hegel, books celebrating German art and culture, including books by Jewish authors like Werfel and Zweig, now shunned. Only their isolated location permitted this display. It was frightful what the world was coming to, if one allowed oneself to think of all this.

Anna pushed these thoughts aside now. Many genuine good wishes had come their way too. Wishes for a "quiet and harmonious marriage," wishes for "sunshine and no worry," wishes for everlasting happiness. Anna had to laugh, now, looking at some of these naive slogans. Her close friends had fewer illusions, and yet, they too saluted their decision to marry. Rereading their letters, especially Mumm's, brought Anna to tears. Anna could feel her mother's pain again about being unable to attend the wedding. She wrote how she had dressed up and was sitting in front of the family photographs, which she had adorned with green leaves and violets. "Don't exclude God from your marriage," she admonished them. "Man's wisdom is not enough." Anna had smiled then, but now wished she could share her mother's faith.

Since it was Sunday, her mother, still here visiting, was sleeping in, but she'd be up soon. Anna heard Erdmuthe gurgle in her crib upstairs. She was grateful her mother had come to help with the baby. She played with Erdmuthe, washed her diapers, helped with the cooking. But now her visit was drawing to a close and soon she would go back to Silesia to take care of her brother. Watching how her mother had looked on in horror when she and Michael fought worried Anna, but she could not talk to her about their struggles.

EASTER
*April 9, 1939*

Finally another holiday! The first holiday since the beginning of the year. The magic of Christmas Eve and the hopeful spirit on New Year's Day have long faded, Anna thought, sadly. She often thought back to their courtship days, and the letters they had written to each other. "A day off!" Anna said to Michael, when she entered the *Stube*. "I am going to put all our letters in one folder and organize them by date."

In the evening, after the stable work and their simple supper of potato soup, Anna put the heavy *Leitz* ring-binder on the table, and by the warm light of the kerosene lamp began to read some of the passages to Michael that had caught her attention while sorting the letters. They both needed to be reminded of their earlier sweeter days.

"Our letters were so loving, full of longing and full of life," Anna said. "We wrote about so many things that moved us, about books we read and places we visited, about becoming farmers, about Catholicism and dreams, about nature and great works of art and architecture. Our writing was so beautiful! Listen to what you wrote when you were in Freiburg:

> In the evening I sat at the Schlossberg, until the trembling delicate latticework of the cathedral tower, shaped like a pyramid, turned into a dark and heavy mass. Then I wandered through the streets and lanes, under arches, along singing rivulets and later the cathedral tower came to life again in the moonlight, when it was of even more unearthly delicacy than during the day.

"I remember how intensely you could look and see. Once you wrote a long, long letter about clouds, a sunset and a storm over the Penzing lake! Remember?" She turned the pages to find this special letter of February 1935. "Here! You said these were unforgettable images of the soul. Your writing was so incredibly poetic. You described the translucent clouds that looked like a bowl:

> At the time I thought of the beauty of the grail, that this had to be the grail that was being pulled by sky horses, and how blessed I was to witness it. In the end the "bowl" glowed. It grew more and more delicate, as though it tried to reflect the very last glimmer of the light. The "horses" pulling the bowl had now turned to a very cold grey white. And then the bowl dissolved. For days I surrendered my life to this experience and I still often look at this image inside me.

"Listen, what we wrote about our vision, our lives as farmers. We were so unrealistic. We were looking forward so much to working together on our own farm! In the summer of 1935 you wrote this:

> How will it be when we will work together the whole long day. How different it is when one does this cooperative work with the person one loves, when one helps the other, when many times a day the work brings us together . . . Dearest, I can't wait! I simply can't imagine that we might not get along. Although I try to imagine what is essential for you is different from what is essential for me . . .

"And I wondered whether we would be able to pull the whole world into our house and our farm, whether we would be able to find the great big whole in the small and limited. We wanted to determine our work and not let the work determine us, and now look what we are doing! Only eight months ago I wrote to you:

> We must not forget over our daily life which will often overwhelm us what's essential, our spirituality and all that connects us to the secrets of existence.

"We intended to combine farming with our intellectual life, and now we are too exhausted and stressed for time to even read a book! We are eaten up by the work and there is no spirituality and life of the mind. We are failing miserably with what we intended to do. We were such free spirits and now look what's happened! Remember how you loved to ride your bike, all the way from the Baltic Sea to Bavaria, how you loved to be on the road and wrote:

> I often feel the lure of the outdoors, the desire to get my bike and fly along, all by myself, farther and farther away, leaving everything behind, again and again, with every meter, riding further and further away.

"I loved that desire for freedom in you," Anna said. "But most of all I miss how we used to love each other! We had such a deep longing for each other and our child to be. Each of us felt incomplete without the other and this love helped us overcome all the difficulties we encountered. And we had so much trust in the future. Every time we met, our love and understanding deepened. You said it so beautifully in a letter before I came to Bavaria to start our new life:

> The path we shall walk should be beautiful and long. The forest toward which we are walking will stretch far and wide. It stands for the unknown. We ourselves, it seems, are the goal of the journey."

*How did it all change,* Anna wondered. *Did the troubles already start before we came here?* She reread parts of the letters they had exchanged during the past autumn, when Michael was getting the farm ready for her and the baby and she was so impatient for news. Michael had fought about her purchases when she was in Berlin shopping for household goods. *We did have difficulties already then,* Anna thought, *but the wellspring of our love was deep and we always found tenderness and forgiveness after our fights.* "We have to try to keep the magic alive," Anna finally said out loud.

They sat next to each other on the bench around the table and Anna leaned on Michael's broad shoulder. He wrapped his strong arm around her. *The struggle of the last year has aged him,* Anna thought. *His hair is thinning and his forehead is furrowed. But he is even more handsome now.* While she had read to Michael his face had softened, his forehead had smoothed, his eyes had mellowed and there was a smile playing in the corners of his mouth. "We have gotten to where we wanted to be," he said. "Let's make it work, Anna," and then they sat there, quietly, for a long time, in the light of the lamp.

# THE GARDEN OF PARADISE
## Spring 1939

The old grandmother, Theresia Klausriegler, stood in the doorway of the *Oberhias* farmstead, entranced. She took in the sight and breathed deeply. As far as her eyes could see: blossoms! The cherry tree blossoms were fading, but the tall pear trees with their long-stemmed white blossoming bundles were in full bloom and the pink apple blossoms were just about to open.

"Like the Garden of Paradise," the old *Oberhias* grandmother said aloud, although there was no one within earshot. Looking at this beauty spread out in front of her made all the hardship of the many years she had lived on this farm fall away. It was her annual reward. For her a new year did not start on January first, but it began in late April or early May when the orchard bloomed. Every year she waited and watched, observed the buds grow fat and white, until they finally burst open. And every year it seemed like a new miracle. *Yes, indeed*, she thought, *like the Garden of Paradise. Now I am able to last another year . . .*

The old grandmother relished a clear, bright spring morning like this one. She let the sun warm her wrinkled face and listened to the jubilant bird song and the bees nuzzling in the blossoms. *Unless a night frost comes, it will be a good harvest and there will be plenty of cider and plum brandy. Plenty of work too*, she thought. *But today is Sunday and I will rest, at least until everyone comes back from church.* She sat down on the *Hausbank*, the bench on the east side of the house, next to the entry door, and smoothed out the long black dress she wore on Sundays. The walk down the mountain had become too difficult, but she did not mind. Her Sunday service was right here, in the midst of this beauty God had created. And she enjoyed the few hours alone, when her hands could rest for a bit and she could be quiet and think.

*Spring is such a hopeful time,* she thought. Her son Konrad, for many years now the *Oberhias Bauer,* had mowed the first green grass early this morning — a good thing since the hay was getting low — and soon the young cows would be driven out to pasture. The fields were planted and growing and there was new life growing in her daughter-in-law's womb. Klara was expecting her third child in August, after quite an interval. Maridl was already going on eight and Resl, named after her grandmother, was a year behind. Maybe this time Klara would have a boy, a son and an heir for Konrad. After all, she was thirty-nine and time was running out!

And there was new life at the neighboring farm, the *Unterhias,* as well. For some time things had not looked good there. The *Oberhias* grandmother was relieved that new neighbors had bought the farm, even though they were Germans and not farmers from birth. It remained to be seen how they would fare in these harsh farming conditions. But anyone was better than the old Buchmann who had set his own farm on fire, with his cattle barricaded in the stable so that all the animals burned to death. She could still hear the screaming of the cows! Somehow he got away with this insurance fraud and was able to rebuild. She was glad when he rented out the farm, so that she did not have to look the scoundrel in the face, and she was not too distressed to see the tenant run the place quickly into the ground. Served Buchmann right! She was delighted when Buchmann finally gave up and sold.

Now the Dempfs were farming next door. The *Nachbar,* the young neighbor, had come last fall on his motorcycle to check out the place and was able to buy it, after somehow scraping together the money. The *Nachbar* had worked from morning till night, preparing the fields, whitewashing the walls, getting the house ready for his wife. She had felt sorry for the poor man, struggling all by himself, but she could see the place was in no condition for a pregnant city woman, and a fragile one at that. The wife had finally come in December and you could tell from her accent that she was definitely not from here. His Bavarian accent sounded similar to theirs, but her language was something else. When you looked at the *Nachbarin's* small-framed build you could not imagine how she'd be able to do all the hard work on a farm like this. But then she had helped felling trees a few weeks before the baby was due! It might have been foolish, but one could not help admiring her. It was good to see the farm in the hands of people who cared and made an effort to bring it back to life, although it would take time. And it was heartwarming there was a young child next door, a cheerful little girl, who would be a playmate to her soon-to-be-born grandchild. A new spring, and new life all around!

Klara Klausriegler, the current *Oberhias* farm-woman, wife of Konrad and mother of two daughters, was on her way home from church. Her husband Konrad had stayed back at the *Gasthaus*, the village inn, as was the custom, and the girls had run ahead to pick wild primroses and anemones. So Klara had a rare moment to herself. As she climbed the steep Ebner hill she was getting hot in her woolen Sunday best. She relished the cool woods on top. Coming out into the open she was stunned by the sight, even though she saw this view every Sunday on her way home from church. But at this time of year the landscape that lay in front of her was more beautiful than at any other season. The meadows, an intense spring green, looked like velvet, and the two farms at the bottom of the Rieserberg were clothed in a veil of white. Everywhere she looked she saw blossoming trees! It felt like she had entered a fairyland, or the Garden of Paradise, as her mother-in-law always said. How beautiful it all was! A compensation for their isolated setting.

At least now, she thought, they were not entirely alone, with new neighbors next door. She had felt alone the last few years, with Buchmann as a neighbor and then tenants who did not care about the farm or about being neighborly. She was glad they had neighbors now who seemed reliable, for one depended on good neighbors. It looked like these people were more compatible, although they came from far away and the wife, the *Nachbarin,* was Lutheran. Klara appreciated that the *Nachbarin* asked how things were done around here when she was unsure. Seemed like her husband was a bit too proud for that. *Men,* she thought. She liked the *Nachbarin* with her energetic resoluteness, although she still had not quite gotten used to her brisk North German accent. And she was happy there was a baby next door, although the name Erdmuthe was a bit strange and sounded like those newfangled Nazi names. It meant earth mother, the *Nachbarin* had said. Poor child, being cursed with such a lofty and foreign sounding name. She herself preferred the old-fashioned names from the monarchy, like Klara, Maria or Theresia.

Only three more months, and her own baby would be here. She noticed she was getting bigger and her shortness of breath was bothersome as she slowly climbed toward the farms. She remembered how amazed she had been when she saw the *Nachbarin* for the first time, seven months pregnant and barely showing, and now, only two-and-a half months after the birth, you'd never have known she had been pregnant, so thin she was! It would take a bit longer for her to regain her original shape, Klara thought. But she was grateful she did not have the tendency for obesity like her younger sister who had never lost her weight after giving birth. She was glad the girls would be old enough to help with this baby, at least after school. She could not wait for them to be done with that, although that was a few years off. Maridl was eight now. She'd have six more years of schooling.

Before anything else, she had to worry about Maridl's First Communion. Getting her a white dress would be a big expense. But what could she do? At least Resl could wear it again next year. And who knows, if this was a girl, she'd get more use out of a dress that was no good for anything else. Although, that was not a sufficient reason to wish for a girl! They needed an heir for the farm and that would have to be a boy. She was nearing forty and didn't think another pregnancy after this one would be a good idea, although you never knew what God had in store. She wasn't overly worried about the birth. This was her third baby and with all the work she was doing outside, she was in good shape. She would have it at home, in her own bed like the other two, not in the hospital like the *Nachbarin*. The midwife would come to help. That was preferable to a doctor. The midwife had born children of her own and knew what it was like. She had helped a long succession of children come into the world. No, she was not worried about the birth. But it would be good when it was over and the baby was healthy, boy or girl.

Klara was glad the old grandmother was still around. It was evident she was getting weaker. She could not work outside anymore. But she would be able to watch the baby when she herself would have to help outside. Later, in the winter, Grandma could mind the child while doing the spinning and knitting work. After that the first few hard months would be over. It would be hard for the *Nachbarin* when her mother left. She had come all the way from Silesia to help for the first few months. *Maybe after she is gone, Konrad's mother can watch both children,* she thought. As she rounded the corner she found her mother-in-law sitting in the morning sun, her worn hands in her lap, asleep on the bench in front of the house.

As he started for home, Konrad, the *Oberhias*, was animated from drinking several glasses of hard cider at the church *Gasthaus. My own cider is better*, he decided. The rich blossoming of the trees promised another good harvest. Especially the plums looked good; they would be able to replenish their supply of plum brandy. Whatever was left over from the year before would age and could be kept for the lean years that were bound to come. A frost at the wrong time, and all was for naught. He kept his fingers crossed. So far so good.

It was high noon and getting hot. Good his broad-rimmed hat kept the sun out of his face. He took off his grey *Loden* jacket with the green edging and the silver buttons. The wool cloth was beginning to get shabby. Pretty soon he'd have to buy another suit and relegate this one for less formal occasions. There wasn't much surplus money and Maridl needed a First Communion dress. *Maybe I should not wait any longer and get a new suit, with all the talk about a war,* he thought. *Who knows how hard it will be to buy clothes then and for how long. I have had this suit for a long time. I bought it before the fire . . .*

The fire! Every time he thought of it, the memory sent shivers down his spine. It was as though it had happened yesterday. The storm, the crashing thunder, lightning brightening the sky, the pouring rain. Then suddenly a sound like an explosion, the smell of smoke and flames shooting out of the wooden upper story filled with hay and roofed with straw. Klara grabbed the baby and ran to the Reitner farm, since no one was next door and the nearby Rippen farm had burnt down two weeks earlier. He and his father and mother ran into the stable. The cows and oxen were screaming; they knew something was wrong. They opened the doors, untied the animals and let them run. They saved the pigs too and the calves. But nothing could save the house. It fell victim to the flames in no time at all. Meanwhile Klara had run into the pitch-black night, finding her way by the intermittent strikes of lightning. She got to the Reitner's drenched and put the baby Maridl, only a few months old, on the table. No one paid much attention in all the excitement until they heard the child scream. She had rolled off the table and no matter what her mother did, she would not stop screaming. Later they realized her spine had been injured and permanently damaged. *She'll never make a good farmer's wife,* her father thought now. *That was a high price to pay for getting a new house . . .*

All the neighbors had come to help rebuild. Some gave labor, others materials, some both. And there was enough money from the insurance to build a house much better than the one they had had. Instead of a dirt floor they now had wooden floorboards; instead of the open fire in the kitchen a tiled hearth was put in. The wooden hayloft over the living quarters was eliminated and three extra rooms and a large hallway were built there, in stone. Instead of the straw roof they now had red clay tiles. It wasn't quite as fancy as the house next door, but Konrad was satisfied. The new neighbors might consider his house more primitive than theirs, but he was proud how far they had come since he had taken over the farm from his father.

Now all he needed was an heir. Of course there was no guarantee it would not be another girl and if it came to that he'd have to live with it. At least his wife was able to have children, unlike her older sister. She had married a farmer in the flatland, and now they could not have children. They had been talking to them about giving them Resl after she'd finished school, so she could some day take over their large farm. Klara wasn't quite ready to think about that, but to him it made sense. After all, only one of his children could take over this farm and arrangements would have to be made for the others. Well, time would tell. It was doubtful Maridl would marry one day. She'd probably have to stay at the farm after his youngest took over. For now it was good the girls were getting big enough to help, while his mother was less and less able to pitch in. It seemed there were never enough hands to do all the work. The girls were in school much of the day and Klara would have to depend on his mother to watch the baby when he needed her to guide the oxen and help with the harvest work.

With all these women folk, he sometimes wished for a male companion, even if it was only a farmhand. But there wasn't enough money to pay a *Knecht* and they'd have to make do. What could he do but accept things as they were, the hard times and the better years, the good harvests and the bad, rain or shine. It was all in God's hands and they'd have to make the best of it. He was not going to worry. In the end things always worked out. Today was a beautiful day and Konrad was going to enjoy walking home in the spring sunshine.

Anna's mother, Mumm, missed going to church. Everyone here was Catholic, not Lutheran, like her people in Pomerania or Silesia. And the walk down to the valley where the medieval onion-towered church stood on a steep hill, was long and arduous. She decided a walk on this spring morning among blossoming trees would be a fair substitute for a church service. This would be her way of honoring God. What a glorious morning this was! She walked toward the Rippen farm on a path under a row of tall pear trees and looked into the blue sky through branches bent with the weight of white blossoms. Bright blue forget-me-nots bloomed under the trees. Anemones, and the last primroses were still out. Without realizing, she hummed her favorite song "*Geh aus, mein Herz, und suche Freud*: "Go out, my heart, and seek delight," Paul Gerhardt's song in praise of the beauty of nature.

*Yes,* she thought, *God's gifts are great and give me joy!* But at the same time her heart was heavy. She worried about Anna and Michael, about Anna's tenseness, about their endless fighting, about Michael's melancholy and moodiness. *Here they are, finally on their own farm, in such a beautiful place, with a new healthy and cheerful baby girl, and they are making their lives miserable!* She could see how the relentless work exhausted Anna and how thin she was, only two-and-a-half months after the birth. She could understand Michael's worry about money. They had poured all their resources into buying the farm and now lived without any margin. She knew they both had no time for leisure, recreation or intellectual pursuits. "But I still can't understand why they have to make their life worse by wrangling over every minor detail," she said aloud. After a bitter exchange of words Anna would often rush out in anger, banging doors. And she could see Michael's heart closing after such a scene and his face becoming hardened and numb. She worried about her little granddaughter, Erdmuthe. How would all this affect her? She was sure such outbursts of anger were harmful for such a young child, still so close to paradise. And how much harder would things be for Anna after she left? Now she could at least help, wash diapers, do the dishes, cook. How would Anna manage without her? And yet, she would have to go back to Silesia soon. Her brother Paul did not do well by himself. She did not want to think of the mess she'd find when she got back. She'd miss Erdmuthe's smile and gurgling sounds, and she was sad she'd be unable to see her grow, to watch her learn to turn over, to observe her sitting and walking, to hear her say her first words. *How I'd love to experience all that! But there is no way around it. I'll have to leave soon . . .*

*At least Anna takes joy in the child,* she thought. The hours she spent with her several times a day, feeding and changing her little daughter, talking and playing with her, took her away from all the strife at the farm. She always looked more relaxed and happy when she came out of the baby's room to go back to work. But it seemed to her that Michael often begrudged Anna that time and only reluctantly released her. Apparently he could not understand how much energy was needed to take care of a baby. How lucky that Erdmuthe was such an easy child to raise. She hardly ever cried. Usually she entertained herself until someone came and paid attention to her. Sometimes she felt sorry that there was so little time to attend to the baby. Now she could look in on her, sing a song, talk to her; but after her departure, the child would be left to her own devices much of the time. Good that Michael had at least set up a little wagon for her, so she could be taken to the field with her parents. That was better than leaving the child alone in her room. That way the baby would have fresh air and lots of activities to watch. *If only I could stay longer*, she thought. As she turned back toward the farm she saw the old neighbor grandmother sitting on the house bench. *I'll go and say hello*, she decided.

Michael sat at the large, square larch-wood table in the *Stube* and wrote in the leather-bound journal, the book that would trace their story, the story of their farm and of their daughter. Only a few months ago he had begun writing with so much hope. But by now he had lost heart. He looked out the window at the blossoming trees and for the first time ever the spring blossoms did not give him joy. *The white of the blossoms might as well be snow*, he thought. *Cold white snow. The old neighbor grandmother spoke of the Garden of Paradise, but for me it feels more like a frozen hell. How has it come to this, so quickly?* he wondered.

He thought of the hard first weeks alone in the cold and dirty farmhouse, the long lonely days full of anticipation. The house was empty then, but it held so much promise. After Christmas their furniture had arrived and Anna had begun to set up house. How excited they had been when they installed the picture of their Madonna and child! And they hung the photograph of the Pergamon altar frieze of the child who had been raised by a lioness, another chubby-cheeked baby that made them long for their own. Now they had their own child, but everything was different from the way he had dreamed.

While Anna was happy unpacking her crated treasures, he had felt embarrassed before the locals about their possessions. The neighbors had helped cart up sled-load after sled-load of their belongings — house wares, linen bedding, furniture, books, all the things that had arrived at the village station from Berlin, Silesia, and Bavaria. Between felling trees and milking cows, Anna hung curtains to soften what, to her, looked like barren rooms, while he thought they had way too much, especially compared to their neighbors who made do with the bare essentials.

Of course he had known Anna needed more comfort than he. He could accept that, but he did have trouble living with their quarrels. Why did she think she knew better than he how to go about their daily work, when he had so much more experience? Why was she so unwilling to yield, to let him take the lead? Klara, the neighbor's wife, did what her husband wanted. Why couldn't Anna? True, she knew a lot, she had studied longer than he had, she was older and often wiser, and she had helped him find his way. He owed much to Anna, maybe too much. But she knew less about farming than he did! That was his realm. Why did there have to be so much contention about every decision, every task? All he wanted was to live simply and peacefully, in love. If he could not do that, what was the point of it all?

Not even the child could make him happy, he realized, while Anna could find solace and joy when she was with the baby.

Erdmuthe's happy nature, her bright eyes that looked into the world with such curiosity, her cooing, her rosy cheeks — nothing could cheer him. All of that did not give him joy, but pained him. He felt cut off from the beauty of nature, the vibrancy of his child, even the anger of his wife. *Nothing seems to reach me*, he realized. *How can I retrieve my hope for the future? How can I find the golden mean I am yearning for? How can I be more content? Why can I not be at peace, like the neighbors?* He did not even feel like going out into this bright spring morning and saying hello to Klara, who was just coming into view on her way home from church.

Anna looked out the window of the nursery while she was bathing the baby. The apple blossoms in front of the house would open any day now. In the fall she would plant tulip and daffodil bulbs, and next spring their bright reds and yellows would add color to the delicate whites of the blossoms and wild flowers. She wanted a flower garden like her mother's in Silesia, even if Michael cared more about vegetables and thought flowers were unnecessary. There had to be room for things impractical and superfluous, for joy and beauty!

Right now Erdmuthe gave her the greatest joy. How perfect and complete her little body was, how smooth, soft, and pink her skin! Her blue eyes looked at her with such intensity, taking in everything around her. This afternoon she would put her buggy under the pear tree out back so she could look up at the white blossoms and the blue sky and hear the bird song and the humming of the bees. There was no danger in that, unlike the time Mumm had put Erdmuthe's buggy under the roof and an avalanche of snow had buried the baby. It was a miracle she had not suffocated!

Anna sat down in the stuffed chair Michael's father had given her for nursing and put Erdmuthe to her breast. How eagerly the child opened her mouth, grabbed the nipple and sucked. Anna enjoyed this sensuousness, being so connected to her child, nourishing the baby with her body. What a perfect system nature provided! She could see Michael's pain and sadness when he talked to his little daughter, and Anna could not understand why her innocence and joyfulness could not penetrate his melancholy.

Oh, how had it come to this? How often did she ask this question. The circumstances of their current lives seemed to overpower them both. The grinding work, the scarcity of money, their insecurity about the farm work — everything seemed to conspire against them, drain their energy, their tenderness, their joy. Now they quarreled during the day, and at night they lay in each other's arms, spent and desperate, full of the wounds of the day and afraid the next might destroy the love they still held in their hearts.

Anna felt exhausted, just thinking about it all. She felt her own optimism weaken, and she was angry with Michael. He seemed not to notice how difficult this was for her and how hard she tried, how much she'd had to give up. It was not easy for her to get up at five in the morning, not to have time for reading books or writing letters, to scrub the wooden floors on her hands and knees, to forgo any kind of luxury, to be stuck up here on this mountain farm, away from her friends and family. Now, at least, her mother was here, and her help and company were invaluable. But Anna tried not to share her problems with her mother. She was afraid she'd worry her too much and Michael would feel that she was stabbing him in the back. She longed for her friend Friedel from Berlin. She could hardly wait for her arrival this summer. Today was Sunday and she would take time to write to her friend, to let her know how things were here, so she would be prepared. Anna knew she would feel better, sharing her sorrow with a friend of many years.

Erdmuthe had fallen asleep at her breast. Anna gently laid her into the crib, her grandfather's crib, which Michael intended to paint with their initials and garlands of flowers. He too needed more time to nurture his creative talents, she knew. She was happy he took time to write in the journal on this glorious Sunday. Writing gave him an opportunity to express his thoughts and feelings. She was glad his writing was honest, although reading about Michael's growing depression pained her. But at least she knew what was going on inside him, now that it had become so much harder for them to talk about such matters. She suddenly realized they had begun to use Erdmuthe's book as a means of communication with each other. They used it to talk back and forth between them, trying to sort out the problems in their relationship. Although it did not seem to influence their unhealthy interaction, at least it helped them understand each other better.

Still, amidst all this pain was her joy over their child. When Erdmuthe laughed at her, when she saw the baby sleep so peacefully in her bed, when the child vigorously sucked her breast, life was good and rich and Anna temporarily forgot her troubles. *I'll go out into the sunshine for a few minutes, breathe the fresh spring air and take in the beauty around me*, she decided. *We must not forget how beautiful it is here!*

# BAPTISMAL DAY
## *July 23, 1939*

"Too bad Mumm is not here to enjoy this day," Anna said to Friedel, as they made their way down the mountain. "She would be so happy we are finally baptizing Erdmuthe, even if it's in the Catholic Church. She was so worried about the welfare of her soul."

*This has to be a most unusual baptismal procession*, Anna contemplated. *Four Lutherans and two Catholics; two women and four teenage boys. No father. No grandparents. Different, like everything else in our lives here!* "The birth of the calf is a lame excuse," she suddenly blurted out. "Michael knows perfectly well that calf is not due yet!" Anna knew he had made up this excuse because he did not believe that a child's soul needed to be purified. But could he not have come for her sake? Anna was angry and hurt that he was not willing to make this sacrifice.

But, Anna was determined not to let Michael spoil her joy on this beautiful summer day. She was glad Friedel, Erdmuthe's Godmother-to-be, was with her. Michael's cousins, the two Catholics in the group, had dressed up for the occasion: nineteen-year-old Walter wore handsome *Lederhosen* and Mandi, two years younger, a fancy jacket/ pant combination. The Wedel boys, who were chasing each other down the mountain, had no such clothes and had come in shorts. But Friedel wore a *Dirndl*, a rather pompous Austrian folk-costume, and Anna had put on her white dress with the colorful embroidered Ukranian border. After all, occasions to dress up were rare here, so why not exploit such an event, Anna thought. Of course, Erdmuthe was the fanciest of them all in her lacy gown which Mumm had hand-sewn so long ago for Anna's own Lutheran baptism. And her sister Hilde had worn it after her. Hopefully they'd have other children who could wear this lovely dress. Even boys could get away with it for a baptism.

*What will the priest think of the name?* Anna wondered. It certainly was not a traditional Catholic name, or a name familiar in this region. Michael's cousin Manfred had objected in his letter after Erdmuthe's birth. "Why Erdmuthe?" he had written. "In such a thoroughly Catholic place, in the land you have settled, one of the old names would be more appropriate. A name like Barbara or Elisabeth, Magdalena or Theresia." Anna was annoyed when she thought about it. Who was this cousin to criticize them like this? But Michael had laughed it off. "What does he know," he had said.

They took turns carrying the child, and by the time they reached the church on top of a steep hill — an hour's walk from the farm — Erdmuthe's dress was a bit crumpled. At least she was still in good cheer and that was the main thing. They did not want to disgruntle the village priest — the *Pfarrer* — with a screaming baby and draw attention to the unusual circumstances of their party. He did not have to know the Godmother was not Catholic, or that the father was missing, Anna thought.

Anna had gone to the parsonage a while back to sort out things with the *Pfarrer*. Now she saw the inside of the church for the first time. It was a bit overloaded with kitsch for Anna's taste. A nineteenth-century Mary of Lourdes statue and a Heart of Jesus figure especially drew her attention, but the Gothic vault overhead was beautiful and unspoiled. If Michael were here he would like these arches, Anna knew. The sanctuary was cool and quiet and their small group made the place feel almost empty. Anna regretted this was not a community celebration, as baptisms were supposed to be. She felt a pang of homesickness for the simple white Protestant church in Silesia, where her uncle Paul was pastor, although she detested his condescending attitude toward his parishioners. At least this *Pfarrer* seemed kind and friendly, she thought, as they shook hands and encircled the baptismal font.

"Let us begin," said the priest, and invoked the initial exorcism, asking for this child to be set free from "original sin." Anna cringed. This was what had kept Michael away, she knew, and she felt torn herself. The swearing off of the devil, his evil works and pomp, the pouring of holy water and marking a cross on the child's smooth forehead, all left Erdmuthe unperturbed. Anna was relieved the ceremony would soon be over, when unexpectedly the *Pfarrer* asked for the father to come forward. Young Walter, not yet twenty, looked at Anna, then valiantly stepped forward, thus ending the consternation and tension. The priest did not move a muscle, although he must have realized this young lad could not possibly be the father. Anna burst into tears and had to restrain herself from running out of the church, while the rest of the group snickered. Once outside, they could not contain themselves and gave in to loud laughter, when they assembled in the *Gasthaus* for coffee and cake. Anna was not amused. Michael would get to hear an earful from her. She could not decide what was worse: her embarrassment, the pain over his absence, or the callousness of her companions. Even Friedel had joined in the laughter. Anna felt utterly alone.

Although he did miss the presence of his little daughter, Michael enjoyed the peace and quiet at home. He was happy everyone was gone and that, on this free Sunday, he had time for contemplation. As always when he was alone, his thoughts circled around his questioning of their life on the farm and his growing despair. While he worked, his thoughts went round and round. Now the journal helped him focus. He wrote to his child, not yet half a year old:

> No summer before have I felt as little as this year! How different this summer is from earlier ones! How many burdens have been unfamiliar to me until now, how easy was everything before, and how many opportunities have we squandered. The fragrance of elderberries did not tickle my nose this year; the intense green of the Steyr river had less power than formerly a small puddle had. Only rarely did the rich fruit tree blossoms strike me as more than a meager late snowfall. Suddenly the grass had grown to its full height and I had not noticed the sprouting of the blades and flowers . . . How hard it is now to master the world around me. I wonder whether the time will ever come that everything will run more smoothly and become easier? Will you eventually grow into this life and contribute your part? I keep asking myself, whether the goal I had in mind and toward which I

keep moving can be justified? How often I ask myself that when I play with you, often too briefly. One day, I assume, you will answer this question for me. Oh, my little Erdmuthe, how much do I ponder the foundations and opportunities that offer themselves. Often these reflections are more than I can bear, and yet I can't avoid them.

Michael had lost track of time. Soon the baptismal party would return home, and he had not written anything about this particular day, why he was sitting at home rather than participating in the ceremonies. He was glad he was not in church in a suit he hated to wear. Mostly he was satisfied that he had refused to participate in a ritual he could not accept. "I am happy you don't yet understand this whole affair," he said aloud, returning to the present. "I hope you'll never understand it. What sins should have to be washed away from your life, or ours!" He did not think such an innocent child should have to be purified. And he did not want to wonder whether there were sins committed by them, the adults.

When the home-comers told the story of Walter as the "father," Michael laughed like everyone else. That infuriated Anna even more. But in the end she was powerless against all this laughter. *If only I could join in,* she thought. But she could not overcome her hurt.

## MICHAEL'S BIRTHDAY
### *August 17, 1939*

Anna had looked forward to Michael's birthday, always a special day for them. They had first recognized each other on this day, so long ago, in Helsinki. They had met in beautiful places in Germany to celebrate. *And now we are together and don't have time to mark this occasion,* Anna thought sadly. Unfortunately the birthday fell on a Thursday and they could not take a break from haying. Their celebration would have to wait till Sunday.

They were haying on the steep slope adjoining the forest. Michael set the wagon up at a precarious angle, too far down, Anna thought. "We should put it further up, where the ground is flatter," she suggested. But Michael did not listen. It would take too much time to haul the hay further up, he said. This would work. Anna was convinced he was wrong, but she was tired of arguing and obediently climbed up on the wagon to stack the hay Michael was heaving up to her. Suddenly she could feel the wagon slide and jumped off, just in time, before it tipped over. "That was lucky. Now let's place it higher up," Anna said and felt vindicated.

But Michael refused. Anna had to climb up again. By now she was getting angry, and afraid. Of course, the predictable happened and the wagon tipped again. Anna did not make it off this time. She felt a crack and an intense stab of pain. "I broke a rib." she said. "Are you sure?" Michael asked. Anna was sure. It had happened to her once before, a long time ago. "I have had enough of this. I am going back to the house," she said, in tears. "Then I'll have to do the stacking myself," Michael said angrily.

Anna watched, in pain, from the back of the house as the wagon fell a third time. In the end, Michael had to give up. They had lost considerable time righting the wagon three times, and they had been lucky nothing worse had happened. When Michael finally came back, Anna waited for him to admit she had been right. But he could not bring himself to say it and Anna was in no mood or physical shape to bake the birthday cake she had promised Michael, Mumm's *Sandkuchen*, the pound cake he so loved.

Why was it so hard for Michael to admit to failure, Anna wondered. And why could he not acknowledge that she made sacrifices? She was willing to do what needed to be done, like spending evenings after all the farm work, sitting by the kerosene lamp and darning socks. She did not enjoy this task and the outcome was not pretty. But it saved money and they had no cash to spare. She wished Michael would give her credit for such efforts and for all she was giving up — cigarettes, for instance. "You can't smoke here!" Michael had declared. "Your Prussian accent is bad enough! A smoking farmer's wife is unacceptable." "You are so stingy!" Anna retorted. "I bet the expense bothers you more than what the neighbors think."

When Michael had returned from the hay incident, he knew very well he should apologize. Why couldn't he just say she was right and he was sorry. He knew it would clear the air. Instead, he was silent and let Anna seethe. But Anna was equally stubborn, Michael felt. If only she could see that sometimes the work had to take precedence over everything else. But she just did not get it. For instance when the mailman came. Anna was ready to stop whatever she was doing, sit down and read her letters, sometimes two or three! But you just could not leave the oxen standing there, in the middle of plowing! "Why not?" Anna would ask. "What's the rush? Look at the neighbors. They take their time too." She would be miffed for the rest of the day and punish him with her silence. "May I read my mail now?" she would ask, pointedly, after the work was done. "Maybe you are jealous, because you don't get any," she had said recently. That hurt, maybe because it was true.

Michael often felt at the end of his wits. It seemed to him, no matter how hard he tried, he could not live up to Anna's expectations. For instance when he was readying the farm before Anna's arrival and had slaved to get the place ready for her and the baby. He had worked from dawn until he dropped into bed late at night. He had whitewashed the blackened walls, scraped the grimy floors, plugged the drafty windows, repaired the smoky stoves, plowed the fields and mended the pasture fences. The house was cold and uncomfortable and he ate only bread soup and potatoes to save time. He worked and worked and worked, and Anna scolded him for the brevity of his letters! The only letter she had enjoyed, she had written, was the one with his drawings of the layout of the rooms.

They were both good at hurting each other and at accumulating grievances, Anna had to acknowledge. Sometimes her outbursts were a result of her fatigue. Michael was so much stronger than she, he simply could not see when she was physically spent. And Anna found it difficult to let him know before she was at the end. Then she'd throw herself into the grass, kicking her legs, crying and screaming: "I can't do this anymore!" leaving Michael to wonder whether she was just making a scene, or whether she had truly reached the end of her rope.

The thing that enraged her most was Michael's stinginess. She could not bear to hear the word frugality one more time! The other day she reached the limit of her endurance when Michael did not let her pick some of the early good eating apples. "What do you mean, you want to sell *all* the eating apples?" she objected. "What about us? What about your daughter?" But Michael carefully packed the fragrant, ripe apples into wooden crates to ship to Berlin. "I guess, I'll have to steal apples like you had to when you were a child," Anna screamed angrily, and stomped out of the *Stube*. When she got to the bedroom, she burst into tears. She felt so utterly helpless. Here they worked day and night, and they could not even eat their own apples! Sometimes she just wanted to pack up and leave, although she knew that was not the solution.

*I wish we would not hold grudges*, Michael thought. He could recall incidences when Anna would go off like a cannon. He often did not know when something he said or did would provoke Anna. He felt she had absolutely no sense of humor and would misinterpret things he'd say in jest. He remembered how once he joked with Friedel, when they were taking a break from their haying, while Anna was on the agreed-upon kitchen duty. "Well, you seem to be having a lot of fun," Anna said cynically as she joined them in the courtyard, "and I slave in the kitchen to cook your supper." It did not help when Anna saw Friedel roll her eyes and Michael smirk. "You two can just cook your own dinner," Anna yelled, disgusted, and left. When Friedel and Michael came in later, tired and hungry, Anna practically threw dinner in their faces.

If only she could figure out what lay at the heart of their troubles, Anna thought. *Maybe we both need too much confirmation from one another. Maybe we need to find ourselves more fully before we can live in peace with each other.* Anna knew that in the early days of their relationship Michael had lacked self-assurance and the ability to see his own strength, that he needed her to find his own center. Maybe this was still true. And maybe this was true for herself also: *Does my life only mean something when it is grounded in the love of another person?* she questioned. *Is that the center that influences everything? Do we expect too much from each other instead of taking charge of our own happiness?*

"Ach, Michael," Anna said at the end of the day they had not honored properly. "Why do we make our lives so difficult?"

# WAR
### *September 3, 1939*

It was a mellow September day. The cider fruit was falling from the trees early and splashing on the ground, and wasps got drunk on its sweetness. War again, the *Oberhias* grandmother thought, as she was changing her little granddaughter Klari's diapers. *Poor little thing, just a month old, and now she'll spend her first years growing up in war time. No matter whether she'll remember or not, it will affect her.* For herself, this was the second time around, and the last war had ended only twenty years ago. *Another war! What lunacy. All those names on the memorial by the church! Isn't it terrible enough that millions died in the trenches the last time around?*

She was still mourning the end of the monarchy, and the loss of the *Kaiser*. She loved that old emperor! He was a true ruler, not like that Hitler who thought he was more powerful than a king and maybe to prove it he has started another war. Who knew where it would all lead. Good thing this little grandchild was a girl. Even if she was not the desired heir, at least she couldn't be drafted into war when she grew up. And how fortunate that Konrad had injured his hand in the last war, not so badly that he was crippled and could not do farm work, but badly enough so that he could not pull a trigger! They had sent him home. He was only twenty then.

War or not, she thought, not too much would change on their farm. The seasons would come and go as always and the work would never stop. They had already drafted the young neighbor, several days before the war had officially started! How would all the work there get done now? They had had a steady stream of visitors next door, all summer long. City people from Berlin had come and relatives from Bavaria. They had come to help, but it seemed no one knew how to use a scythe or rake properly. Still, they got the work done. The neighbor had bought a new German machine for mowing and turning over the hay. He had all kinds of modern ideas how to make the work easier. But such machines cost money and who could afford such investments up here in the hill country! He had talked about getting electricity and a system for spreading the liquid manure on the fields. She did not quite know what to make of such improvements. The old ways of doing things were good enough for her, she thought. To do the work by hand took longer, but with many people it got done in time and no cash was needed. Of course they had fewer hands over there. Now that everybody had left after it became clear there would be war, there were only the two of them, the *Nachbarin* and sixteen-year-old Gabriele, the *Nachbar's* cousin from Bavaria. Thinking he might be drafted her brother Walter had left for home too.

She sometimes missed working outside, but she could not take the heat any longer, and there was enough to be done in the house, especially with the new baby. She better make a big pot of milk soup, she thought, before everyone came in to eat. Now, at cider making time, all hands were needed to collect the apples and pears from under the trees. Maridl and Resl were doing their share. They were good at filling basket after basket for their father to haul in and mash in the huge vat. The whole entry hall where the large cider press stood smelled of fermenting fruit. She loved those rich fall fragrances of ripe fruit and decaying leaves, those earthy smells before all would be covered by snow and the time of darkness began. Little Klari started to cry. She must be hungry, her grandmother thought. Oh, what was in store for her, for all of them, with this new war?

Klara worked outside again for the first time since the birth a month ago. She breathed in the autumn air and relished the sunshine. Good the baby was safe with her grandmother. She needed to be out here now, for when the fruit fell it needed to be picked up. Otherwise it would rot. She got tired bending down, but there was no other way to do this work. Even the neighbor who always thought up labor-saving devices had not come up with any easier way to collect the cider fruit.

What would become of them all now that there was another war? she wondered. Her husband was safe, thank God, but there were men on all the surrounding farms in the valley. She feared they would all be drafted eventually and then the hard labor would fall on the women. Work already filled their days, with feeding and milking the cows twice a day, putting meals on the table, washing the laundry, scrubbing the floors. Once a month bread had to be baked, at Easter and Christmas a pig was slaughtered, and the meat readied for smoking. And the baby wanted to be fed! The girls would have to pitch in more. Thank God they still had the old grandmother's help. Klara prayed God would keep her well and healthy for some time. Hopefully the girls would be out of school by the time their grandmother became feeble and needed care.

Klara worried about the neighbors. They had had a hard enough time as it was. She just could not understand all their quarreling. Especially how the *Nachbarin* sometimes yelled and carried on. What good did that do? Men were apt to shout once in a while, but responding in kind just made it worse, she thought. She did not like it either when Konrad came back from his Sunday outings late and a bit drunk, but it would never occur to her to yell at him. After all, he was the man in the house who did the hardest labor. Who was she to tell him what to do? Of course she had her own ways to put him in his place. She just gave him the silent treatment and did not speak for the rest of the day. That told him his behavior was not acceptable, without making a fuss.

She knew he was a bit disappointed that this baby — hopefully the last — was a girl. He never said so, but she knew! But why would it have to be a boy? Why could not Klari inherit the farm? That would give Konrad extra years to remain in charge. They'd probably give Resl to her sister after she was finished with school, although they would lose her work power for all the years until she got married. She did worry about Maridl. She could only hope she and Klari would get along one day so that she could stay on the farm. At any rate, there was no sense worrying now. Who knows what would happen by then, especially considering this war. At least they would be spared bombs here in the countryside and they'd always have enough to eat, despite requisitions that would surely be levied on the farmers. And city folk would come begging for food. She was glad there was such a bounty of fruit this year. They'd be able to make a lot of plum brandy and that would come in handy for bartering if things got tight.

So what they had all feared had come to pass: another war! Only this time he would not have to go, Konrad Klausriegler thought. He remembered the last war. He was only eighteen when they drafted him to fight in the Balkans. Maybe the injury to his hand had saved his life. Maybe otherwise he would not have come home, like so many others. But what was the use to think what might have been? The people were powerless in these situations. The rulers decided and there was nothing anyone could do. Only, he wished he had bought a new suit. Now it surely would be more expensive, or not to be had at all.

Good thing there was all this work to do to keep him from worrying. He liked making cider. He hauled basket after basket of fallen fruit into the cider press room. The fruit needed to be crushed before he would fill it into the press. He enjoyed tightening the spindles more and more until the golden liquid ran out and was caught in wooden buckets. It was not hard work, compared to plowing a field or stacking a hay wagon, but everything had to be clean and orderly and one had to proceed step by step, until the oak barrels in the cellar were filled, ready to ferment. By Christmas the cider would be ready to drink. The girls loved the cider making too, he knew. They'd catch the sweet golden flow in pitchers and usually ended up drinking too much and then spending extra time in the outhouse!

War, he thought again, unable to banish the images that came to him. How many would not come back this time? It would be a lot harder for young women like his daughters to find husbands, and there would be a new batch of widows! And even if the men did come back, the women would have to do all the work while they were gone. Look at the *Nachbarin*, she is struggling already, after only a few days. He'd have to try to help her, when he could, he thought, although he knew it would be hard to make the time. At least they'd be fairly safe here on their mountain, safer than city folks.

He was irritated by it all. *I think I'll take a break and smoke a pipe,* he decided. He usually only smoked in the evening, after all the work was done, but today he'd make an exception. After all, it was not every day that a war started. He could grant himself this little pleasure. Who knows, tobacco might become scarce too. He would enjoy it while he could.

Although Anna had expected it, she was shocked war had actually begun. And especially, that Michael had been drafted, even before it was official. "When will I see you again, my little daughter?" Michael had written into the journal before he left. And how would she manage to run the farm, all by herself, Anna worried. It had all happened so quickly.

The summer had been full of visitors and hard work, and although there were rumors war would come, she had had no time to worry about it. So many people had come to the farm, some as paying guests, which meant extra work, but also extra money. Others had come to help, although that was sometimes questionable. Michael's cousin Mandi, for instance, always found ways to get out of work. Anna had a hard time being realistic about these visitors. She had still not shed her ingrained Pomeranian sense of hospitality. Guests were to be pampered and taken care of. And yet, she depended on their pitching in here. On the one hand Anna felt guilty, but on the other self-preservation required her to be hardnosed. Yet Michael carried that to an extreme and exploited their visitors more than necessary, she believed.

In the end, even her friend Friedel who had spent four months on the farm with her two teenage sons, had disappointed her. Anna had been full of anticipation. They had been such close friends for so many years. Anna had witnessed her divorce and affairs, her trials as a mother, and had helped get her writing published. She had always appreciated Friedel's acerbic humor, her honesty and directness, her ability to analyze people. Anna had so looked forward to talking over the problems of her marriage with Friedel, to reminisce about old times.

But then when Friedel was at the farm, everything was different. There was so much work to be done they hardly had time to talk, and they had lacked the necessary privacy. There were conflicts over the boys, who were fussy eaters and sometimes downright impertinent. To top it off, both Anna and Friedel preferred to work outside, and the one whose turn it was to do the cooking and housework tended to mope. But what bothered Anna most was Friedel's disparagement of her outbursts and anger toward Michael. One night they both stayed up late and Friedel told her what she thought: "The scenes you are making are simply demeaning! I can't watch you like that, when you scream and thrash about, slam doors and carry on. These excesses show such utter lack of self-control! And often it is about such unimportant matters!"

Anna was shocked how Friedel perceived her. Instead of receiving the longed-for support of a woman friend, Anna felt abandoned and alone. And now this! Anna had just cleaned out the guest room the Wedel family had used and found the bedding black with grime and the chamber pot filthy. She was near tears with frustration.

In the larger scheme of things this was, Anna knew, simply a minor annoyance. She'd get over it. What did it really matter, when one considered what might lie ahead? Even the quarrels with Michael all summer long, Anna felt, were insignificant now that there was war and Michael was gone, already drafted. He had been training at nearby barracks for six days now and there was a chance that tomorrow, on Sunday, he might come home for a day's furlough.

Anna found it more difficult than she had expected to get the work done without Michael's physical strength and without his oversight. Not so much the routine tasks, like the stable work, but all the other work, and there was so much of it this time of year. Three fields needed plowing, the potatoes and the turnips had to be harvested, the fruit to be dealt with. How on earth would she get all that done with only the help of Gabriele? Michael had made a calendar that told her what to do when, but she still could not see her way through it. Besides, much depended on the weather and that was entirely unpredictable.

Anna had so wanted to surprise Michael with a plowed field, in case he came home, but so far they had made little progress. She could not believe how challenging it was to guide the plow, to make deep furrows, to turn over the heavy, dark earth. It had looked so easy, when she had seen Michael do it. But now she realized his skill and muscles were irreplaceable. Yesterday they had taken Erdmuthe to the neighbors, so they could plow. Alas, they had hardly gotten the harness on the oxen, a much more cumbersome process than she had realized, when Maridl came back with the screaming baby. And that was the end of that.

But what preoccupied her more than anything else was the letter she had received from Michael. She pulled it out of her apron pocket to reread. He had written it shortly after he arrived at the barracks. "Now that peace seems impossible," it said, "I do wonder whether we should consider moving East, where one can expect the army will create a *tabula rasa* in order to 'free' it for others."

Anna was so stunned that at first she could not quite grasp what he was saying. They had only just begun here, bought the farm less than a year ago. They had hardly given their life here a chance and he wanted to leave? Worse, he was considering taking over someone else's farm in Poland or the Ukraine! Hadn't they come here to get away from Hitler, from his idea of expanding eastward in order to create more *Lebensraum* — new living territory — for the Germanic race? And now Michael wanted to participate in this travesty! Was he that unhappy that he had lost his judgment? *If he comes home tomorrow it will be more important to talk about this than to plow the field,* Anna decided.

"KAUFTAG": FIRST ANNIVERSARY
*October 24, 1939*

The valley lay in thick fog, while the Rieserberg was bathed in October sunshine. The yellow tamaracks, lining the pastures and set against deep green spruce, glowed golden. The sky felt like a deep blue bowl over the autumn landscape. Heavy walnuts dropped from the tall tree near the house, their green coating splattering on the ground.

For Michael the return of the *Kauftag*, the day they had purchased the farm a year ago, was the most important date of all the special days he commemorated. *A year ago we bought* Hirschengut, Michael remembered, proudly. He sat in the *Stube*, thinking of their blessings and trials. They had survived the first year of farm work better than he had feared. The military had released him after two weeks, still in time to plow and get in the potato and turnip harvest. Good thing, too, since Gabriele had left for home after all and no other help was to be had.

*We brought in many loads of hay,* he thought with satisfaction. *We turned over the earth, and we had no major disaster.* True, much remained to be done — a silo needed to be built and the cellar repaired. But he felt less urgency about such improvements than he had in the beginning. Not everything needed to be done at once. Actually, he was quite pleased with himself, and surprised he had proven to be more adaptable, more capable and more persistent than he had expected.

He had put aside the thought of leaving for the Eastern territories. Not only because Anna had been so angry that he had even considered such a possibility. Her reaction had made him realize they had not given their life here enough chance. After all, it was possible their daily tasks would eventually become routine, that they would demand less energy and time. *Look how calmly the neighbors get things done,* he thought with a pang of envy.

And their child was thriving here! She was full of exuberant wildness, trying to escape the confinement of her playpen. He expected she would be hard to control when she got older. For now Erdmuthe spent many hours entertaining herself alone. He was touched how she sat quietly in her wagon, still, like a Buddha, yet missing nothing.

Summing up the past year he entered a hopeful thought into the journal:

> The more carefully we concentrate on our daily demands, the better we will be able to fulfill them. As the farm will take on shape over time, our lives will gradually expand through the years of our growing and become rich and wide enough for us, within given limits and firmly rooted in the foundation we will have created.

He still was trying to hold on to his vision of becoming a successful farmer, although he knew the war could change all their lives in an instant. Without radio or newspaper they knew little, except what penetrated to them through letters. Poland had surrendered after only eighteen days and was now occupied by the Germans. Food rationing had begun at home, although on the farm there was no danger of being hungry. There had been German air attacks on Britain. But life on the farm remained undisturbed.

For now at least, it seemed the draft spared farmers. That was something to be grateful for. But Michael had to admit, he had not suffered during his two weeks of training. He could imagine being a soldier. The simplicity of barracks life suited him and he enjoyed the comradeship with his fellow soldiers. He did not mind the physical exertion; on the contrary, he found it energizing and satisfying. He realized he was in much better shape than city men. And there was spare time in the barracks. He had had more time for reading, thinking and writing letters than on the farm. And there were men he felt he could talk to. After the gloom at home he enjoyed the jocular atmosphere among the men, the teasing and ribbing each other. Nonetheless, he was glad he was back home now, beginning their second year.

While Michael contemplated their first year at the farm, Anna wrote a letter to her mother who was probably worried about them after having witnessed their struggles.

> Please, don't think we are miserable. I experience the joy of physical labor, the calm and satisfaction it gives, the happiness derived from the fact that we participate in the production of what we need to live, that we are able to do it on our own land. I believe, farming provides the chance to live a much more complete and rounded existence than other professions.
>
> True, we are not able to do this work with the same self-assuredness of someone who is born a farmer. We are in constant high gear, physically and mentally. We have become more realistic and sober, but we have a much closer relationship to nature than any city person could imagine. After all, it is nature that determines the course of our days and work.
>
> The simplicity of our life is as much an enrichment, as it is a limitation. Despite all our work, I feel a rare sense of inner peace, contentment, and happiness. Maybe that is due to the child, but it is also because now we have our own home that we longed for, and the farm is so beautiful, or, at least, has the potential to be.

*We should take more time to look at the big picture*, Anna thought, *and not get bogged down in our daily struggle. We forget too often why we came here and the good things about our lives here.* This letter helped her put things into perspective, and hopefully it would put Mumm at ease as well.


THE TRIP

*May 14, 1940*


In April Anna's tulips had come up and added bright reds and yellows to the pervading white of the blooming orchard. On the hillside above the *Oberhias*, the yellow balls of *Trollblumen*, the globe flower, swayed in the breeze. Lilies of the valley opened under the lilac bush and the lilacs sent their fragrance into the house. Anna was pleased the vegetable garden was coming along nicely too. Radishes and field salad were ready to harvest. Carrots and peas had sprung up. Anna could not wait for fresh greens.

Today was Anna's birthday, the second she was going to celebrate at *Hirschengut.* But as it turned out, she would not be at the farm for this special day, after all. Her sister, Hilde, had come to visit and taken her away for a little trip, and Anna had a glimmer of hope that this brief reprieve might dispel the depressive mood that had settled over them and the farm. The neverending struggles with Michael had begun to wear her down, too, and the toll of their private war terrified her. She was beginning to doubt that there was any chance for a good end. *After all, we are not evil people, neither of us,* she thought, *and yet this brings out such harshness and viciousness in both of us.* She could understand it less and less. Sometimes she just wanted to flee. Thus Hilde's birthday present of a short trip came like a godsend.

Maybe a change of scenery was all she needed. A brief getaway, time away from each other, might clear their minds, Anna hoped. She and Hilde had not gone far. They stayed in a little *Gasthaus* in the nearby lake district. Anna was grateful her sister was treating her, for Michael surely would have resented such an expense. They hiked, ate, slept and talked. The two sisters enjoyed each other's company, unlike in earlier times when Hilde had stood in the shadow of her older sister. Now, at thirty-one, Hilde lived a successful life as a single woman. As a chemical engineer she felt sorry for Anna's deprived circumstances. She was glad she could give her sister a few days of calm and luxury.

Anna relished this reprieve. What bliss not to have to get up at five in the morning! And although she missed the child, Anna savored not being responsible for Erdmuthe for a little while. Her father was perfectly capable of caring for her for a few days, she knew.

Anna looked at this vacation as a short break from hard work. But Michael sat home, brooding and poured his doubts and deepening despair into the journal:

> So many special days have passed and I have not written into this book. Even though I have thought about all that is unresolved, on these days and all days in between, I have not found clarity. Not about what is now, not about the course of our fate in the future. What will happen? Today I write down this question, because today it is more burning than ever before. Today I write down this question even though it tears me up more than ever before. Today I write of this because I am more perplexed and helpless than ever. For today Anna left, for several days, for many reasons, all of which are compelling and force her away from here . . .

Michael felt utterly abandoned — abandoned like when his mother died after his birth and left him behind. Why could he not trust that Anna's trip was just a little vacation, a desire for a bit of rest? Anna seemed to think nothing of her departure. She had left, full of anticipation and joy. She had not even written him a postcard from her trip. He had no idea where she was staying, how to reach her, should anything happen. Surely she was having a good time, while he wondered whether this was the beginning of the end.

# THE OPERATION
## October 24, 1940

Anna lay in a hospital bed in Steyr, wearing a new nightgown she had bought with her mother's gift money. Michael had thought her old nightgown would do, but Anna wanted to treat herself to some luxury before her ordeal. She could see a bit of sky from her bed, but no trees, and she missed Hirschengut and the autumn smells of decaying fruit. She resented lying in a hospital bed while the world went by without her. Potatoes and cabbage would be harvested, cider would be made on the farms, the last asters would bloom in the garden and she was not there to partake in any of it. It was true, Anna was permanently exhausted and would not have minded a short vacation, a few days of rest, a bit of time away from the farm, like she had had in May. But being in the hospital would hardly restore her.

From the very beginning of her second pregnancy — Anna did not know why — she had felt something was wrong with this child. And now, four months later, they had learned that their child was growing in the wrong place and would not live. Anna was about to have an operation to end her ectopic pregnancy. Both she and Michael were immensely sad to be losing this child, a much desired child, their problems notwithstanding. But at this point Anna was more concerned about her own survival. It was very late for this operation her doctor had said. There was no guarantee. The thought of Erdmuthe motherless was almost unbearable. Wasn't it enough that Michael had lost his mother? Still, Anna wondered whether it might be better for Michael if she died. At least it would be a resolution to their seemingly unsolvable difficulties. He would have to find another wife to help him raise their little daughter.

*No, Anna thought. I can't have such morbid thoughts. I will need my strength. I want to live. Maybe this turn of events will shake us out of our destructive patterns, bring us to our senses, help us start over. The best I can do before they wheel me off is to write a letter to Michael.* He had brought her there and was taking a walk to break the tension before the operation.

She wanted to remind him how much happiness they had given each other in the past, that she had not always been such an ogre, that in earlier times he had admired her while now he only seemed to notice her failings. But more than anything else she wanted to tell him that she still loved him and wanted to be with him, no matter what: "I want to tell you that I love you no less today than at any time before, and that I want to see you happy again, and that I want to be the person you can be happy with." Anna wrote, then lay back in her bed. Now she was ready for whatever was to come.

Michael was back on the farm, leaving Anna to recover in the hospital. Thank God the operation had been successful, and Erdmuthe had finally fallen asleep. She missed her mother and Michael could not get her to eat, no matter what trick he tried. Now that the child was in bed, Michael could finally write the report about the farm that he had resolved to write every year on this special day. Strange, he thought, that Anna's operation would happen on the second anniversary of the purchase of the farm.

When he thought back, in many ways this second year had been easier than the first, and yet, at the same time harder. The work had been less trying, probably because they were now more familiar with their tasks. They had had more hardships this year: the water pipes had frozen in January, the summer had been rainy, they had lost pigs to a strange disease, the fox had stolen numerous chickens, a cow had died ten days before she was to deliver her first calf. The potatoes, cabbage, and turnips had grown poorly. And yet, they were less unnerved by such setbacks. Somehow they knew by now that, in the end, things would work out, more or less. Erdmuthe was healthy and full of life, and that counted more than anything else.

Out there, away from their life on the farm, a war was raging. It reached all the way to Scandinavia now. Paris was occupied by Hitler's soldiers. Bombs were falling in Berlin and Friedel and her boys were spending time in air raid shelters. But the war affected them little here. They were safe and the army had granted him another reprieve. In the midst of a war they had enough to eat. Anna had survived her operation, their child was happy, they had good neighbors. They had so much to be thankful for and yet, aside from the work, things had gotten more hopeless. *We are the unhappiest people imaginable, although still not so unhappy that they could not become even more miserable,* he thought, and wrote:

> Here we stand in the middle of our lives, and what do we have to show for it: That we have learned nothing for our difficult task, a task that requires cooperation and too much labor, sacrifice and frugality, and allows for too little contemplation, especially if one has not grown up with this kind of work and deprivation.

Michael reread what he had written and was not happy about his summary. But it was a realistic appraisal, he knew. Even the letter Anna had written in the hospital gave him little hope. He was more pessimistic than Anna, but he felt he had to respond honestly, Anna's ordeal notwithstanding:

> How bitter this farewell was again, like so many others. I wonder whether we will ever again be able to get along.

It is not that the good will is lacking. But each of us has a different viewpoint. And although we stand next to each other, our desires go into different directions, like two streams dividing . . .

Michael did not look forward to the next few months. After Anna's return from the hospital she and Erdmuthe would leave, go to Pomerania and Berlin to get away to recuperate. He would have to cope by himself. He knew Anna needed this period of healing, and maybe it would give them needed distance from each other to re-evaluate their situation, an opportunity to regenerate and a fresh impetus to start anew after Anna's return. He knew, were she to stay she'd feel compelled to pitch in, seeing all the work that needed to be done. She had to leave, but he did not relish the thought of a long lonely winter by himself. True, Ingeborg, Anna's young Pomeranian cousin would be here to pitch in, but it would be very quiet without Erdmuthe's shouts, her joyful little voice.

ANNA'S RETURN
*February 14, 1941*

Today was Erdmuthe's second birthday and Anna still was not here. Michael had looked forward to her return, longing to celebrate this day with his wife and child. But now Anna had postponed their arrival for another week. Didn't she know how important these special days were? He could not quite believe that it was so impossible to get here! Anna had been gone for three months now. Enough was enough. He had been patient and understanding and did not begrudge her the time with friends in Pomerania and Berlin. He had been glad to hear she had renewed her newspaper contacts and been able to make extra money by writing book reviews. He knew Erdmuthe had been ill, and yet, he suspected Anna had not made an all-out effort to get home for her birthday.

*It has been too long,* he thought. Not that he did not have enough to do. He needed to cut wood in the forest and make repairs, for which there had been no time during the hectic summer and fall months. In the evenings he had made blocks for Erdmuthe and painted the crib in which both he and his father had slept. He was pleased with the outcome. It had the jumping stag on the front, his and Anna's initials surrounded by flower garlands on both ends and on the drawer his and his daughter's birth dates. He had not fixed the loose dowel he had enjoyed turning as a child, just like Erdmuthe did now. He hoped his artistic efforts would please Anna. And that soon another child would lie in this crib.

He looked at his daughter's little chairs and her toys and tried to remember her small face, her shiny eyes, her spiky hair, her high-pitched voice. It was all beginning to get hazy. Sometimes, when he walked through the empty house with heavy footsteps, he momentarily forgot she was gone and was afraid he might have awakened her. But reality caught up with him quickly and now he was worried she might not recognize him when she returned, that she might have forgotten her father. He was thinking of little else but the three of them and their life together!

At Christmas he had been overwhelmed with longing, longing for one single celebration of total harmony, when everything would flow together: their work and leisure, their worries and their joys, what they were given and the sacrifices they had made. He wrote to Anna, in a thirty-two page long letter:

Such a celebration would be a heavenly festival, like the glow in Erdmuthe's eyes, a glow we too could have, if only we were not so stubborn and blind.

Michael had poured out his heart in this Christmas letter:

> I want nothing more, but to live with you in peace, and if that is not possible, I want to live with you anyway. If I had a choice between riches, opportunity, friends, beauty, everything imaginable I might desire, and one single hour of peace with you and after that a life of only sorrow and anguish, I would choose to be with you.

Anna was mistaken if she thought there was a time when he had loved her more. On the contrary, he realized, she had become more important to him now than at any time before and he did not wish to see anything they had experienced undone. But that did not diminish his longing for peace between them. "I want to make you as happy and content as I want to be myself," he wrote. "Let at least the first few days after your return be good and beautiful."

Before Anna had left on her long trip she had often marveled at how simple her life had become. All of her concerns rotated around her child, her relationship with Michael, and the farm work. The work dominated everything. It meant she had too little time with Erdmuthe. It meant that she was exhausted and impatient with Michael. It meant there was no time to write letters to friends or read a book, let alone write literary reviews. She forced herself out of bed in the morning. She fell into bed at night, spent. True, often her work gave her satisfaction. She was proud when she made her first pound of butter and sent it to her mother. She felt a sense of triumph when she stacked the hay wagon well and Michael approved. She looked over her lined-up jars of canned vegetables, fruit and meat with a sense of accomplishment. She felt pride over a cleanly scrubbed floor. Still, the relentlessness of it all sapped her joy. Work never let up. She had to steal from her sleep to keep a neat house. There was no time to rest, and still she got less done than she thought necessary. No wonder she had been so very weary.

While traveling home, Anna thought about how different her life had been these last few months. She had worn her former city clothes, silk dresses a Berlin seamstress had made long ago, jewelry that had sat in a box on the farm. But more importantly, she had had time for conversation, to read and write. Her mind had opened up again, her thoughts were not limited to her life with Michael and Erdmuthe.

At the farm she had forgotten there was a world out there, and a war. When she visited her friends in East Prussia, Stephan had come home on leave and told terrible stories about crimes the German military had committed in Poland. He told of summary executions of the Polish intelligentsia, of abductions and rapes of women, of village after village set on fire. "This will remain an unerasable stain in the history of us Germans," he had said.

And then there were the Jews. Anna was in disbelief when she heard what was happening to them. She should have known better, she thought, after what she had seen during the shattering *Kristallnacht*. And now it seemed that was only the beginning of things to come. During her Berlin visit she read the Nazi paper *Der Stürmer*. There it said in black and white: "Now judgment has begun and it will reach its conclusion only when knowledge of the Jews has been erased from earth." "Erase," it said. "Erase." And apparently they systematically worked on this campaign. Friedel, who still lived in Berlin, had told her about all the restrictions imposed on the Jewish population. They had to wear a yellow star. There was a curfew. They were not allowed to own radios, bicycles or cameras. Their valuables were confiscated. They were only allowed to rent from other Jews. They were forbidden to use public facilities: parks, swimming pools or libraries. Jewish doctors were only allowed to treat other Jews. "The list goes on and on," Friedel had said. "Who could, has left, others have disappeared. I hear there are now deportations, Jews picked up in the middle of the night and sent to who knows where. And people just pretend nothing is happening."

The mental toll of the war, Anna realized, was enormous for everyone. Her longtime friend Felizitas, also visiting in Berlin, had told her that ten of her husband's cousins had been killed in two years of war. "How can you be so wrapped up in your personal life, when such things are happening," Felizitas had asked Anna, full of reproach. "Our entire future will be destroyed through this war!" Only her art restoration work, which, to her, dealt with eternal values, kept Felizitas going. She saw the war as horrifying and murderous. "The foundation of our former lives is gone," Felizitas had said. "I always thought that we could preserve lasting values as individuals, but I don't anymore. One needs all one's strength just to endure." Anna was thunderstruck. On the farm she had not had time or energy to think about such things. Without radio or newspapers on her mountain, she hardly knew what had been going on elsewhere.

Despite these revelations Anna discussed the issue of resettlement with people who might be able to give advice, as Michael had asked her to do. She herself was beginning to look at the idea more favorably. Maybe they would be able to handle their lives better on a farm that was easier to work? But everyone dissuaded her, especially in regards to settling in the Warthegau, a province in German-occupied Northern Poland. Maybe there would be better prospects in Alsace, the region that had long been switching back and forth between Germany and France, someone suggested. At the same time, Anna wondered whether by settling elsewhere they might jump from the frying pan into the fire. Maybe they should change their approach on the farm they had now, instead of resettling.

Being away from the farm gave Anna more perspective on her life there. After her return things would have to change, she decided.

There was no reason why they had to work themselves to death. She had written to Michael what she was willing or unwilling to do:

> You have to allow me the absolutely necessary time for housework, without constant bickering: that means the rooms in use need to be cleaned once a week, and the laundry needs to be attended to. And I can't work outside, take care of the house and do the cooking as well. Your expectations of me are entirely unreasonable. I can't work as hard as other farmers' wives. I am just so discouraged.

He had to understand. Things could not go on as they had. She hoped she would keep her resolve once she was back home.

Anna found Michael's lack of gratitude hard to comprehend. She felt he could not fully appreciate that she had come through her medical emergency, that she had survived at all. She could not understand how he took for granted that she was still on this earth. After all, she could have died. She remembered how she had felt in the hospital garden after she was able to go out into the sun for the first time. How deeply shaken she was, how she experienced being alive as a great, beautiful gift. She knew it was her responsibility not to let this gratitude pass without learning from it, without making a change in their lives. *We can't change the past,* she thought, *but can't we change the future?* There was so much she had to tell Michael when she got home. Felizitas was right, they were too isolated on their mountaintop. They had to find a way to let the rest of the world in.

She was touched by Michael's long letter regarding their relationship, moved that he would not want to change the past. "Our relationship is truly strange and powerfully absolute and unconditional," she had written back. "We can hurt each other, so that we can hardly bear it, and yet, nothing can drive us away from one another."

# EASTER
## *April 13, 1941*

*This is such a busy and festive time of year,* Klara thought. She loved
all the customs, rituals, and tasks, although the days were a bit hectic.
A week before Easter Konrad made a beautiful *Palmbuschen* for Palm
Sunday. That Sunday the church filled with the fragrant, colorful
bundles decorated with apples and ribbons, and, as usual, theirs was
one of the best. The farmers would not admit it, but she knew they
were competing with each other. Konrad took pride in his handiwork,
putting together all the special greens. Cedar, holly and juniper grew
in front of the house for this very purpose, but for the ivy and the
purple *Seidelbast* flowers he had to climb the hillside, and the willow
and hazelnut grew along the little stream down in the hollow. He had
been pleased the *Seidelbast* blossoms were so fragrant and perfect.
Sometimes they were not open yet, and other years they were done
blooming! "This year they are the way they are supposed to be!" he
had said, happily. Konrad made a number of small bundles, each one
containing a sample of all nine required greens. Then he wound them
into one large "bush," that formed their *Palmbuschen*. After church
Konrad took the individual bundles apart and put one each on the
fields, in the stable, and in the rooms in the house, in the hope that they
would have a good harvest and be protected from calamity.

Then they slaughtered a pig. They would have a great big pork
roast for Easter Sunday, but most of the meat hung in the smoke
chamber, being slowly converted to *Speck*. All those smoked bacon
shanks would now last till Christmas. The *Nachbarin* had shown
her how to can meat, like they did in Pomerania, and how to make

sausage, but somehow she did not have the courage to try. Maybe later. For now she felt more comfortable to preserve the meat the way she was used to.

After the slaughter came the big spring cleaning. Konrad put new whitewash on the walls and added green stencil patterns and Klara and the girls had polished the windows and scrubbed the floors, brushed away the winter cobwebs, swept the courtyard and cleared away accumulated junk. They washed the bedding and hung it out to dry in the fresh air and put away the winter clothes until fall. Everything was fresh and clean and Resl even brought in a bunch of wild primroses and set them on the table.

For the ceremony on Saturday night Klara put together a nice basket of food: smoked bacon, boiled eggs, and braided brioche bread, to be blessed in church. She put a red and white cross-stitched cloth over the top. It was not necessary that everyone should see what was inside. After church they would have a rich *Jause*, an elaborate, well-deserved cold meal after the long time of fasting. She was ready for Easter!

But what was going on at the neighbors? Klara wondered. First the *Nachbarin* had been gone for months while the *Nachbar* struggled by himself. She could understand that the *Nachbarin* needed time to recover from her operation. After all, she had almost died. But that long! And now she saw the *Nachbar* leave. Where would he be going carrying a backpack? Seemed like one or the other over there was always on the way to somewhere else, she thought. Seemed they had trouble staying put. She could not imagine what it would be like to be on the go like that. She had only slept in two beds in her lifetime: the one in her childhood home across the valley before her marriage, and the one here since then. She would probably die in that bed. When you had a farm and animals there was not much room for wandering and she had no desire to explore the world beyond this valley.

Anna was distraught. Their fights had continued after her return. They had not had a belated Christmas celebration or honored Erdmuthe's birthday a week late, as they had envisioned. Michael's wish that their the first few days together be peaceful had not come true. And now she had driven Michael away from the farm! She doubted he would find much solace in Wasserburg. She herself had at least friends like Felizitas, to whom she could flee, but Michael could only go to see his parents and she knew they had no comprehension of his situation.

Now it was Easter and she had not even dyed eggs for Erdmuthe. They had done nothing to prepare, while the neighbors' house was turned inside out. But she just could not think of such matters since their fight on Good Friday. And she could not even pin down what it was all about. She hated her impulsive temperament, that she just could not stop when she felt hurt and then became mean and abusive. This time it had gotten so bad Michael had hit her and she could not even blame him.

Since Michael had left, she was melting with love for him and thought of him gently and yieldingly. If only she could live by these feelings when they were together! She had to write him how proud she was of him. He needed to hear that. It was too bad she found it so difficult to tell him in person. She took his abilities with farm work for granted, she thought. She should tell him how much she appreciated how skillfully he was able to work with his hands, making toys for the child, building a bookshelf in their bedroom, fixing tools that were broken. She herself was so inept in such matters and she admired him for his many skills, and yet, in her pride, she found it hard to tell him. *Why is it so hard for me to admit that there are things he can do better than I? Why did we feel such a need to compete with each other?*

Anna knew he suffered more than she did after their fights. She exploded and then she could go on. He buried the hurt inside where it festered. And she knew sometimes she could have avoided such scenes. She had to write him at least that much.

## PARENTAL VISIT
### *September 10, 1941*

After the long trip from Wasserburg — they had changed trains three times — Anton Dempf and his wife Agnes struggled up the mountain. In his youth Anton had loved to climb the Dolomite Mountains in South Tyrol with his first wife, Elisabeth Schwarz, Michael's birth mother. But now, at sixty-nine, his girth had expanded, helped by his sweet-tooth wife who served him coffee and cake every afternoon. His shirt was drenched with sweat, as he climbed the Ebner hill, the steepest part of the path, relieved that Michael carried his suitcase. He would have preferred bringing a rucksack, as Michael had suggested, but his wife, worried about wrinkling her dress, had insisted on a suitcase. He knew her dress would be too fancy for this mountain visit, but there was no use pointing this out, since her city wardrobe lacked clothing suitable for an excursion into their son's more primitive living conditions. At least his lederhosen, the Bavarian leather pants he wore at home and his checkered cotton shirt, were not out of place here, he thought.

Agnes, fifty-eight, flabby and short legged, breathed heavily, her heart pounding. She wished she was back home where it was cool and comfortable. Why in the world had Michael chosen a location like this, she wondered. Taking up farming was a crack-pot idea to begin with, but if he could not be persuaded otherwise, why not at least pick a farm closer to Wasserburg, a farm on flatter land, a farm where one could be successful? A place where one could visit one's grandchild.

This was the first time they had attempted to see for themselves how Michael and Anna lived. Agnes was not distraught that they had not seen their daughter-in-law for three years, ever since the wedding. She was not looking forward to this encounter. She had never hidden her dislike of Anna but she knew here, on Anna's territory, she had to be a bit more civil. She could not retreat to her bedroom and ignore Anna, as she had during Anna's first visit in Wasserburg. But she doubted she'd ever make another visit. The long train ride and this uphill hike were just too much for her. She had underestimated how difficult it would be. At least, at the end of their three-day stay, they would be taking Erdmuthe with them. But Agnes already regretted she had let Anton persuade her to come along. No electricity, no running water, no heat. After all, September mornings could be chilly! It was beyond her how people could live like this! The poor child, she thought, growing up in such isolation, in such rustic ways! Every time Erdmuthe came to Wasserburg, she had to work at civilizing her. Last time they had to take her to the hairdresser, who cut her spindly braids and gave her a decent haircut, only to be scolded by her ungrateful parents.

"How in the world did you get all your furniture up?" Agnes finally asked, panting. "We did it in winter, on sleds, when the ground was frozen," Michael explained and pointed out the steep forest road the oxen had taken up to the farm. "It was quite an undertaking," he laughed, remembering how they had had to whip the oxen to get them to pull the heavy carved oak chest from Schleswig Holstein that now sat in their bedroom. Finally his parents would realize what was involved in living up here. That all the staples they needed had to be carried up the mountain, that the packages of food they sent had to be lugged to the post office or train station in the valley, although he figured he might earn their disdain, rather than their admiration. Be that as it may, Michael was glad they had come. He felt it was important for them to see what they had spent their money for, whether they approved or not. Hopefully they would not only see the hardship, but also the beauty of this place. His father might, but his mother? Michael had his doubts that she would see beyond her own discomfort. Actually he was surprised she had come at all.

Seeing her disapproving face brought it all back to him: her disgust when he had decided to give up the law. Her disdain toward Anna, a hated Prussian. She had not even put sheets on Anna's bed when she visited in Wasserburg for the first time, an insult beyond imagining, especially for someone from Pomerania where hospitality was of utmost importance. And during his stepmother's visit to the farm where Anna apprenticed, she had called Anna, who had a doctorate, "a mere servant girl"! She seemed to have forgotten that she herself had been a "mere" shop girl when his father married her after the death of his first wife. She had boycotted their wedding and had held out to the very end when he had asked his parents to help pay for the farm. These times of strife with his parents had been terrible years. But Michael had always been convinced things would improve once they were grandparents. And now they had agreed to come to the farm, even if primarily to fetch Erdmuthe.

Michael was worried about Anna, whether she would be able to hold back her long-standing resentments toward his parents, especially Agnes. Maybe her pride would help. Anna had gotten out her best linen from Berlin, fancier than the Wasserburgers'. "I want them to see we don't live like backward peasants," she had said. She was going to set the table with her mother's Pomeranian porcelain and crystal glasses. "There is nothing to be ashamed of," she had said to Michael, gleefully. Anna had conflicting feelings. She wanted to show off her riches, but also was pleased her mother-in-law would have to do without a bathroom and other comforts. "It will be good for her," Anna had said, laughing with satisfaction." She may think I am a servant girl, but she'll also see how hard I work and that she herself could never do such heavy labor!"

In the end, Erdmuthe's unreserved joy about her grandparents' appearance helped make the visit a success. She proceeded to show them everything in her little kingdom on the farm. First she took them to her room and showed them the crib her father had painted so beautifully. "I once lay in this crib," her grandfather said. Erdmuthe looked him up and down, then looked at the crib and shook her head. He was too big, she seemed to think. "I was a baby once too," he said. Erdmuthe shook her head again. That seemed hard to imagine. Her grandparents were amused. Then she showed them where the chickens laid their eggs, the stables where the pigs and the cows lived, the tree with the sweet plums, the place where the hot pink cyclamen bloomed. She picked a bunch for her grandmother with her clumsy little hands and made her smell their intoxicating fragrance. Her grandmother was enchanted and began to see her granddaughter in a new light, but she still cringed when she came in with dirty hands and presented a cake made from garden soil.

Michael took his father to the neighbors because he knew he would be interested in some of their folk art treasures. He admired the carvings on the huge cider press in the entry hall and the tile work on the stove in the *Stube*, with the ceramic angel on top. But most of all he was intrigued by the reverse glass paintings in the *Herrgottswinkel*, the sacred corner above the table. There were four pictures from the famous village of Sandl near the Bohemian border: a Flight to Egypt; Saint Florian, the protector against fire; St. Leonhard, the saint of farmers depicted with a bull; and the crucifixion. "These are beautiful," Anton Dempf said to the neighbor. "I would not mind having them in our museum in Wasserburg. But be sure never to give them to a collector. They belong on your farm." The *Oberhias* was surprised to have a treasure worthy of a museum. They had protected the farm because they were holy pictures, but he had never given them a thought as works of art.

It was not too difficult to keep the parents occupied while Anna and Michael had to work. Michael had set aside small repair jobs for his father: a lamp needed to be fixed and a bookshelf needed work. And there was many a chance to use his photographic skills and take photos of their beloved grandchild and her intimate relationship with the farm. Anton had brought film, hard to come by these days, and would take the exposed roll back to Wasserburg to develop and to make prints in his darkroom at home. Agnes had brought her embroidery work which kept her occupied and made her feel virtuous, for she was putting red cross-stitch stags on a linen table cloth for the farm.

Anna thought Agnes needed to see what Pomeranian hospitality was like and presented herself as a gracious hostess. She had put a vase with fall asters into the guest bedroom and selected particularly pretty linen towels. And she pointed out that everything they ate came from their farm: Anna had made the butter herself, potatoes came from their field and coleslaw from their own cabbages. The pork was canned by Anna after the spring slaughter. The jam came from their garden strawberries and the apple sauce from fruit on their trees. Agnes had to admit the food was tasty and wholesome. She made no comment on the table setting, but Anna could tell she was surprised by the elegance. She did say: "You sure have a lot of books," but then could not stop herself from adding: "Too bad you have no time to read." But Anna let it pass. After all, it was true.

When the grandparents departed with Erdmuthe, Michael and Anna felt a sense of relief. Everyone had been civil and no major faux pas had occurred.

## AT THE ABYSS
### *November 9, 1941*

Michael sat at the kitchen table, lost in his thoughts. The summer had been so very hard and the fall too. He had not even written into their book in October, on the third *Kauftag* anniversary. Three years . . . Hard to believe that three years ago Anna was not even here yet. She was in Berlin then, shopping. That's when *Kristllnacht* occurred, Michael remembered. So much had happened since then, here at the farm and out there. Anna had left the farm twice in these three years, and now she and Erdmuthe were gone again.

Although he knew it was just a short vacation of a few weeks, he felt as though Anna was never going to return to him or he to her. But by now it all hurt less. He was simply numb. Somehow he had lost touch with reality. He felt nothing at all. He felt no joy, no curiosity, no vitality. He felt an immense emptiness. He realized more than ever before that the only way he could live was being surrounded by Anna's love, and not having her love meant his death, It would be better to be dead than to live without what was most essential to him.

He felt no reproach toward Anna. He had no expectation, no hope, no anger, no demands. He simply knew the flow of love in their daily life had dried up, although the soil in which their happiness could grow was still un-poisoned. He believed that not everything was irretrievably lost, but their life together was too painful and he had no strength to do anything about it. In his great emotional vulnerability he did not even have the will or desire to wish that things would change. He felt that he stood at the edge of an abyss, ready to let go. He wondered when the point would come that a return to life was impossible. He knew he was close. As it was, he felt like a living corpse.

Ingeborg, Anna's Pomeranian cousin, had kept Michael company and helped with the work during the long months of Anna's absence after her operation and again now. But in his current despair Michael had hardly been aware of her presence. Now she was done with all the work of the day, had washed and changed out of her work clothes, combed her hair and was going to help Michael with the slicing and stringing of apples. The last few evenings they had hung up a bunch of such strings, crisscrossing the *Stube*. The drying apples emitted a subtle fragrance. It was tedious, but calming work.

She watched Michael, as he sat across from her. "Anna writes, she is proud you are so capable and that we have accomplished so much. She says I should make sure you are not working too hard. It's been a long day. Wouldn't you rather read a book now? I can do this by myself," Michael said. "No," said Ingeborg, smiling. "I'd rather be here with you doing this." Michael did not say anything after that. She was getting good at slicing, she thought, pleased.

It seemed to her that he was becoming gloomier and gloomier. He hardly ever spoke to her. She could tell he was usually somewhere else with his thoughts and unless there was something she had to ask regarding the work she kept quiet. He was such a strongly built, handsome man, she thought, but so very sad. He was only thirty, but he looked older. Maybe grief did that to people. She was twelve years younger, but she felt, since she had been coming here to the farm to help, she had grown up quite a bit. At first it all seemed so glamorous. She had been surprised that her cousin, Anna, had given up her job in Berlin to become a farmer. Then, after Ingeborg had finished school and the war had started and they had so little help here, her mother had suggested she go and pitch in and absolve her *Pflichtjahr* — the compulsory year of labor after school — at the mountain farm in Austria. Why not do her year of service with her relatives who needed help so badly, and this way she could see a bit of the world and travel all the way from the Baltic Sea to the Alps. There was nothing to keep her in her Pomeranian hometown Köslin. So she had come.

But it wasn't what she had thought it would be like. Yes, the place was beautiful and the house was quite grand, even if a bit primitive without electricity. But the work was hard and oppressive. She hardly had time to read or write home. They had no radio or newspaper here and she had little idea what was happening elsewhere. And it was painful to listen to Anna's and Michael's quarrels. Terrible how they tore each other to shreds! Usually Anna started and then they went on and on, until they both seemed destroyed. Then impenetrable silence followed. She was always glad when she could do some work away from this tension.

She did like to play with Erdmuthe and help with her care and that was something that cheered Anna too. Erdmuthe was such a sweet, alert and happy child. Now she was with her grandparents. Ingeborg missed her and was looking forward to her return. She wasn't so sure she was looking forward to Anna's coming back. It was nice to be here, alone with Michael, although she wished he would not be quite so silent.

"Are you homesick?" Michael asked into the silence. "No," she said. "I like it here. But I miss Erdmuthe. Don't you?" He did not seem to. "I have so much else to think about," he finally said. *Must be about Anna,* Ingeborg thought. They hated each other when they were together, and missed each other when they were apart. What a tragic love. "That's enough of this work," Michael said, finally.

*I could make him happy*, Ingeborg thought, smiling. *I'd like to kiss away those deep furrows on his forehead and brighten that sad, pained smile. Maybe he'd like to take a bath.* "Would you like me to heat water and prepare a bath," she asked. Michael looked at her, surprised, and she thought, pleased. "I have often wanted Anna to ask me that," he said, "but she never has. "Yes," he said, "that would be wonderful." *How did she know*, he wondered. How did she know that that's what he had been thinking: that he felt miserable and that one thing he'd like was for someone to make him a bath.

Michael helped Ingeborg carry the tin tub into the kitchen. There was a good amount of hot water in the wood-stove water container, but they'd need to heat more in the two large canning pots, so there would be enough to fill the tub. There were enough embers left for Ingeborg to make a nice hot fire. "It will take a while for all that water to heat," she said. She was tired and it was getting late. But now she had promised, she'd stay up. True, he could pour the water into the tub himself, but it seemed to matter to him that someone else did it for him. She was not going to disappoint him now. "I'll get my book," she said. "I'll read till the water is hot." He had a book to read also and so they sat quietly in the *Stube*, under the light of the lamp and read.

Ingeborg went several times to put more wood on the fire until finally the water began to hiss and steam. The pots were too heavy for her to lift alone and Michael seemed engrossed in his reading. So she used a smaller pot to transfer the water, pouring and pouring until the tub was full enough. She was careful to leave enough room so that the water would not spill when he immersed himself. She hung a large towel on the rod by the stove and fetched the soap from the wash basin by the faucet. The kitchen was warm and steamy. She opened the door to the *Stube*. "Ready," she said. "I can empty the water tomorrow morning. I think I'll go to bed now."

Michael looked at her. *She is so young and quite beautiful,* he thought. He started taking off his shirt and pants — she had seen him stripped to shorts many times. She knew he hated wearing clothes, if he could help it. Now he dropped the last piece of clothing and stood in front of her, "Would you stay and scrub my back," he pleaded. "Sure," she said, and knew she should not.

He slid into the water, then sat up. His back was broad and muscular, still brown from summer sun. She soaped his neck and shoulders and scrubbed with a cloth. "Scrub harder," he said, "and further down." She had to reach under water for that. She let the cloth drop into the water and touched him with her hands. His skin felt smooth and sinuous and she rubbed his back from the neck down and from side to side. "Too bad the tub is too small for both of us," he said. "I'll be fast. Will you wait?" He washed down quickly. *It is a shame not to linger in this hot water,* he thought, *but this moment will not return.* He stepped out, dripping water all over the wood floor, threw his towel over his shoulders and, wet as he was, embraced Ingeborg, who was standing in the middle of the kitchen. It was as though a stroke of lightning shot through her. She could have left earlier, but now it was too late.

When Ingeborg awoke in Michael's bed the next morning, her body felt tingly all over. Michael was gone, probably milking the cows. "Anna can't know about this," he had said, before they drifted off to sleep. But how could she hide it? Anna would see through this, she was sure. She had to leave before Anna came back! She'd have to find a convincing explanation to give to her parents, why she was home for Christmas early. For now she would not think what all this meant for the future. She was happy and she had one more day with Michael! One more day . . .

Michael knew when he woke up that he felt different, that he was not at the abyss anymore. Somehow the intensity of his sexual experience with Ingeborg had released him and given him a new desire to want to live again. Anna would come back in two days and Michael realized he had to let her know something. So he wrote her a veiled letter:

> You must believe that I stood on the ultimate brink. But for the first time after these two-and-a-half years which robbed me of all ability to act, I know now I will not return to where I have been. Take it as the gift of grace it is for me. I will not again be the person you left: a living corpse.

He did not tell Anna what had restored him to life. Maybe she would guess why Ingeborg had left. Michael knew, that despite the transformation he was experiencing, Anna would have to change too, if they were to go on together. Anna would return in two days. He would live again, no matter what would happen, Michael knew. Ingeborg would go home for the time being. He had no idea where all this was leading, but he would live this last day with Ingeborg to the fullest.

## THE REVELATION
### *February 14, 1942*

Already three months since she had come back, Anna noticed. Not easy months! She had not known what to expect, after she had received Michael's letter. When she arrived, although she could see the dark cloak around Michael had lifted, things were not much better, at least not initially. Since Ingeborg had gone home, the two of them had time alone, but she could see Michael was somewhere else. Then Friedel and the boys had come for Christmas. Anna relished being able to talk with her friend, having guests when there was not so much work to be done, celebrating a real Christmas, especially for Erdmuthe's sake.

She had to smile, when she thought of it. How excited the child had been when she saw the candles on the tree all lit up. How slowly and carefully she had opened her gifts. The Christchild — the *Christkind* — who Erdmuthe believed had brought the tree by flying down from the Kruckenbrettl, was part of her daily consciousness now. When Anna picked her up from her playmate Klari's house next door, she would look up at the sky and say "Up there is *Christkindi* and the angels and the moon and the stars!" Her world already included celestial bodies and spiritual beings! How amazing it all was.

Then, two weeks ago, Ingeborg had come back from her Christmas vacation. The day before her return Anna had decided to move out of the bedroom into Erdmuthe's room. She just could not sleep next to such a distant Michael anymore, and it seemed a natural progression since they were discussing their potential separation. Anna felt it was better to make the change before Ingeborg's arrival. This way there would be no fuss.

After Ingeborg's return Anna noticed a new familiarity between her cousin and Michael. There were glances between them and situations that made her wonder; for instance, when Ingeborg slept in the *Stube* because of her cold and Michael would go to his lonely bed long after Anna had gone upstairs. But then she thought, *No, that can't be! If there is something between them, they would tell me.* And she had given Michael ample opportunity to talk when they had discussed their future, together or apart. *No, it simply can't be*, Anna thought again. *They would not be so callous.*

Yes, they had talked about their future, she and Michael. Anna had told him of Felizitas' father's offer of a caretaker job in one of their houses, should she decide to leave. She had asked Michael what he intended to do, in case she and the child left the farm. He'd have to find a new wife, he pointed out "one needs a wife on a farm," and he'd want to have more children. Strangely, they had felt close and intimate, as they talked about this. They were able to talk quietly and at length now, almost as in old times. And they had fewer rows.

Today was Erdmuthe's birthday. She was so excited about her cake, the three candles, the set of blocks from her father, the bracelet from Figa, as she called Friedel, the new book from Ingeborg. The *Nachbarin* brought her an egg and Klari came to play and have hot chocolate, such a treat these days. Erdmuthe was anxious for someone to read her the birthday letters from her grandmother in Silesia and her grandparents in Wasserburg. Michael stayed in all day, read books to her and played with her. How Erdmuthe relished being pampered by everyone, and she deserved it, her mother thought. She had to entertain herself alone often enough while they worked outside. This day was so much better than last year, when she was traveling with Erdmuthe and Michael had been so disappointed they were not home. Such a peaceful day!

Everyone had gone to bed and Anna enjoyed sitting in the *Stube*, thinking about it all. She would turn in too, Anna thought, when she saw it: a letter in Ingeborg's handwriting, sticking out from under Michael's book. It was not her habit to read other people's mail, Anna thought, but she had to look. This would bring her clarity, she knew, and she had a right to know!

She pulled it out. Anna herself had received many a letter from Ingeborg in the past. Her handwriting was pointed and stiff, not soft and flowing. Anna had never liked it. It lacked personality, she thought. But that was beside the point. "My dearest Michael," the letter began. Anna had to force herself to go on reading. Her throat closed, she could hardly get any air. Her heart started racing. The letter spoke of plans for the future, marriage, children, Ingeborg's dowry which could help on the farm, the fear of her parents' disapproval. *My God, things have progressed that far,* Anna gasped. *My God, how could I be so trusting and blind, so stupid!*

After the worst pain was over — she felt as though she was close to a heart attack — Anna grew angry. *How could they!* she thought. Not, how could they do it, that was not surprising, considering the state Michael had been in, considering that she had trustingly left them alone together at a time when they had to work inside. She knew it was partly her fault this opportunity had arisen. But that Michael had not told her! Had not told her when she asked what his plans for the future were, when she had given him the chance to be honest, when she had shared her own thoughts about leaving him and the farm. When they had always been honest with each other, even when he had had an affair shortly after their wedding.

Anna sat there, the letter in her hand, and wanted to scream. Suddenly her whole world had collapsed, her meager hopes that they might salvage their marriage after all, her trust in humanity, her belief in truth and honesty. She was so stunned she could not even cry. She would have to go to Michael and tell him she knew. She could not live with such a pretense, like Michael and Ingeborg had. Now that she knew she would not participate in this ridiculous charade. And she was not going to make it easy for him and simply leave. It was good it was out in the open. It was up to Michael now to make a decision, to decide between her and Ingeborg. She was not going to help him and decide for him. She was going to wait and see what was going to happen, Anna thought grimly. And she knew, this was Michael's Achilles heel: he was incapable of making decisions, at least in regards to their tortuous relationship. If any good could come from this it was that he was now forced to take a stand. She stormed upstairs, then slowed her steps, quietly entered their bedroom which she had deserted two weeks earlier, and woke up Michael.

## ANNA'S TRANSFORMATION
### March 14, 1942

The morning after finding out about Michael's affair Anna had moved back into their joint bedroom. That was four weeks ago, Anna realized. How long and yet how short those weeks had been. Spring was finally on the way after a long and ferocious winter. It had snowed and snowed. Michael had shoveled the meter-high snow off the roof and burrowed tunnels through the drifts behind the house, to Erdmuthe's great joy, for she loved to jump from the top of the "snow fortress." Fortunately they had had enough wood to keep warm. Today a warm *Föhn* wind came down from the mountains and made everyone light-headed, bird song filled the air and carpets of blue hepatica stars covered the forest floor. Michael was on his way to Wasserburg, to see his parents, to deliver their child for a visit to her grandparents, to flee the farm and see a therapist. Anna was finally alone and could think.

*Ingeborg has no guts,* Anna decided. *She does only what is best for* herself*! She can't stand playing second fiddle and that is what it has come to. So she left and lied to Michael that her parents needed her help.* In her mind Anna recapitulated all that had happened during the last few months. How Ingeborg's parents had found out what had occurred here. How they had been furious with their daughter, and yet written a damning letter to Michael, pushing all the responsibility on him and blaming him for having led their innocent, inexperienced child astray! Of course Michael bore the greater part of the guilt — Ingeborg *was* very young, Anna admitted. But, surely she was not that innocent, considering how conniving she had been when it came to deceiving Anna. Ingeborg's mother, Anna's aunt, had dissolved in guilt and apology. Once home, Ingeborg had written that everything was her fault, that she was worthless, that she had ruined her own future and she hoped, not theirs too and that it had all happened for Anna's and Michael's sake. Anna had to laugh out loud at such a ridiculous assertion! She had no idea whether Ingeborg really believed all that or whether her parents had made her feel more guilty than she already felt. She was sure that, thanks to their simplistic interpretation of Christian morals, they did consider their daughter evil and worthless. But that was their problem. Anna had enough to worry about. At any rate, Ingeborg was back home and had broken off contact, at least for now.

Anna's main worry now was the relationship between her and Michael; that she wanted him to be free to make his decision without pressure from her. Michael had said that at this point he felt nothing for either Anna or Ingeborg. That sounded a bit too simple to Anna. Maybe it was simply that he could not decide, that he protected himself from the pain of having to give up or hurt one or the other. Anna wondered whether what Felizitas had written was really true, that Michael was incapable of choosing between the two women and that Anna would have to leave the farm to give him space, to truly set him free, that her very presence at the farm made it impossible for him to decide what to do.

But how could she leave now that they were not fighting anymore? Now that they were living more harmoniously than they had for a long time. Anna felt no urgency now and wanted to wait patiently to see what would happen. She had given up struggling and her main concern now was Michael's happiness. If he could be happier without her, she was willing to give him up. But she thought it would be tragic if she lost him now, when she could finally be the kind of wife Michael had wanted: gentle and pliable, without aggression. She herself was quite amazed about her transformation. She had finally been able to become less selfish, to think more of him than herself. Why hadn't she been able to do that earlier? Maybe now it was too late. Oh, how she missed him! If he only could get some clarity in Wasserburg!

Actually Anna was glad the situation had reached this climax. At least there was movement now, not standstill. And whatever would happen, Anna knew she would survive, that she was the stronger of the two, that she would go on. If only Michael would come out of all of this healthier and happier! If only they could find a way to stay together!

Of course Anna was also scared and had her low moments. She often was near tears. In those situations Erdmuthe was her greatest solace. The child seemed to sense when her mother was distressed. She often came up to her now and said: "Let me give you a hug," and then she would embrace her with all her might. Recently, when Anna had run crying into the library room, she found her daughter standing outside when she came out again. "Is mummy good again?" the child had asked, throwing her arms around her.

Anna remembered how, a few days earlier, she had banished her daughter to the library after Erdmuthe had been naughty. She had told her: "You may come out when you are good again." Anna had waited outside and after a while the child opened the door and said: "I'll be good now."

Erdmuthe was such a loving and sensitive little girl. Anna hoped that the conflict between her and Michael would not dampen her spirit. *God give that she'll remain healthy and happy*, Anna prayed.

# WAR AND PEACE
## Summer 1942

They were in the midst of summer now. Michael loved these long warm days, when he could wear nothing but shorts, when he could work outside all day long, with the sun burning onto his back, when the evenings were mild and the stars shone brightly, when the hayloft was fragrant with fresh hay, when the rye field slowly turned yellow. He sat in the shade, under the pear tree out back, and looked over the valley.

Things were going well, Michael thought, except for the disaster at the beginning of the summer when they had to slaughter their best cow and her two calves. Kussi had been expecting her third set of twin calves and all seemed well until the time for her delivery had come. When Michael realized something was wrong and the first calf was stuck, Anna ran to the neighbors in the middle of the night to summon help. It seemed to take forever for her screaming and knocking to rouse the *Nachbar*. He came running in his nightshirt, reached into the birth canal and his face became more and more furrowed as he tried to turn the calf. In the end, attempting to save the mother cow and her second baby, they had to cut the stuck dead calf to pieces inside the womb. But it was too late. The second calf was dead too, and the mother also succumbed in the end. In the morning three carcasses hung in the courtyard and they had all their hands full to process the meat. It was lucky Mumm had arrived two days before and could help make sausage and can meat. In times like these Michael wished for electricity and refrigeration. But such an expense was impossible amidst war time scarcity. At least, the unexpected supply of meat helped feed the many summer visitors, especially an array of hungry Berliners, among them Anna's friend Friedel and her teenage sons.

Felizitas, too, had come, and had chastised Michael and Anna. How could they be so oblivious of the war and let the events in the rest of the world pass them by. And it was true, Michael thought. They lived unscathed on their mountaintop, wondering about their marriage, while Russian civilians were starving in the Siege of Leningrad and German soldiers were bogged down on the Eastern front.

With increasing food shortages, their farm work was becoming more and more valuable. They could help feed people, and at the same time make money. Anna had made a list of friends and relatives and was sending packages in rotation. She sometimes thought their prices were too high, but their friends had money and were willing to pay. Depending on supplies, she sent everything conceivable: eggs, smoked meat, sausage, butter, apples, potatoes, cabbage, homemade cookies and cake. She was good at packaging, and relished the thankful responses. Shipping materials had become more and more precious. Bottles and boxes, sacks and baskets, string and cartons had to be sent back for re-use. All this meant extra work, but it brought in money.

Aside from added income Anna's food packages provided opportunities for barter. Anna had sent out appeals for items not available to her, such as sewing needles, good soap, and especially film. With increasing war time scarcity, film was particularly difficult to get and Anna was thrilled when she found an unexposed roll in the returned packaging, or when a visitor brought such a treasure.

It was so peaceful here on their mountain one could almost forget war raged elsewhere, were it not for procurement problems of items needed for daily life, or all the death notices of people like the Rippen neighbor. He had been called up in the fall and was dead by Christmas. And almost every letter brought painful news. Anna's former boss had lost three of his four sons in Russia. They had heard from Felizitas about the destruction of the ancient Baltic city of Lübeck the night before Palm Sunday. All its famous churches, historic civic buildings, and old streets with their patrician houses had burned, leaving only one of the city's seven spires standing. "I am ill thinking of it — one of our most beautiful cities gone forever," mourned Felizitas, and Anna had cried reading her letter.

Such news made Mumm, at the farm the second time, very restless. She wondered what was happening in Silesia. "Why don't you stay here?" Anna pleaded. "Who knows how long this war will last? We could use your help and you would be able to see Erdmuthe grow, spend time with her and teach her the names of all the wildflowers." But Mumm could not overcome her sense of duty toward her brother. "I can't leave Paul fending for himself," she said. Anna suggested he come too, even though she knew it would be hard to put up with him. But Mumm knew he would never leave his former parishioners. "I'll have to leave soon," she sighed and kissed her granddaughter.

While their friends in the cities endured hunger and bombings, their days here were calmer than in a long time. Michael had to acknowledge that Anna had mellowed. He felt that the turmoil of the past months over Ingeborg had purified them both and helped them cast out their harshness toward each other. He still did not know what lay ahead. He felt he could not shape the future himself, although he knew they'd have to make a decision eventually. But how could one make any decisions at all in times like these! What was true one day, could be different the next. Who knew when their luck would run out and when he would get drafted? Maybe he should speed things up and volunteer for the front and let fate decide. On the other hand, maybe it was best to do nothing and simply continue with the work as best they could. It did seem to him they had overcome the worst. They were in limbo, but that did not stop them from savoring the new flow of love between them.

# "KAUFTAG": FOURTH ANNIVERSARY
## *October 24, 1942*

Michael sat over the journal. The year before he had failed to write on this day, and since then he had made only one entry, on summer solstice. But he must write, he knew. His annual accounting was a sacred duty. He kept many special calendar dates throughout the year in mind: their birthdays, the day they met, the day they decided to become a pair, the day Anna came to the farm, the day she "abandoned" him — special days strung like a necklace throughout the year, often only noted in his mind, not in the book. But he could not let this day, the day he had bought the farm, pass by without writing. The fact that he had not marked it last year, showed him what state he had been in. Thank God he was past that. He noted that it was important to him to commemorate this day as the *Kauftag*, the day four years ago when he had purchased the farm, rather than the anniversary of Anna's operation and survival two years ago.

What he remembered most when he thought of the year past was the most glorious blossoming of the trees they had experienced thus far, and that he could enjoy their beauty again. Thankfully, no frost had ruined the bounty and the fruit harvest had been abundant, especially for the eating apples. They had sent crates full to Berlin and boxes to their friends, but he had let Anna keep some for themselves too. Karl Korn, Anna's former *Berliner Tageblatt* colleague had just sent them a note of thanks:

> What a celebration the arrival of your fragrant apple package was. What fertile and rich soil, what penetrating sun you

must have in your orchard to produce such glorious fruit. I could not restrain myself and ate them all at once!

Yes, the apple harvest had been spectacular, but the slaughter of the cow and her twins had been their worst loss ever! They had lost pigs and chicken and sheep in the past, but never at once three animals so essential for their stable. You just could never get ahead in this place. If one harvest was good, the next set you back again. It was such a struggle! Sometimes he felt like they were treading water.

And then the long-delayed land transfer tax had come due on top of this disaster and they did not have the money to pay. In desperation Michael decided to ask for help. "I am sure nothing will come of it." he had said to Anna. "But what do we have to lose?" To his surprise the officials at the provincial agricultural department were receptive and listened to him. He guessed they were not used to an enterprising young farmer like him, someone who had come to farming by choice and deliberate training, not by birth. Someone who had innovative ideas and was not stopped by tradition. They likely assumed that the *"Blut und Boden"*[5] back-to-the-land movement with its emphasis of rural values had led them to become farmers. Their efforts could easily be misinterpreted as Nazi ideology put into action. But if that brought them financial aid so be it, Michael thought.

Five days after Michael's visit to the provincial office two men appeared on the farm to investigate. They were sufficiently impressed to cancel the debt and gave them a goodly amount of money for investments, enough for some of the improvements Michael had dreamed of for years. *We can start a silo now, repair the cellar and order a liquid manure fertilizing system*, he rejoiced. Anna and Michael could not believe their good fortune. Maybe things were finally looking up.

But that's not where it ended. "You must apply for a *Neubauernschein*,[6]" the government advisors suggested. "Fill out the application to become a new farmer, a *Neubauer*," they encouraged him, "and we will help you to get assigned to a farm in the East!" So here it was again, the idea of resettlement in some German-occupied territory, the idea that had pursued him from the very beginning, but then been abandoned over relentless daily demands. Now the officials had left forms and instructions for picture taking.

Anna considered the picture taken for their application quite hilarious. They stood behind the house, Michael muscular and bare-chested, a strapping young farmer. Anna wore a *Dirndl*, the traditional folk costume the Nazis loved and Erdmuthe stood between them, blond and erect and straight-faced, holding hands with both of her parents. Weren't they the perfect wholesome "blood and soil" family? Confident and forward-looking! Little Erdmuthe provided the required proof they could have children, a prerequisite for German colonizers.

Filling out the forms and answering all the questions about their heritage required research into ancestral records. It was a good thing he had already completed his *Ahnenpass*, the record of the family tree, Michael thought. It was obvious that pure Aryan heritage was a pre-requisite for their application. Well, if the intent was to Germanize the Eastern territories it was no wonder they wanted good German stock, Michael reasoned. He and Anna avoided talking about this issue.

The most difficult question, by far, was where they would want to settle. Michael was willing to go anywhere where farming would be easier, even to Poland or the Ukraine. But Anna objected. "Let's try Alsace," she suggested. Over the past few years she had written and talked to many friends and acquaintances who had opinions about this matter, or personal experience. And everybody had said:

"Don't go East! There are too many historic barriers, too much hatred accumulated over centuries. Nobody will want you there." The question was, would anybody want them anywhere else? *Well, the wheels are in motion. Who knows where we will be next year,* Michael wondered.

## ALL SOUL'S DAY
*November 2, 1942*

Klara Klauriegler looked with pleasure at the blooming chrysanthemums in her garden. There were bright spiky yellow blossoms, rust-colored blooms shaped like small balls, and white ones that almost looked like daisies. Of course the main purpose of her garden was to provide vegetables and more variety in their diet during the summer months. All the produce had been harvested and for the winter it was back to onions, carrots, potatoes and sauerkraut.

Still, a few flowers did no harm! She did enjoy the cheerful bunches of daffodils in spring and her fragrant heritage roses — little pink balls — in summer. These chrysanthemums were the last splash of color before snow fell and that could be any day now. Klara did not grow these flowers only for her own pleasure, but to adorn the family grave for All Soul's Day. What a climb, she thought, up the steep cemetery to their family grave near the top! A week ago she had pulled the last weeds and made a cover of fir branches for the winter. Today she'd cut the chrysanthemums to brighten the grave before the first snow, and, she would set out and light a candle for all her dead loved ones.

It was good to have a day to remember the dead. Her father-in-law, whom she had taken care of before he died, her parents, and now those who had not returned from the war. She liked to walk through the cemetery, read the inscriptions, the names of neighbors, the families of school mates, all the people she had known in the village and on the surrounding farms who had died. It was a coming and going. New generations began, the old ones slowly vanished. She and Konrad were now at mid-life. They had a new child, and a grandmother still living with them — three generations living under one roof on their own farm, as it should be. But the war was causing havoc, disturbing the order of things. Children lost their fathers, wives their husbands, mothers their sons, and the bodies did not even come home to be buried. She wondered how many of the dead soldiers had graves in far-away Russia. Maybe they were just left to rot in a ditch by the road. Maybe they were left frozen in the snow, or maybe they decayed in some god forsaken swamp. Death notices were now arriving in rapid succession. All one could do was put their names on the gravestones and remember them. Sometimes she just did not understand what the world was coming to. She'd put a vase of flowers on the grave of the Rippen *Nachbar* also, she decided. Almost a year since he was gone! What a shame it all was . . .

Anna was distressed to see her neighbor's flowers cut. Maybe she should plant some chrysanthemums, too, to have a bright spot when everything else was done blooming. Her flower garden edging the vegetable plot was slowly coming along and that made her happy. In spring she had snowdrops, daffodils, hyacinths, and tulips. For the summer she planted cheerful annuals and her mother had sent her dahlia roots. Their magnificent blossoms lasted into the fall. Chrysanthemums were not a bad idea. But she would not cut them. She did not have any grave to tend here anyway.

Anna was saddened that her father's grave and the graves of her grandparents were so far away. She thought of the black crosses cast in iron in the cemetery of Pollnow, her hometown, of the cobblestone market square surrounded by linden trees, of the prominent, majestic Dahle house. Since her mother had been booted out after her father's death in 1922 and Anna had gone to Berlin at age sixteen to support herself, Pollnow was not home anymore. She had gone to Pomerania after her operation, but not to Pollnow where her father lay buried. She had visited Karwen, her uncle's estate, now run by her cousin Werner where she felt more at home. Who knew when she'd be able to visit again.

She liked the steep graveyard here, where the dead looked down onto the village and the church. Michael too thought it was a good place to be buried. But the many soldiers killed were not buried here. Their graves were far away, likely untended. Although, she had seen a grave of two Russian WWI prisoners of war here in the churchyard, and someone was taking care of it. So, who knows . . .

Michael thought mainly of his mother on this day. He thought of the cemetery in Wasserburg and how beautiful it was in the evening, when candles burned on the graves, when people walked quietly on the gravel paths, visiting each other or communicating with their dead loved ones, while trumpets sounded from the church tower. He remembered the old city wall, overgrown with ivy, surrounding the cemetery to make it an intimate, protected place where people felt at home with the living and the dead.

Michael realized that he used to like to be there on All Soul's Day, because it gave him a chance to think of the mother he had not known at all. His father had never talked of her, maybe because of Agnes's jealousy. There were no pictures of her in the house. At one time he had discovered photographs and put them into the family album he had put together before he left Wasserburg for good: pictures of his mother reading, climbing in the Dolomite mountains in long skirts and fancy hats, of his mother as a young lady companion, traveling in Croatia. She seemed a lot more adventurous than his father's second wife, and more educated. Not having known her was a black hole that could never be filled. He would have liked to be in Wasserburg on this day, although he had no desire to see his parents. But it would warm his heart to put flowers on his mother's grave and to go down the list of ancestors engraved on the family crypt.

## MILITARY CALL-UP
### *January 8, 1943*

The Christmas season was over and a new year, the fourth since the start of the war, had begun. Everyone was assembled in the courtyard for the slaughter of the pig, late this year. Michael and Anna had just filled the troth with boiling water and heaved in the dead pig, so the bristles could be scraped, when the mailman arrived. *Here it is,* Anna thought, turning white when she saw the official-looking envelope. Michael ripped open the letter, and said: "Five days, I have to leave in five days." Erdmuthe wondered where her father would be going. "To the soldiers, child, I have to leave and be a soldier now."

It was a bad sign they had begun to draft farmers, Anna thought. The war was not going well on the Eastern front. She had heard that in Russia malnourished and inadequately outfitted German soldiers perished in blizzards and froze to the ground. The Germans had had to give up Moscow and were now desperately fighting to hold Stalingrad. Propaganda at home told of glorious battles and victories, but the truth was leaking through. No one knew how many soldiers died daily, but it was clear the army needed replacements. It was evident the number of men not in war was dwindling. So now they were drafting farmers, Anna thought bitterly.

They forgot to scrape the pig and had to start over when they came to their senses. Anna and Michael had known this day would come, but they had chosen not to think about it. "Damn," said Michael. "Why now, after we have sent in our *Neubauern* application?" He had contemplated what it would be like to get the call and even considered volunteering, so the waiting would be over. But now he was not ready!

Anna was in a daze. There was so much to think about. She had briefly run the farm by herself before, but this was different. Now it would be open-ended. And who knew how long this war would last? At least it was winter when work was less pressing. The work in the woods that Michael usually did around this time of year could wait. Thank God they had enough cut firewood to stay warm, unlike friends who lived in the cities in partly demolished apartments, without windows, and with leaking roofs. And at least it was only training for Michael, not yet the front, Anna reassured herself. Znaim, in German-occupied Czechoslovakia, was not too far from Vienna. Maybe they could meet there, maybe Michael could come home on furlough during sowing and harvest periods.

But she'd definitely need help and with farm hands being drafted, the only help to be had were foreign workers, prisoners of war from the occupied territories, from France, Poland, and the Ukraine, and those people were not easy to work with. After all, they were not volunteers, but placed on farms against their will. At least she spoke French and that had helped with Francois, a Frenchman who had been assigned to work on their farm earlier. He had come from a farm at home and understood the work, even though he had his sensitivities. Speaking with him in his language was against the rules, but Anna knew it made Francois feel less like a prisoner. And it was fun for her to revive her language skills and use her mind. She hoped there was a chance he could be re-assigned to their farm, now that they were short of labor.

They had had their share of foreign workers sent to them for seasonal support in the past. A Ukrainian had been on the farm in 1941 and last year alone three Frenchmen and a young Polish girl. Poor Krishka! Hers was an especially sad case. Of course they had difficulty communicating, but Anna realized right away something was wrong with the girl. It took her a while to figure out where the bed-wetting came from and why she seemed so distressed. It turned out she was only seventeen, had been abducted and raped by German soldiers and now, so far from home, was pregnant. Anna went to the authorities. "This is unacceptable," she said. "This girl has to be sent home!" At first they only laughed at her. "This is war time, lady," the official said. "Forget it." Usually such unwanted babies were forcefully aborted. But Anna persisted, and Krishka was indeed to be sent home, just now, when Michael was leaving too! She'd leave two days before him. Anna almost regretted her fervor to help this girl, now that she would need her so badly. But she did know it was the right thing — at least one good thing she had done in these uncertain times, besides sending all the food packages to friends and family.

It would be hard without Michael, Anna knew. Especially now, after they had had a relatively peaceful time, after Ingeborg was out of the picture. They had had almost none of their nerve-wracking rows. And she had to be grateful she had Erdmuthe, while Michael would be all alone, amidst strangers, getting ready to fight. *Every time things look up, some disaster happens,* Anna thought. *Just when you think you have a little bit of control over your life, things get overturned.*

# ALONE
### *April 2, 1943*

After long days of winter darkness, fog, and drizzly grey weather the days finally lengthened and the warmth of the sun gained strength. Light and shadow played on the hillsides and white clouds floated in a blue sky. Daffodils budded in the garden. The fruit trees worked their annual miracle. Violets opened on embankments, and Anna's spirit lifted, finally, for the first time since Michael had left almost three months earlier.

She felt she had been on a roller coaster ever since his departure. During the day Anna struggled to keep the farm going with the help of her workers. At night she wrote long letters to Michael, asking questions about when to fertilize, how many potatoes to put in, what to do about the pasture fences. Recently she had written him, full of elation: "I bought a good pair of oxen, and the neighbor says at a decent price!" But no praise had come from Michael, no word of recognition, no personal word to her at all. *If only he cared more. If only I knew he was looking forward to our reunion. How much easier it could then be to bear all these responsibilities, to cope here alone,* Anna thought.

But he seemed so far away. When they had met, briefly, in Vienna, she had been unable to reach him. He had been kind and gentle, but so very absent! To combat her loneliness, Anna had begun reading old letters, hers and his, and all the feelings of love had re-awakened. Today was their wedding anniversary, the fifth Anna suddenly realized. How very long ago that seemed! She sat down and wrote Michael how she remembered their wedding day:

It was such a glorious day and we walked so calmly through the meadows toward the little church. And after the ceremony we went so quietly up to your room and you held me so close and warm and tight in your arms. We were very still together, but very close. Later you were sometimes blissfully wild and crazy, but then, on our wedding night, we were like we had been husband and wife for a long time. That's how it was. Oh, if it could be like that again!

No matter how hard she had tried, there had been no echo from Michael to her many loving letters. He had written hardly at all. Anna was afraid this letter would not reach him either.

At least Erdmuthe was a source of consolation. She was so tender! Anna was moved by how the child tried to console her when she was sad. She soaked up her daughter's warmth. And she was grateful for the neighbors, their empathy and their help with tending Erdmuthe when she had to do errands in the village. She was particularly touched how the *Nachbar* had taken her under his wings, how he was teaching her to break in the oxen, for instance. "He is more personal with me, these days," she had written to Michael.

Now that things at the farm were going more smoothly, she was beginning to enjoy her independence. She realized she was more capable than either she or Michael had assumed. She was lonely, but it turned out, she could do this by herself if she had to! After the first few months of trial and error she now felt a sense of pride and accomplishment, even without Michael's praise.

If only this war would end soon! The news, limited as it was, that penetrated to the farm was hard to bear alone, especially the news of Stalingrad. Several hundred thousand Germans had died or surrendered. Two divisions had come from this very region. The boy from the nearby Reitner farm was one of the dead. Francois, their French worker, gloated, convinced this was the beginning of the end.

Anna had enough trouble enduring Michael's emotional distance. Bad news about the war in addition was almost too much! Berlin and Munich had been bombed and lay in rubble. Sometimes Anna felt so utterly desolate she wished for one more good day with Michael and then death. Sometimes she wished she had died after her ectopic pregnancy. But she could not stay with such feelings of despair too long. Earlier today spring had been in the air and she felt the wind in her hair and the sun on her bare arms, and now the stars glittered brightly in a velvet sky! What a blessing that such beauty could still console her.

Michael had not forgotten what day it was. He remembered every detail five years earlier. But how far away all that seemed and how long ago. Anna had sent him so many letters, pleading, longing letters, letters about the past, the farm, their child. Some angry letters too. He wished he could respond, write something meaningful to her, tell her what his life was like here, but he could not. Sometimes he sat there, for a long time, and no matter how hard he tried, he could not get beyond answering the questions about the farm. He knew his silence pained her, and yet he could not do anything about it.

She said she understood how this experience was changing him, how he was entirely engrossed being a soldier, but in reality she had no idea. It wasn't even her fault, since this was such a male world and he had told her so little. When they had met in Vienna, he had felt tender toward her, but afterwards he had wished he had not gone to see her. It was too hard to go back to his troop, to deal with the distance he felt after his absence, his sense of estrangement when he returned to his comrades. He realized he could not switch back and forth between his life in the barracks and his life at home. Trying to encompass both worlds would make his new life more unbearable. He could not understand how others could do it.

*Anna simply expects too much from me,* Michael thought, disgruntled. She needed reassurance and love; she wanted him to think of the past and the future. Could she not see that she could expect absolutely nothing from him in this situation? If only she could understand that he was unable to write the kind of letters she yearned for. If only she could see that he had to concentrate on learning how to shoot, that he had to deal with congestion and lack of privacy, with sixty men sleeping in one room. If only she could understand that there was no quiet here to think.

Only when he had a chance to explore the town he felt within himself. The medieval city of Znaim was beautiful. The steep embankment of the river reminded him of Wasserburg, his hometown, built into the loop of the Inn river. Znaim had a mighty fortress and the steep Gothic roof of St. Nicholas Cathedral rose high above the houses of the city. The handsome market square of this Moravian town looked like many places in the former Austro-Hungarian monarchy, generous and comfortable. Michael felt almost at home walking in the narrow lanes, amidst the walls of these historic buildings.

In ten days he would go home, on leave, to help with the sowing, to see his wife and child. He knew he should be happy, but he was anxious and dreaded it. Once he was settled somewhere he did not like change, he noticed, and he realized he was beginning to settle into this new life of a soldier. Anna thought he was throwing himself into soldiering so he could prove himself amidst all the uncertainty of their personal lives, but he had learned he could simply not live two lives at once, and this was the one he was living now.

For the first time in many years, maybe since the hectic days when they had rebuilt the house after the fire, the *Oberhias* felt stressed. He did not know where to start. His help was needed at both neighboring farms. The Rippen *Nachbarin* had first lost her husband, and now her farmhand Karl had left for the front. Since his departure she seemed entirely lost and expected his help for everything! And being a neighbor had its obligations — he simply could not let her fend for herself. This meant that sometimes their own work did not get done on time. "You always think of others first," Klara had grumbled yesterday. "What about us!"

And the *Nachbarin* next door! She was so brave and she was trying to manage with her foreign workers as best she could. But it was not easy. These people were overly sensitive! Even though she spoke French with Franz, he did not seem to realize how lucky he was. Instead he gave her a hard time and threatened to leave, just because she had said that he would not get his evening meal before five-thirty. The gall this man had! Although he had to grant him that he was a good worker. Just moody. But that was trying enough for the *Nachbarin* who had so much on her hands.

*What will become of all these farms, if the men don't come home? And how much longer will this war go on?* Konrad wondered. As it was, the government requisitions of butter, eggs, meat and other agricultural products had risen constantly. How much more could they give? True, they were lucky to have food and did not have to worry about being hungry. But it seemed that besides feeding themselves and the nation nothing else was left these days. And now he had to work for the neighboring farms in addition to his own!

Although, he had to admit, he liked helping the *Nachbarin*. She was spunky. And how could she possibly break in the oxen on her own? This work was too dangerous for someone like the Frenchman who was used to horses and did not know enough about oxen. And if something happened to her workers, the *Nachbarin* would get into trouble. These people were prisoners, but you had to be careful how you treated them. They could be quite uppity, especially the Poles. The new Polish girl over there had given the *Nachbarin* enough trouble already, and now she had run away! It was a crying shame, the husband drafted and then all this trouble with foreign workers. The least he could do was to help wherever he could. It was touching how grateful the *Nachbarin* was. And she did her share to help whenever there was a chance, especially when they needed anything written on a typewriter. She knew what was going on in the world and told them about the latest catastrophes. They had gotten the news about Stalingrad from her, and about the bombings of Munich and Berlin. All these people living amidst rubble. *Sometimes it would be better to know less*, the *Oberhias* thought, *to go about your work as best you can and not worry about anything else. But that is difficult these days when your neighbors get drafted and maybe killed.*

## A FULL LIFE
### *May 14, 1943*

Anton Dempf sat in his paneled *Stube* with the bull's-eye glass window, the carved chandelier above the table and the grandfather clock with its loud tick and sonorous chime. He breathed in the rich fragrance of his morning coffee and considered himself lucky he could still enjoy such a luxury, thanks to his business connections. He wore the clothes he always did: leather knickers and a Bavarian *Janker*, the traditional jacket people here had worn for centuries. He felt most comfortable and well-dressed in this Bavarian garb and saw no reason to own a suit. This morning he granted himself an hour of peace and quiet before his busy day ahead.

In two days he would celebrate his wedding anniversary, already the 29th. How the years raced by! The trauma of his younger days, the death of his first wife, the war in which he had served the last two years, from 1916 to the end, the hardship years of inflation, all that seemed long ago. Now, at sixty-seven, his life had reached a calm routine. His health had stabilized and his work was satisfying.

The printing presses on the ground floor of his large house put out the daily gazette, the *Wasserburger Anzeiger*, and small publications — a monthly history magazine and regional brochures and pamphlets. That gave him the opportunity to publish his essays on local history and folklore and to print photographs which he developed in his own darkroom. He enjoyed researching the history of his town and the surrounding area and roaming the countryside in search of items for *Heimathaus*, the local folk art museum he had helped found. Only yesterday he had picked up a beautifully painted chest at a nearby farm for the extensive peasant furniture collection he had assembled. He was happy that the study of folklore, and thus his own work, was receiving new impetus and appreciation these days, that folk and fatherland were valued again. He looked forward to the tour he was to give this afternoon to two soldiers, home on leave. Nothing gave him more pleasure than such a guided tour to highlight the museum's treasures. He had long tried to foster understanding for folk art, especially in young people, and he appreciated the interest of these soldiers.

Yes, life here was full, although new worries had now replaced the ones of the past. There was a possibility his press might be closed, as many already had, to melt the metal of the machines for weapons. At least his daughter, Lily, was finally settled and had married into a well-to-do Munich family of hoteliers. They owned a large hotel near the train station and he needed to worry no longer about her future. But the lives of his sons were endangered. Lutz was in the army and who knows where he'd be sent to fight next. True, a lucky star seemed to guide his life and his carefree spirit seemed to protect him. He had come back from the invasion of Poland unscathed, and had escaped Stalingrad by getting seriously ill and being sent home to a military hospital to recover while his troop was entrenched in Russia. Maybe he'd wiggle his way through the dangers of this war.

He was more worried about Michael, who had a wife, a child and a farm to attend to. Their relationship had been difficult for many years. He had struggled against his son's life plan, but recently he had become reconciled to Michael's unconventional ways and had relinquished his own expectations and resentments. He was happy he had reached an understanding that as a father he simply needed to support him. He had had such difficulties reaching Michael's heart. But today it seemed easy. *Maybe I should write him a letter and tell him:* "Son, I love you and I only want your happiness. If we don't agree on the path to reach it, that should not divide us." *Yes, I will write him today,* Anton decided. Michael probably could use a boost during his military training, not knowing where this war would take him.

This war! Lately it seemed the German war effort had reached a stalemate. He had felt so uplifted by the Führer's vision for Germany, by the economic surge his country had experienced and all the military victories. But now the news was worrisome and he looked with greater skepticism at the photographs of his Führer gracing their rooms.

He prayed nothing serious would happen to upset Agnes. His wife had a tendency to get unhinged easily. If a path did not run perfectly straight, it turned into a frightening thicket for her. If the sun did not shine she experienced life as a dark storm. She simply could not deal with the vagaries of existence. Thus he kept his worries to himself.

He hid his fears, his occasional lack of courage, his physical fatigue. He believed he always needed to appear cheerful and optimistic. Sometimes he felt a need for comforting consolation himself. But he could not turn to his wife for that. He was glad for the friendship with Otto Geigenberger, the painter, whom he visited daily around noon. He could talk about his concerns and worries with him.

But, for now he would put his worries aside. After all, he had Erdmuthe's visit to look forward to. He had not seen his granddaughter since the fall. In January, when she was scheduled to visit to help celebrate his birthday, her father's military call-up had interfered. But now she was coming. Lily would pick her up and bring her on Sunday. She'd be here for the wedding anniversary celebrations. He could not wait. She was such a bright spot in his life, his greatest joy these days, such a source of happiness. He'd take her to the river to build sand castles; he'd read bedtime stories to her; he'd let her sit on his lap to play *"Hoppa hoppa Reiter!"*, the bumpety-bump rider game. He'd listen to her stories of her life on the farm. They'd go on walks together and he'd take her to the museum. He was sure he'd find things there she'd enjoy — looking at the wax figurines she knew from home or a painted crib or cradle. And he would take photos of her and develop and print them. He knew Anna would be happy if her daughter came home with new pictures. Anna was not the kind of daughter-in-law he had hoped for. But she had given them this grandchild! *In two days Erdmuthe will be here!* The clock chimed and he had not noticed how many times, since he had started to reminisce. *A full day of activities ahead,* he thought. *I better get going.*

It was already seven o'clock, when Anton returned from the museum. *He looks tired,* Agnes thought when the two of them sat down for their supper of blood sausage and meatloaf. "Let's drink a beer," Agnes suggested, hoping it would relax him. Anton had seemed anxious during the day and had experienced trouble with his eyesight.

They went to bed early and Anton decided not to read, as was his habit, to give his eyes a rest. At 1:30 Agnes awoke, roused by Anton's pacing. He was short of breath and when he had a coughing fit, Agnes called the doctor who came quickly and gave him an injection to speed his heart beat. But Anton became unconscious soon thereafter and his blood pressure fell precariously. The doctor suggested she call the priest and at 2:45 Anton was pronounced dead.

He had died, as he had wished, unexpectedly and out of the fullness of his life. He left behind an uncomprehending wife, a heartbroken daughter, a stunned granddaughter, a shocked community and two sons called home from military duty. Michael, who had the task of taking care of funeral and inheritance matters, regretted his father, always a humble person, had stipulated there be no eulogy. He would have liked to do his father the honor, especially after he read the still unmailed heartfelt letter he had written to him on his last day on this earth. Anna came to the funeral, more than anything to see her husband. She did not bring Erdmuthe, thinking that would lessen her sorrow over losing her grandfather. Left behind with the neighbors Erdmuthe grieved. She could not understand why she now was unable to visit in Wasserburg for the second time, and why she could not see her father, who she knew was there. Only when she visited Wasserburg later during that summer and her grandmother pointed out her grandfather's name on the family crypt, did she understand that her Wasserburg visits would not be the same from now on.

# HARVEST LEAVE
## August 14-18, 1943

While one German city after another sank into rubble, Anna endured endless rain and the discontent of her workers. When she thought of Michael, she wavered between hope and despair, while Michael stubbornly concentrated on learning how to become a good soldier. Their few and brief meetings, on the farm and elsewhere, began in love and ended in pain. It seemed they had reached a stalemate in their struggle, when unexpectedly to them both, a correspondence began which made them listen to each other and open their hearts again.

They wrote honestly about everything: their bliss in the past and the pain they had inflicted on each other since they had come to the farm; the meaning of their child in whom they saw their best handed on into the future; the desire to have a son; whether they would stay together or not; the meaning of the affair with Ingeborg which restored Michael's will to live; the bond between them that they believed could never be torn, no matter what would happen; and Michael's wish to re-establish communication with Ingeborg.

Over all this lay the shadow of a war which might decide matters without their doing. But Anna did not believe the war would determine their future and wrote to Michael:

> Never, never did I think that fate should relieve us of making a decision. My greatest wish is that you could come back to me freely, joyfully and with hope and love. If I have to lose you because that is what you decide, I will cope with that. I know you will not leave us needlessly, and only if you see no other way. But you can't die like this! How could I ever live happily again? We simply are not finished with each other.

Thus they waited for Michael's two-week harvest leave in August with longing hearts and renewed hope. To the delight of his daughter who had been making preparations to celebrate, Michael arrived three days before his birthday. During their courtship, they had celebrated that day taking in the exuberance of baroque Bavarian monasteries, or romping in the dunes of Spikeroog Island in the North Sea, places of natural beauty or exquisite architecture which nourished their souls.

Now they would celebrate here, in this beautiful place, their home, away from the chaos of war, together with their much loved daughter who cheered them both. In spring Erdmuthe had picked pink pearly everlastings on the hillside above the farm and Anna had made a birthday wreath from them for Michael. "A very small one," according to Erdmuthe's instructions, so he would be able to take it with him to wherever he might have to go to fight. And, as in peace time, Anna made her mother's pound cake, which Michael loved and, although the day fell on a Tuesday, they did only the work that was absolutely necessary: feeding and milking the cows.

They had set the day aside for a walk up the hill to look down into the valley and far into the mountains, to relish the height of summer and breathe the fragrance of the wildflowers and herbs. Before she went to bed, Erdmuthe thanked God for bringing home her *Vaterle*, as she affectionately called her father. After the child was asleep, Anna and Michael continued the dialogue they had begun in their July correspondence. In order to soothe their injured hearts and not inflict more pain, they avoided the issue of their possible separation and concentrated on their desire for another child. Anna had received fertility shots and their open and intimate letters had made their bodies and minds receptive to each other. After the long dearth of the past months, and their current willingness to consider the needs of the other more than their own, they were more ready for loving each other than they had been for years.

In Michael's arms, Anna forgot all her tears and anger. All she wanted was to make him happy, without consideration of the future, to feel his strong body, to be one with him, to be the undemanding wife he desired. It seemed easy now and she could not understand why she had been so harsh and stubborn during the past few years. Michael was gentle with her and giving, and it seemed to Anna that serving in the army had strengthened his wounded self-confidence. Even though the front was awaiting him and their future together seemed uncertain, they were happier than they had been in a long time. It was not the shining happiness of the early days — melancholy surrounded them both — but it was happiness, nonetheless.

They loved each other, not with total abandon, but in hopes for another child. Michael said he wanted a child, whether or not they would separate, so he would always have a part of Anna, and Anna was willing to let him take this child — they envisioned it would be a son — with him into his new life, whatever that might be. This child, Michael thought, would be different from Erdmuthe, who he felt was the pure and harmonious combination of them both in happier times, without the grief they had experienced later. "Anna," Michael said, "*this* child will be a symbol of reconciliation, a proof of the vitality of our relationship, evidence of our strength, not our weakness!" He felt he could now give the kind of strength to this child that he had lacked in the past.

Anna wanted this child too, but she sometimes wished for the fate of her favorite painter Paula Becker Moderson, who had left her husband, then returned to him and died at thirty-one, after the birth of their child. "Maybe that would be best," Anna said, "to be once again truly happy with you, to bear you a son in the midst of this happiness, and then to die, to leave this bliss, forever. But I would not want to be aware I would die, for the farewell from the children would be too painful, even harder than saying goodbye to you."

Michael too felt a sense of mortality. He said it would be easy to leave and fall in battle, and yet the fact that their time together might be measured made these days with Anna particularly precious. He was grateful that the new life force that carried him now did not solely derive from Ingeborg, but included Anna and received nourishment and strength from her as well.

For Anna things were simple. She wanted to be with Michael to the fullest and not worry about the future, whatever it might bring. She knew she wanted to share her life with him, even if it might mean pain. But she wanted him to feel free to decide, and thought she was ready to accept whatever he needed to do. She wanted him to be able to go to the front as securely as possible, unburdened by any expectations on her part.

Michael's situation was more complicated. He felt torn and unsure about a future with Anna. He still thought something was missing, despite the intensity and closeness they currently experienced. But he could not define what that something was. He did know he wanted to contact Ingeborg after this leave. Whether he would be able to see her, what would come of it if he did, remained to be seen. After a year and a half without communication he needed to find out where things were with her and him. And yet, he said: "How could I leave Erdmuthe? How could I survive, Anna, if one day your arms were not open for me anymore? I could not bear that."

Such were Michael's conflicted concerns amidst the harvest and farm work. But nothing lessened his joy over Erdmuthe, who was determined to spend every available moment with her father. She showed him everything she had learned or acquired during his absence. Michael had unrealistic expectations for his four-and-a-half year old daughter: He expected her to be able to count in tens. He wished she would draw better, but he did appreciate her stories of her time spent with Klari at the neighbors.

The little family had two weeks, two short weeks of work and play and love, before Michael would return to his garrison and prepare for the front. He had decided to volunteer to fight in Russia. Erdmuthe could not understand why. "Why are you going to the Russians?" she asked. "Why, if they are shooting at you?" Was it because he could not decide what to do, Anna wondered. She could not imagine that he might not come home from the war. She had written him already in July:

> I do believe, with great certainty that you will return from this war. I believe that life lets go of one only if one has lived it to completion. And your life has not only been unfulfilled, you don't even see the path yet. You won't die in uncertainty, without clarity, I am convinced of that. I am thinking so very much of the fact that you will soon be going to battle. For the first time this happening takes on reality for me, with all the hardship, endangerment and toil it means for you. And still, I continue to believe you will come back. And you must believe it too. Death is a strange phenomenon. One cannot bring it closer or hold it back. You will return in order to fulfill your life, and also because I have to drain this bitter cup.

Anna firmly believed that Michael would be protected, as long as they were not finished with each other. And after their bright August days she believed the tide was turning in her favor. Thus, to her own surprise, she was not perturbed that Michael intended to see Ingeborg. Seeing him go off was painful. But she was buoyed by two weeks of joy and the hope that she was carrying another child.

# ORION
## *Christmas 1943*

Erdmuthe cried bitterly after her father left. But she had a gift of including him in her daily activities, whether he was physically present or not. "I have to tell that to *Vaterle*," she would say frequently, when something happened she wanted to share with him. Or: "I have to show this to *Vaterle* when he comes," setting aside a pretty feather she had found, or a stone. She asked her mother to write him every detail about her illness, how her throat hurt, what nightgown she was wearing, that she was sleeping in the warm *Stube*. And she was unshaken in her faith that he would come back for Christmas, especially after she found out about Orion.

A soldier friend of Anna's had sent her a poem about Orion he had written for his son:

> Orion hoch am Himmel stand
> Den Gürtel um die Hüfte wand.
> Drei Sterne sind der Gürtel sein,
> Die leuchten hell in klarem Schein.
> Mein Kind, wo wird Orion stehn
> Von deinem Fenster aus zu sehn?

(I see Orion high in the sky. He winds his belt around his waist. It is made of three stars. They shine brightly. My child, where do you see Orion, looking out your window?)

When Anna read the poem to Erdmuthe, the child was entranced. She wanted Anna to show her Orion and she learned the poem by heart for her father. She was full of excitement after she had seen the constellation. "Is it all right to ask God to send *Vaterle* home for

Christmas, so I can show him Orion?" she asked her mother and from then on she pleaded with God every night to bring her father back for Christmas. When indeed he appeared on the night of December 23rd and looked in on her, Erdmuthe woke up and sleepily started to recite the poem. "God made it come true," she said, and went back to sleep.

On December 24th Michael and Anna did no farm work. Michael read the forest fire book to Erdmuthe and the book about Herr Urian who traveled the world. Then he went to the woods and came back with a pretty little spruce tree. "The best I could find," he said, "not crooked like our first tree here." Erdmuthe waited anxiously in the kitchen trying to play with the blocks her father had made for her the year before, while her parents helped the *Christkind* set up the tree. When the bell rang she stood in the entry door, overwhelmed with all the candle lights. Then she took her father's hand and walked inside.

They had a sweet Christmas Eve, the three of them. The stars were out and Erdmuthe and her father together found Orion in the sky. "Wherever I will be," he said to her, "I'll be with you when you look at Orion. Even if you can't see me, I'll be here with you, don't forget that."

On Christmas Day it snowed. Flakes fell softly and landed like feathers on Michael's military cap. Anna took a picture of him and Erdmuthe looking over the fence. Erdmuthe wore her checkered woolen dress with the lace color and looked sheepishly at her father. She knew he'd be leaving now. "Don't be sad," she said. "I will be with you when you look at Orion. We will be together."

And then Michael was gone, walking down the mountain, to see Ingeborg before embarking on his journey to the Russian front.

Anna had tried not to put expectations on Michael. She had let him know that although she wished for a life with him after the war, she would be able to go on, should he decide to leave her. That she would be able to find meaning in life without him, if for no other reason than taking care of their daughter. She wanted him to go out into this war unburdened by any responsibility toward her. But she also wanted him to know there was a home for him to come back to, if that was his choice.

Despite the pain of the farewell, Anna was calm and full of hope. She and Michael had had a blissful day. The August weeks had not brought them their desired child. But it was not too late. Maybe next month her blood would not flow. Maybe this time new life would be growing inside her. What consolation that would mean, while he was out there fighting. But of this she was sure: he would come back to fulfill his life plan. Hopefully he would come back to her and their daughter. *He will return,* she told herself, *and one day this period of testing will be over.* She felt everything was in God's hands and nothing coincidental could happen from now on.

## LETTERS
### January - April, 1944

In early January Anna sat down and wrote to Ingeborg's parents in Koeslin. They had been upset and anxious about the renewed contact between their daughter and their niece's husband. "Don't worry," Anna wrote. "After the good time Michael and I spent together in August and at Christmas, I am convinced, that he will come back to me and that he will realize Ingeborg would not really make him happy."

When her parents showed Anna's letter to Ingeborg, not long after she had seen Michael, she was speechless. It was complicated enough to carry on a correspondence in the midst of war, when letters got lost, when soldiers got transferred and mail never caught up with them. It was distressing enough that, thanks to her own carelessness, her parents had found out that she was back in touch with Michael and they were trying to interfere in her life, again. And now this!

She had been so happy when Michael had written to her last fall, after the long silence. She was almost in disbelief that he wanted to see her before going out into the war, to see whether they had a chance to make a life together after all. He had come twice, each time after spending time with Anna and Erdmuthe. But he had come, and he had given more days to her than to them! They had loved each other and spoken again of the possibility of joining their lives after the war. Everything had been better than the first time. She was older, more confident about a future with him, and he was more self-assured. But they both knew nothing could happen until the war was finished. If only this war would end so they could go on with their lives!

Since his visit after Christmas she had had only one letter from Michael, and now this! She found herself reading Anna's letter again and again. How could Anna feel so sure Michael would return to her after the war? It all sounded so different from what Michael had made her believe. Was he playing a double game?

*This is it,* she decided. *I will write one more letter to Michael and then no more.* Not because her parents wanted her to break off the relationship. No. She would tell him she would be there for him once he had left Anna for good, but not before. She realized being out of touch would be hard, but she could not write to Michael when he seemed so ambivalent. At least she was not yet pregnant, she thought gratefully. And then her anger and dismay gave way to tears.

Anna tried to run the farm with the help of her foreign workers, Vicek, the gentle young Pole, and Kathi from the Ukraine, who was feisty and rebellious. Anna was grateful the work was less pressing in winter and left her time to read fairy tales to Erdmuthe. But mostly she lived through letters.

In the past she had had to wait till evening to read her mail, so as not to interrupt her work. But now that Michael was not there to stop her from reading letters when they arrived, she ripped them open as soon as she held them in her hands and read them on the spot. At night, by the light of the kerosene lamp, she re-read them, answered and filed them. After Michael's departure she had dug out the many folders of their correspondence. She could quickly locate specific letters and knew many almost by heart. Now alone, letters, not only from Michael, but from others as well, had become an essential life-line, she realized.

Every day she waited for the mailman. Would there be a letter from Michael? Would she hear from Friedel or Felizitas? Who would be bombed out in the cities, who would be killed in action? Would her mother and Uncle Paul in Silesia have enough to eat? Was her sister Hilde still alive amidst the rubble in Berlin? The news most of these letters held was terrible. Still, Anna was almost addicted to receiving mail. She needed to know what was happening to her loved ones. Letters told her what her friends were experiencing, how the war was progressing, who was dead or alive.

There were also rare letters from soldiers, letters relating what they went through. In one letter Michael's sister Lily described her experience in Munich with Lutz, their half-brother, while on home leave:

He was completely churned up inside, destroyed . . . His joy about being home was intermingled with the impressions of the war and he was shaking with sobs. The whole evening he was haunted with what he had experienced. He pulled me close and did not want to go to sleep, because, he said, a bed was much too clean and special for him. I had to sit by his side for a long time and he said, beaming with joy, how much he was looking forward to returning home, and how he felt like a prince in this bed, and then he broke down crying again. The next morning he went to Wassserburg and there he pulled himself together so that mother had no idea what was going on inside. I can't tell you how much this all tore at my heart.

Anna found dealing alone with all the war news painful. There was news of the houses of close friends totally burnt out, houses in which she had spent time in the past. In Leipzig 80 percent of the book business was destroyed; Berlin lay in ruins; Frankfurt was being bombed. Her friend Miechen's husband was in a prisoner-of-war camp in Algeria. Hans Haecker, who had written the Orion poem, missing for months, was finally discovered in captivity in Egypt.

Anna did not know where Michael was. She was yearning to hear what his life at the front was like, what he was thinking about her and about Ingeborg. She felt suspended, living in the past or the future, rather than in the present. "I am waiting, waiting like every soldier's wife," she wrote to Michael, "and in addition I am waiting to see what will happen to us." Contemplating the possibilities had seemed easy when they were together. Now it was excruciating.

Anna had had two thoughtful letters from Michael, one written on New Year's Eve, the other on New Year's Day, special days for them both. "The Macedonian mountains here shine white, just as the ones at home do," he had written. "The war seems far away."

They had been kind and reflective letters, but now — and it was mid-January — she had had no news for a week. Why wasn't he writing? Maybe she was ungrateful, but she was getting impatient and was torn between worry and annoyance. She had written fourteen letters since his departure on Christmas day and longed for a reply, finding it difficult to muster patience. Anna did find solace in the thought that Michael would always be part of her life, no matter what their decision would be. "I am so full of life and happiness," she wrote to him. "The deepest reason, I think, is that since Christmas I know I can't lose you, or you me, no matter what will happen." Anna knew her friend Felizitas could not understand how she and Michael could still be so engrossed in their personal lives. She had written:

> Thinking of all that is happening in the cities, it seems rather ridiculous that people complicate their personal lives, just because 'something' is missing. My God, Michael needs to experience the true harshness of life, he has to realize that the main thing that counts now, is to get through these times halfway decently and responsibly and that everything else is of lesser importance.

Anna could understand Felizitas' view. Her husband had died of lymphoma before the war even began and she did not have to worry about losing him. Maybe it was true that they were still living too much in their own little world, Anna acknowledged. But Felizitas could rest assured, Michael would be getting his reality check at the front. Anna was convinced of that.

After much waiting, a letter came from Michael from somewhere in the Balkans. "It is so peaceful here that one could have the impression of being on vacation," he wrote. There was not enough to do and he longed to be in Russia. He too was waiting for mail. Of the numerous letters Anna had written since Michael's departure, he had received only one.

Even though she knew it was unfair, without the desired resonance from Michael, Anna could not continue writing such loving letters. Thus she began telling him about the frustrations and progress of the work on the farm and about the sweetness of their daughter. And how the war was getting closer to their mountain:

> Our peace is now gone! Vicek was assigned to carry food to the Grünburger Hütte, where soldiers on skis are stationed. The weapons factory in Steyr has been bombed and 1000 people have died. You know that is only 20 kilometers away! And during a foggy air raid bombs were dropped too early and 72 farms were hit in the neighboring Enns valley. If they had flown over us it could have happened here . . .

Michael wrote more to Erdmuthe than to her, Anna noticed and felt jealous. He was angry with her about the letter she had written to Köslin. *Why did you have to interfere?* he wondered. Mostly, he restricted himself to brief, impersonal notes. As winter ebbed, after months of longing, Anna was beginning to get worn down by bitterness, jealousy and hurt. "I just can't hold on any more. I feel so sad and lost," Anna wrote on their wedding anniversary in early April. "You leave my poor heart naked and alone, freezing, cold and deprived."

Anna had expected Michael might come home on leave at Easter. She and her helpers had prepared for his arrival and even whitewashed the hallways. But Michael had not come. Instead, she learned, he had arrived somewhere on the Eastern front. In hopes he would receive her mail there, she wrote:

> It now seems you have reached your goal. If it can bring you what you desire, your inner stability, then I'll be glad for it. I do know you are in serious danger now, but I am not fearful for you and do hope you will return whole. And maybe you'll return changed. I have stopped brooding about the future. I am here, if you need me and it is good, also for you, that I have distanced myself from the past and now feel freed from it . . .

Erdmuthe too was waiting for letters from her father that spring of 1944. She was proud when the mailman gave her a letter addressed and written just to her and she realized there were many more letters for her than her mother. Sometimes she had to console her mother. She would say: "You'll get a letter next time, I am sure." But then the next letter was for her again and her mother cried.

Erdmuthe was fascinated with these letters. They were written on forms that said *Feldpost* and had a special identification number for her father. They had military postmarks, Hitler stamps, secret codes with eagles and swastikas. They came from strange places, places far away, said her mother, from countries called Albania, Croatia and Hungary and magic places with names like Lumi Smoktina. Some were long letters, others brief notes or postcards. Her father wrote them in careful printing, so she could try to read them. She quickly learned the alphabet and was trying to write letters back, but often she got frustrated and her efforts ended in tears.

The greeting for her birthday was written in large letters: "I hurt my hand," her father wrote, "and can't write well. I remember so well how you tumbled into this world five years ago. You were red like a lobster then and not as pretty as today." Two letters were written on pre-printed stationery: one had images of Christmas garlands with candles, gingerbread men and stars, and the other, amazingly, apples and pears larger than the soldiers who were trying to eat them. Her father said the few apples they got were not big like those on the stationery. "I hope you'll have many apples this year and that some will be a large as the ones on the picture. Oh, when there will be as many blossoms on the trees, as there is now snow, that will be beautiful!"

Sometimes Erdmuthe's father made his own drawings for her: A mountain landscape with a dot and the explanation: "We drove deep into these mountains and are now where the dot is," or a drawing of Hungarian oxen with long horns: "They are so long they would not fit through the door of our stable!" And he sent narrow eucalyptus leaves and told her about the bitter fruit of the olive tree.

Erdmuthe's *Vaterle* asked many questions: "Are you going barefoot yet?" or "Has the calf been born?" "Do you have enough snow for sledding and are you spending time with your friend Klari?" "What are your dolls doing?" "Has *Mutterle* bought lambs already, and rabbits?" "How is your dog?" "Are the little pigs growing well?" "Have you found primroses yet?" "Has *Mutterle* shown you the Big Dipper in the sky?" "Has *Mutterle* put eggs under the hens yet?"

Her father also told her many things about the places where he was: What the people looked like and what clothes they wore, how women knit while riding donkeys and that people carried big bundles of wood on their backs. He told her how much nicer it was at home, and that where he was one had to boil the water before drinking it, and that it had to be pulled up from a deep well, instead of coming out of a faucet. That the rivers were not green like hers and the grass not as thick.

And he told her what it was like to be in a war. How cold and wet it was, how muddy and uncomfortable. How the soldiers had itchy lice on their bodies, worse than hers on her head, and how they lived in underground houses called bunkers, or pointed huts of cloth called tents. How the air pressure blew out the candles when there was shooting and how you had to open your mouth, so your ears would not hurt. He described for her what it was like in some of the villages: "There are small horses, but many are dead and have stopped running around. Almost all the people in the village have left. Only the chickens remain and the soldiers are eating those."

In the midst of such misery, he found beauty. He described a cute donkey he had seen that he would have liked to bring her. "He had really thick fur and his black mouth peeked out from under it." And he told her spring was coming too where he was: "Yesterday was a beautiful warm day and I heard a lark sing for the first time. And I saw two yellow brimstone butterflies."

He talked about all the things they would do together when he came home: "When I come home we'll go swimming together." "When I come home we'll have to look at Orion. I always think of you when I see his three stars." "I can't wait to see how surprised you will be when I come home." "Do you think our dog will recognize me?" and Erdmuthe thought of so many things she wanted to show and tell him. It was hard to write about it all and she hoped she'd remember everything until then. Meanwhile she put his letters into a folder her mother had given her for her birthday and practiced reading, going over the old letters when no new ones came, just like her mother.

Their correspondence had been out of sync ever since he had left, Michael concluded. He had not received the many letters Anna had supposedly written. Anna had started to number her letters, so he could see what reached him and what was outstanding. He knew it was not her fault if he had no mail, but he was disgruntled nonetheless.

"Our problems, yours and mine, seem very distant here," he wrote to her. "The circumstances are against us." Or: "I don't know what I can write from here. If only I was in Russia." Quickly his soldier life took over: "I am very sick of fleas. Please, send Lysol." "I have a horrible boil on my hand and can hardly write." "It looks like we will leave from here again. I doubt mail will be forwarded." In three months he had only received three letters. Then, at the end of March he was finally moving toward his destination. Coming from the Balkans, he was on his way East, toward Russia. His train was rolling through Vienna. He was so close to home, and yet so far. He wrote to Anna about his contradictory feelings:

The sleeping men next to me, the eight horses left and right, the clatter of the train and the total darkness dampen my mood. Everything seems far away. Still, you must not think I am unhappy alone. I am now more content and self-assured than most, because I have no illusions. I am less vulnerable because I have not much to lose . . .

Deep inside he knew that was not really true, that in the end he had much to lose indeed: Anna, his daughter, Ingeborg, his very life. So he added: "Still, I don't think what we had, something so inescapable and essential, can be taken away by external events." Maybe, he thought, he was trying to punish Anna because he was angry at her for the letter she had written to Ingeborg's parents. Thanks to this letter Ingeborg had stopped writing to him and Michael was furious. *Things are difficult enough for all of us, as it is. Why did Anna have to interfere in this unresolved situation? Why could she not wait to see how things would play themselves out?* Michael asked himself. On the other hand, maybe Anna's interference was minor, compared to the impact the war was having on their situation.

On the 17th of April, the seventh anniversary of the day Anna had arrived in Bavaria, a day he felt was as important in their relationship as their wedding day, he wrote to Anna how powerless he felt in these times:

Seven years ago today you came to Bavaria. How many hurdles were put in our path then. You were so courageous, and even though I made your life difficult, everything was so unconditional. Why could it not remain so? Ach, Anna, seven years. What will the next seven bring? I find it so difficult to write to you, maybe because everything is now suspended, maybe because I feel that I have no influence on what will happen, that things happen without my doing. One player that has been added in all this is the WAR . . . Now the troubled waters of these times carry me. I am in their grip and I can't fight against that tide.

146

# CRESCENDO
## *April 17 - 27, 1944*

Michael stood at the shores of the Dniester River and gazed into the water for a long time. The water of this mighty river that flowed from the Carpathian Mountains to the Black Sea was high and milky green from melting snow. *What a great river,* Michael thought. It seemed to him that all the strands of his life were suddenly coming together, here on the shores of this great stream, here at the place where the Russians and Germans would face each other in battle, here in Russia where he had longed to be. Up to now he had felt that he had no influence on what might happen in these uncertain times. But the more he thought about it, there was one thing he could do. He had to write a letter to Ingeborg's mother in Köslin. He had been meaning to write it for the past two years. Now he knew he could not postpone it any longer. Anna had done her part to insert herself into the situation, and now he had to set things straight and protect Ingeborg, no matter whether she was communicating with him or not.

Michael felt he had finally arrived where he belonged. His ambivalence and indecision seemed to have vanished. Everything seemed so much clearer. "I find it possible to write only now and here, where I have a true task and where I am in danger," he began his letter. If only he could make her parents see things the way he did. They condemned Ingeborg's actions and considered her an evil, immoral person and felt this relationship had to be eradicated, silenced and treated with disgust! If only he could make them see that Ingeborg had not wrecked his marriage, that it had already been broken beyond repair, that Ingeborg had actually saved him from the brink!

Most of all, he wanted them to understand, that despite the two years of silence between them, the inner connection between him and Ingeborg had not ended. He felt that like faith, love was a gift. "It is not in the power of man to accept or reject it. Everything we are and have, love included, is given to us until it is recalled — in these times of war more than ever. Our right to make decisions about it lies in the stars," he philosophized. He understood this was a new realization. In the past he had believed the future was wide-open, that he could chose between options. Now he felt that whatever choice he made, the war was the primary factor, that it had taken matters out of his hands, that it was all up to fate, to a power he could not control.

There was one more important matter he wanted to explain to Ingeborg's parents, namely that, thanks to Ingeborg, all the wonderfully rich years with Anna had come alive again. Nonetheless, he felt what he and Anna had lost could not be retrieved. "Something will always be missing," he summed things up. No matter what Ingeborg's parents said, no matter whether they succeeded in breaking off his correspondence with their daughter, he knew he would hold on to Ingeborg. He struggled how to explain it to her parents. How could he put it best? "I can't let go of her because she is the gateway to my current life." He was surprised about this realization.

Michael felt relieved. He had done his part. The final decision might be made by the war, or by Ingeborg. That was out of his hands, but he had done his part. The only thing left was to send a copy of this letter to Anna. He did it with a heavy heart, but he did it, nonetheless.

On April 21st, the day after Michael had found the first spring flowers and seen the first swallows and June bugs, he had his battle "baptism" of fire, 50 km South of Tarnopol. The Russians had made a frontal attack on the Germans who had been holding the bridge. They knocked out communication with the rear by hitting the signal station.

Michael served as a *vorgeschobener Beobachter*, in front of the line, scouting for enemy positions, the most dangerous job of all. He relished the adrenalin rush, the intensity of being in the thick of it. It stopped him from thinking about anything else. *Here I feel alive,* he thought. Unfazed by the danger he later wrote to Anna:

> It was quite a show. I must say I felt as comfortable as during a walk. I heard the singing of a lark more clearly than the hissing of the missiles. I think tomorrow the first leaves will pop. The buds are ready to burst.

Reading this, Anna questioned Michael's bravado. It sounded so different from Stephan's accounts of fighting in Poland, or the reactions of Michael's younger brother Lutz. She could not imagine it was all this harmless. And she resented that Michael seemed not to be suffering out there, while she was struggling, by herself at home, on the farm.

Michael felt, whether you got hurt or not, it was all a matter of luck. A few days later, they were advancing toward the village of Puzniki when Russian tanks obstructed their path. Grenades and bullets started flying and Michael felt something brush his temple. There was no blood. "Something hit me," he said to the soldier next to him. "I better have it checked at the first aid station. I don't think it is bad. I'll be back soon." Michael's comrade was relieved. A minor injury, thank God. He liked this Bavarian. They needed his steadfastness. Michael walked toward the rear. It could have been worse, he thought. *A bandage and I will be as good as new. But where is the first aid station?* He was suddenly confused. Where was he? Michael had lost all sense of orientation and could not think straight. Suddenly everything turned black and he collapsed.

While Michael fought for his life, Anna toiled at the farm. She reported:

> This was a week of hard work, but also happiness. Two calves were born. We have plowed and sown the grain field. Rain came just in time. We raked the meadows, repaired the pasture fences and finished the garden. And I even reviewed books . . . The Reitner neighbors' son Franzl is now also dead. Head injury. Died in military hospital. Everybody mourns him. I was very shaken by this news and it has made me worry about you . . . I wonder where you are? How are you faring? The mailman has now also been called up. We are getting mail only every other day. But I don't give a damn. What I am waiting for does not arrive anyway. Be well, dear Michael.

The copy of Michael's letter to Köslin was on its way and reached Anna on April 27th. Anna was stunned. She found it difficult to send her response out into the battlefield, but she felt she had no choice. "Now the decision has been made," she wrote. "With this letter you have divorced me. You have now answered, simply and directly, all the questions that had accumulated over the many past months."

Most painful for Anna was the fact that Michael said he now felt rooted in a different soil. She simply could not understand why Michael had not told her earlier what he had been feeling. He had always said he did not know what would happen. He had said, at Christmas when they last saw each other, that he was waiting, calmly. He had said their bond could never be severed. He had said and written so many things that made her believe they had another chance! She turned the words in his letter around and around, wavering between anger, tears and disbelief. She wrote:

> Why did you leave me in this uncertainty, when you knew for such a long time? That's why I have to consider this as selling me out. I have now comprehended the main thing: that there can't be a future for us two.

Anna had no way of knowing that Michael had not willingly deceived her, that his feelings had only clarified very recently, as he stood on the shores of the Dniester River.

# THE VISITOR
## May 3-9, 1944

After receiving the copy of Michael's letter, Anna desperately needed someone to talk to, but all her friends were too far away. How she longed to talk with Friedel or Felizitas. Here she had no one with whom she could share such personal matters, to whom she could speak of her sorrow.

And there were frustrations on the farm. Potatoes and grain could not be planted because of bad weather. On April 29th it had even snowed. They were running out of hay. Anna was in a foul mood. She was glad when she heard Michael's cousin Manfred would be coming — Manfred, who had objected to Erdmuthe's name. Even though they had never met, she expected his visit might help, that he might understand her. In some ways she even felt Michael had a hand in his visit, that he had sent him to her.

Anna had no idea when Manfred would be arriving. One morning when she was taking the cows out, she saw a slender tall man walk up the path from the village. When she realized the lanky figure in uniform must be Michael's cousin, she was pleased. They had exchanged a few letters over the past year and Anna had become intrigued with this man. With each letter her fascination had grown and she had been curious what an encounter in the flesh would be like. There was much about him she could not relate to. He was a soldier through and through. He had been wounded numerous times and fixed up in military hospitals. He volunteered again and again to return to his troop, even though he did not believe in the ideological justifications for this war. This world of a soldier was incomprehensible to Anna. She had only recently reread a letter he had written in early 1943 from the Russian front:

> I am deeply satisfied with my life here. I have my company, my men, who are attached to me and for whom I am their 'lord'. I live the life of a feudal ruler of the 16th century. Either there is fighting, and then misery, pain, fear and death, and angels and demons are around me . . . or there is quiet at the front, one has much free time, and one is mostly one's own boss. I have the freedom to spend much time alone, to read, write, listen to music . . . And especially, I can think what I want . . . I think I have overcome the nihilism toward which Western civilization is moving. That's why I now see much that points toward the future, especially here in Russia, in this long-suffering, primeval country. I have learned to love their literature — Pushkin, Gogol, Dostoyevsky, Chekov — and the wide open landscape from which this writing was born . . .

And yet, Russians were the enemy and he had to fight against them, Anna thought, when she read this letter.

They had good and intimate talks as soon as they met. After long days of farm work, they sat up late and Anna told him about her life, of the painful struggles with Michael, their deep abiding love for each other and their inability to live in harmony, about Michael's treasonous letter to Ingeborg's parents, about her farewell letter to him.

She told Manfred she hadn't worked out the details of her future. Most likely she and Erdmuthe would stay at the farm and Michael would leave — an ironic turn of events, since Anna had given up her writing career to follow him and he had made a farmer out of her.

But now her life here felt right. The work was hard, but she was at peace on this mountain and she had discovered that she was capable of running the farm without Michael.

Two days after Manfred's arrival, on May 5th, she wrote to Michael:

> Manfred is here now. His letters have moved me strangely from the very beginning, long before I met him in person. After I saw him face to face, I felt from the first moment a strange familiarity, a mutual understanding. I have no idea whether he experiences the same thing. I rather doubt it. But something special exists. He said this has now become a place where he, the vagabond Manfred, could always set up his tent. It is a spiritual connection, but warm and close. He is like me, only more contained. Alone the knowledge that he exists, calms me. That was already true on the first evening when we spoke of personal matters.

Manfred had not said much during their days of working and talking, but he had listened, carefully, and without judgment. The story had poured out of Anna like a flooded stream breaking beyond its banks. Now she felt full of energy, even happiness. She would turn thirty-eight next week, but after these days with Manfred she felt young and vibrant again, almost giddy like a young girl.

Manfred had been at the farm for almost a week. Anna now realized this was more than a spiritual connection. She was attracted to him in other ways too. She remembered how she had laughed when she had told Friedel about him and her friend had said: "You are already in love with him!" Sometimes others could see more clearly, Anna thought. But now she realized it too.

*Tonight I will seduce him*, Anna thought, as she walked from the clammy entry hall into the bright May sunshine. She was pleased the tulips, only in bud the day before, had opened. How lush their fleshy petals were, how vibrant their reds and yellows! Anna was exuberant, although war had been raging for five years, although Michael was out there fighting on the Eastern front, although she had no idea what the future would bring for her and five-year-old Erdmuthe. *It's a glorious day,* Anna thought to herself, *and tonight I will seduce him.*

Standing in front of her tulips, Anna was lost in these thoughts. *No,* she thought, *there is no reason to feel guilty after what Michael had done to her.* Actually, he had encouraged his cousin to visit and he must have known they would like each other. Maybe, in a way, by bringing them together, he was alleviating his own guilt. Who cares, tonight she would seduce Manfred. But first she would cook a special meal. Although it was not Sunday, she'd serve pork roast and open a jar of her luscious canned pears.

## THE MESSENGER
### *May 9, 1944*

They sat around the square kitchen table finishing their pears. Erdmuthe winked at Manfred, as she was slurping the syrupy juice. She knew perfectly well she was not supposed to do that, and Anna, too distracted, let it go. Kathi, the Ukrainian farm hand, seemed to have picked up the vibrations in the room. She grinned sarcastically, to Anna's annoyance. *She probably remembers my disapproval of her relationship with Vlady,* Anna thought. Although that had to do with the Fascist views of her Ukrainian beau, not with any prudishness on Anna's part. Kathi continued to grin impertinently. *Ungrateful wench,* Anna thought. *She is probably jealous!*

A hesitant knock interrupted the clinking of the spoons against the glass bowls. When no one reacted, the village mayor stuck his head in the door. Anna turned white as a sheet and started screaming:

"No, I don't want to hear it!" she screamed. "No, I don't want to hear it!" again and again. She ran out the kitchen door, up the steep wooden stairs, through the upper hallway and Erdmuthe's room, into the inner sanctuary of her bedroom. Screaming she fell into the pillows and shut out the world around her.

Erdmuthe knew something terrible must have happened for her mother to scream like that. Vicek and Kathi rushed out of the kitchen too, and Manfred sat there, turning his spoon around and around in the empty glass bowl. Finally he looked at Erdmuthe and took her on his lap. "Erdmuthe," he said, gently. "Your father is dead. He won't come back home."

Erdmuthe tried to scream also, but no sound came. She jumped off Manfred's lap and ran out of the house. In front of the garden a cluster of people were gathering around the mayor. Erdmuthe encircled the group, skipping, and out of her mouth came a dirge-like ditty: "My father is dead. He won't come home. My father is dead, he won't come home," she sang forlornly, unaware of her words. The adults looked on, horrified.

Manfred sat in the kitchen, at the deserted table, thinking of all the men he had seen die in battle. This was the first time he witnessed what it was like for those left behind to receive the news. What could he say, how could he help Anna get through this, he wondered. He slowly climbed up the stairs, opening doors to finally come upon her, sprawled on the bed, sobbing in such pain that Manfred found it difficult not to take flight. Then he sat down at the edge of the bed and took Anna into his arms, softly enveloping her. *It is so different from the way I had envisioned we would hold each other*, he thought. All yearning had vanished and he felt like a fatherly friend, not like the passionate lover of last night's dreams.

Anna sobbed and sobbed, hardly able to breathe between convulsions. Then, slowly, she began to calm. *How good Manfred is here,* she thought. *Someone who knows and loves Michael. Someone who can just hold me and not expect anything for himself.* Everything around her seemed dull: the sunshine streaming though the windows, the fragrance of the lilac. "Oh, Manfred," she whimpered. "It is all my fault!" He looked at her uncomprehending. "I should not have written that letter," Anna said, full of self-accusation. "When I told him not to come back I took away his protection against death." And she began to sob again, overcome by guilt and sorrow.

"I told him he would not die as long as we were not finished with each other. And then I finished it and he died," she wailed. Manfred reminded her that it was Michael who had ended the uncertainty and made a decision. "Maybe this was the completion that allowed him to leave this world." Manfred thought of the many soldiers he had encountered in their last moments. "The life of every man I have seen die was fulfilled," he finally said, as much to himself as to Anna. "At that moment their lives seemed fulfilled and they were at peace." The door opened and Erdmuthe came in, in search of her mother. Manfred let go of Anna and Anna took her daughter into her arms. "Oh, my child," she said. "How good you are here." And they cried together.

The next morning the mailman brought Michael's last message. A postcard that said: "How I wish I was at the farm, now that the meadows are green and the trees are blooming as in the garden of paradise." The postcard was stamped on the day he had died. He is there now, Anna thought, at peace, amidst blossoming trees, in paradise. After too many tears, she was beyond crying. She stood in back of the house and watched Manfred getting smaller and smaller, as he made his way down the path. She knew her life had now taken a new and entirely unpredictable course.

*Part II*

# AFTERMATH
## Spring 1944

Anna sent a one-sentence message to her relatives and many friends: "On April 29th Michael fell on the Eastern Front." That was all she could muster. Usually the jumping stag was a welcome sight, but joy quickly turned into grief, when Anna's friends opened the letter. Ingeborg's mother, Aunt Magda in Koeslin, however, felt more relief than sorrow.

It took Friedel in Berlin two days to recover enough to order her thoughts. At first she was just stunned and kept asking "Why?" She realized she shared Michael's outlook on life and had always felt a strong affinity with his often morbid thoughts. Now she was flooded with memories and he seemed very close to her, more alive than ever before. She saw him as they both walked gaily down the hill, or how he sat brooding at the kitchen table. She remembered things he had said and suddenly thought: *Oh, that's what he meant!* Although, she reflected, who could be sure what anyone means.

Her thoughts went round and round: Was he so heavy-hearted because he intuited that his life would be short, or did he die so early because he was so pessimistic and ready to sink? *Or, am I making too much of interconnections that don't really exist?*

Slowly her mind calmed. *I do think he is now content*, an inner voice told her, and the more she thought about it, the more she was convinced he was now at peace. *We probably should not dissect all this too much*, Friedel told herself. *Here a power beyond us humans decided, and how do we know this was not a benign and comforting force? He always lived between dream and reality*, she concluded. *He would never have found what he was striving for. Now his lifelong hunger for the ideal love and perfection he could never reach is stilled. Oh, Michael,* she consoled herself. *I'll always keep you in my heart.*

Then she sat down and wrote to Anna. She wondered what her friend was going through, how she was coping. She asked whether Anna wanted her to come. "Hold on to your memories," she told her:

> They are now your great treasure which will give you insight and strength in the future. And don't be ungrateful for the gift of fate which now allows you to shape your future according to your own needs. Despite your pain it is fortunate you'll be able to decide freely what to do with your life.

Anna might not be ready to hear this now, Friedel thought. But she would realize one day that Michael's death had set her free.

At the farm the mailman was busier than ever, as responses to Michael's death arrived. Letters came from all over, from comrades who had fought at his side, from others who had crossed paths with him: his former high school teacher, the Schleswig Holstein farmer who had taught him, the carpenter who had made his furniture, Anna's old uncles in Pomerania, many friends of Anna's. Anna's Berlin doctor, Frau Huhn, who had spent time at the farm, remembered the beauty of his strong body and the rhythm of his movements when Michael walked across the fields, sowing. A cousin remarked how gentle he had been with his little daughter. All poured out their hearts and mourned his loss.

Some of the close friends who knew of the past marital strife saw this turn of events almost as merciful. Felizitas wrote:

> When I heard of Michael's desire to get to the Eastern Front, it seemed certain and unavoidable to me that his life was about to approach his goal with rapid speed. Maybe this seemed to him, consciously or not, the only solution to a problem he was unable to solve any other way.

Some of these letters consoled Anna; others made her feel even more alone. Did people really know what it was like to lose the person you loved most, especially when you felt you had caused his death? People had no idea!

One letter angered Anna. It came from the local district leader of the Nazi Party: "May you gain strength knowing that your husband gave his life in the service of Führer, folk and fatherland, that he died, so that Germany can live and not be delivered to the Bolshevik hordes."

Bolshevik hordes! How hollow these phrases sounded that were supposed to make a widow like her proud! Slogans like "He died a hero's death, or "He made the ultimate sacrifice for us all," struck her as downright cynical. Still, she was amazed, that even though hundreds of thousands died these days, the authorities still managed to send hand-signed letters to widows or parents. The German military machinery still worked well, Anna thought grimly. It might not keep its soldiers alive, but it managed their deaths very efficiently.

Anna was also angered by a eulogy in the Wasserburg newspaper which his family must have sanctioned. After biographical information came this summary:

> Michael Dempf, the great admirer of local history, the sensitive researcher of folk customs, the courageous German soldier-peasant and homeland defender, the faithful comrade, the loving father and husband, gave his life to his much beloved fatherland. May he be a shining example for all of us to stand for our German homeland with equally unconditional love and devotion, faithful to the very last.

This Nazi terminology made Anna cringe, but finding out the facts surrounding Michael's death helped. Anna received detailed reports from Michael's troop leader and from the operating surgeon in the military hospital. From the various messages Anna pieced together the facts: How Michael was in front of the line as a scout; how a grenade fragment struck his left temple; how the injury seemed minor at first, but then turned out to be life-threatening, given that a piece of shrapnel had entered Michael's brain; how during the operation on April 29th, his heart gave out and he died; how he was buried with military honors on May 5th at the Styrer Park Military Cemetery in Lemberg. *That was the day I wrote to Michael about Manfred,* Anna thought, horrified.

Even though it was painful, she wanted to know everything there was to know. Finding out the details made Michael's death more real. If she had no body to bury, at least she now had images of his last days. Anna told the story again and again, to anyone who was willing to listen: neighbors, acquaintances, and friends. When Erdmuthe heard her mother say: "I want to tell you what happened to Michael," she stuck her fingers in her ears. As far as she was concerned, her father was up in the sky with Orion, not in a grave in Russia.

At the end of the summer the mailman brought a small package of Michael's belongings, mailed on May 8th by the hospital administration. Anna's hands shook as she opened it. There was an inventory and the following items: one pocket watch and chain, one pencil, one eraser, one small notebook without notes, one fountain pen, several razor blades, photographs of Anna, Erdmuthe and Ingeborg, a tiny dried flower wreath, seventy-seven Polish Zlotys and a small wax medallion with an embossed half moon, which Anna had given to Michael at Christmas. Anna's farewell letter was not there. Although Anna had figured Michael could not possibly have received her letter, she was relieved that she did not find it among these belongings. Her letter was returned later, unopened. Nevertheless, this did not alleviate Anna's feelings of guilt.

And finally, Anna received a photograph of his grave from a comrade who had attended the funeral. It looked like the grave was at a spot above the city, similar to their village graveyard. It seemed a peaceful place, surrounded by trees. Not surprising, Anna thought. After all, the German army had created the cemetery for their war dead in a city park. She doubted she would ever get there to see it. But at least she knew he had a grave and his body was not hastily covered up in some ditch, as many others were.

## VICEK
### *Christmas 1944*

Every night after Erdmuthe was in bed, he worked on the doll house. He made the walls from cardboard and the furniture from scrap wood. He realized his table and chairs, bed and chest looked similar to the furniture at the farm, simple and sturdy. He was working steadily to get the surprise gift finished by Christmas Eve. *Bäurin* — farmer woman — as he called Anna, helped him with the more delicate items: bedding, curtains, and table cloths. The blue and white fabric, decorated with flowers and hearts, brightened and softened the rustic quality of his efforts.

"How sweet of you, Vicek, how sweet that you are doing this!" *Bäurin* had said. But it was no chore for him. He was actually having fun. The doll house *Stube* was turning out nicely and he looked forward to seeing Erdmuthe's excitement. He could not help but like the little girl. She was so uninhibited and treated him like everyone else, just like the other people who lived here, the neighbors and visitors. It made him almost feel like he was part of this family, not a forced laborer. Even though he had been sent to work here by the German military, even though he was far away from home, he knew his life might be better here than in his occupied homeland

Poland, where the Germans were wreaking havoc. He was certainly treated better here than some of his compatriots on other farms in the region, he knew that much from his friends.

*Bäurin* had been good to him from the time he had arrived at this place over a year ago. She had been sympathetic when he told her what had happened to his family: After the German invasion in 1939, his parents' farm had been given to Besserabian Germans, and his parents were forced to work as farmhands on their own farm. He and his brother had to work from early morning till late at night on another farm taken over by German new farmers. Thus he was almost glad when he was finally shipped to Austria. True, here he worked for strangers too, but at least he could see how grateful *Bäurin* was for his much-needed labor.

In the beginning he had been terribly homesick, but by now he felt better. He appreciated how *Bäurin* was trying to make his situation as palatable as possible. That's why he tried to be pleasant too, not like Kathi. After all, *Bäurin* refused to lock them up at night, as she was supposed to according to the rules, and she let them eat with everyone else, not at a separate table, as was required. Last summer the village supervisor of foreign workers had come to check up on *Bäurin*. It was lucky he had not caught them eating together. A farmer could end up in jail for such an offense. The inspector's primary concern seemed to be where he was sleeping. "After all, we have to guard the honor of our German women," the man had said. How absurd! *Bäurin* was twice his age and mourning the death of her fallen husband! To satisfy the supervisor, *Bäurin* had suggested he sleep at the neighbors from now on. "Then nobody has to worry about me," she had said, and the neighbor had played along. He was glad no one had checked so far where his bed really was. What he appreciated most was that *Bäurin* had kept him home on the day he had been ordered to attend the public hanging of a fellow Pole who had made a girl in a nearby village pregnant. All the Polish workers in the region were required to witness this execution. But *Bäurin* had said: "No Vicek. I'll take that upon myself. Hopefully the calf will come today. Then we'll have a good excuse." The calf had not come, but no one had inquired why he was not there. He had been anxious that *Bäurin* might get into trouble, but so far nothing had happened.

He was also thankful that *Bäurin* had made sure Krishka, the pregnant teenager who had been raped by German soldiers, was sent home to Poland. Only recently a postcard had arrived announcing the birth of her son. He had happily translated: "I stand under the high gate and look toward the West . . ." she had written.

The other Sunday *Bäurin* allowed visiting foreign workers in his room. When they got a bit boisterous with laughter and dancing, he apologized, but *Bäurin* laughed and said: "It's all right. I know you are young and need to have fun sometimes."

Too bad Kathi gave *Bäurin* such a hard time! She had a foul mouth and when she did not feel like working, she simply pretended to be ill. And she kept getting pregnant and then went to the hospital to get rid of the baby. True, this was not a place to have a child, and the authorities encouraged such abortions, but why couldn't she be more careful! Her boyfriend Vlady was cocky too. Once, when *Bäurin* had scolded Kathi for stealing a blouse of hers, he had threatened he'd denounce *Bäurin* after the war. He would say she had a picture of Hitler hanging in the *Stube*, which was an outright lie. But *Bäurin* was not intimidated. "And I'll tell them, that you cooperated with the Germans in the Ukraine." Vlady had said no more after that. Kathi was a good worker, Vicek had to say that much, if she was in the mood for work, that is. And she was strong as an ox, stronger than he was.

Vicek had felt so badly for *Bäurin* last spring, when the news came that the *Bauer* had been killed. True, the *Bauer* hadn't been as friendly as his wife, but he got on with him during his brief home stays. He could see that *Bäurin* loved her husband despite their quarrels. And he was a good farmer. Running the farm without him now was not easy for *Bäurin*, and he would not be here forever. This war would end! And what then?

The neighbor helped sometimes, but most of the time the three of them kept the farm going by themselves. Mostly they were doing a good job of it. They had no trouble with the birth of this year's calves. They got the hay in despite all the rain. Their potatoes were better than on other farms. *Bäurin* had even ordered new equipment: pipes and a pump to speed up fertilizing the meadows with liquid manure. No one else here had such a thing! So often *Bäurin* had said: "This will be a surprise when Michael comes on leave," and now he would never come back.

This war was lasting way too long! It was true, he was not too unhappy here. But still, he had to wish the war would end soon and that the Germans would lose it. He did want to go back home, be with his family, see the Germans gone from his country. He did not want to think about all they had done to Poland! He had witnessed enough crimes before he came here. He had seen whole villages go up in flames, farm after farm burnt to the ground. He had seen women, in line to buy bread, shoved onto trucks and driven off for forced labor. He had seen young girls rounded up, and rumor had it they were sent to brothels in Germany. Some of them had come back home pregnant, silent about the disgrace they had endured. He had heard of cold-blooded mass executions, of manhunts and pillage and rape. No, he did not want to think of all that had happened in his country. He'd have to hate them all then, all the Germans, for what they had done in his homeland. Instead, he was making a doll house for this little German girl in Austria whom he loved like a sister! *It is all very confusing*, Vicek thought.

He had found a piece of copper in the toolbox. After he finished the doll house, he would make a star, a Christmas gift for *Bäurin*. It would be his way to thank her for her kindness. After all, he could not blame her for all that had happened to him and his country.

## THE RUSSIANS ARE COMING
### *February 14, 1945*

As the months went on, the war became increasingly terrifying. With the end of mail service expected any time — already no packages were allowed — letters arrived at a furious pace at the farm. The news became more and more chilling and Anna dreaded opening the mail.

Anna was most frightened by reports about her former homeland Pomerania and about Silesia, where her mother lived in the village of Niebusch which the Nazis had renamed Bergenwald, or Mountain Forest, in an effort to Germanize the Slavic-sounding Niebusch. In January, she had heard, the Russians had begun their great offensive. They were steadily marching westward, taking over territory after territory. Refugee treks streamed toward the West and the misery was unimaginable. Sister Hilde reported that their relatives in Karwen had left for the West. Anna had spent time at the estate as a child and young woman, and last visited in 1941. Now this place too was lost. Anna had heard horror stories of such evacuations. "Children freeze to death in their mothers' arms," Hilde had written.

*And where is our mother*, Anna worried. She had had no news since she had received a postcard written on February 2nd. Mumm had written:

So far we are well. We have had two orders for evacuation. An endless stream of refugees is coming through here — immeasurable suffering. We hear shooting on the Oder River. I know you must have written, but I have received no news. May God protect us all.

After that, Anna heard nothing more. She knew the Russians had reached Silesia by mid-February. Had her mother left or had she stayed, and which choice was more frightening? Was she alive or dead? Every letter Anna now wrote began: "I still have no news of my mother!" She tried to reach her in every imaginable way, but her letters seemed to disappear into the unknown.

*Maybe we should have evacuated earlier,* Anna's mother, Margarethe Dahle, thought. But she and Paul had decided to stay until they were forced to leave. Staying could not be worse than the misery of the treks. For weeks they had heard the rumble of war in the distance. They had seen the nearby city of Sagan go up in flames, red fire glowing in the night. Now the sounds of war were coming closer and closer and fear of the Russians grew. When would they arrive? What chaos would they cause?

With everyone else in the village Margarethe and Paul waited anxiously, waited until in the late afternoon of February 14th, Erdmuthe's sixth birthday, Russian tanks clattered into Niebusch. One stopped in front of the rectory next to the Lutheran church, the most prosperous-looking house in the village. Several soldiers entered in their muddy boots and dispersed though the house. Some went down the cellar stairs in search of wine and were disappointed to find only vinegar. Others crowded into the pantry, where they only found a few staples. Annoyed, they dumped flour, salt, and sugar and scattered dried beans all over the floor, while Margarethe looked on in dismay. *Tomorrow will be cleaning day,* she thought, naively, and to calm them, offered the soldiers blackberry leaf tea. One, an Austrian prisoner of war, it turned out, said quickly, in a whisper when Margarethe rummaged in back of the kitchen: "Don't worry, I'll make sure nothing will happen to you."

Paul sat in his study, amidst piles of hoarded newspapers, holding on to his Lutheran Bible. "Protect us, O Lord," he mumbled. "Let them leave, before they destroy all our stored food." And, it seemed, his prayers were answered. The Russians disappeared as quickly as they had bolted in.

They had hardly left when Paul started coughing. "Do you smell smoke?" he asked. Then his sister, too, noticed the acrid smell of burning newspapers. Before she could answer, the house erupted in flames. Paul dropped his Bible, grabbed a blanket, and furiously hit the flames, to no avail. Fire shot out from all corners, singed the hair on Paul's arms, sent sparks to his face. "Quickly, let's get out while we can," he screamed at his sister, and finally spying her figure in the smoke, dragged her out the door.

Outside, rain poured in sheets, and yet, it seemed to make no difference to the fire. The two old people stood in front of their house and watched all they loved and owned go up in smoke. "Poor Hilde," Mumm muttered, thinking of her daughter's possessions she had stored in the basement, assuming they would be safer in this isolated village than in bombed-out Berlin. Thank God Anna had taken all her things to Austria, although who knew what was going on there. Mumm thought of her mother's hand-woven towels, the porcelain she had brought from Pomerania, of the dolls she had saved for Erdmuthe, of all the beautiful reminders of an earlier, happier life. Everything was now a victim of the flames. "A good thing we hid that suitcase with our documents and jewelry in the church. At least we can still prove who we are," Margarethe said. "And we are alive."

The two were by now drenched. It was getting chillier and darker, except for the glow of the fire. "We must leave and look for shelter," Paul said, pulling his sister away. But where to go? Disoriented and shivering they tried to find the path to their friends on the outskirts of the village, but soon realized they were lost. Stumbling though water holes, they ended up in a loamy field, sinking in to their knees. Pulling out their legs again and again seemed like the work of Sisyphus. The mud first pulled off their shoes, then their stockings. Rain water ran down their necks and backs. They trembled from the cold and their effort. *Will we ever get out of here?* Margarethe wondered. Maybe it would be best to lie down and die right here. "Hold on," Paul encouraged her, his voice feeble and shaky. "God will show us the way out." After what seemed like many hours, they slid down into a ditch, clambered up an embankment, and found the road.

## WHERE WILL IT END?
### *Spring 1945*

Anna's sister Hilde, an electrical engineer, was stuck in Berlin. To avoid the impression of defeatism, the civilian population was not allowed to leave the city and had to contend with near permanent shut downs of gas and electricity. Hilde had written of shortages of food and water, three air-raid alarms a day, endless hours spent in shelters, and factories working through the night. Frightful stories of rape and plunder by the approaching Russians circulated. "I will flee as soon as I can," Hilde wrote, "if necessary, on foot." After a particularly destructive bombing raid in March, Hilde sent a 'sign of life', a preprinted express postcard that allowed for a ten-word message: "Have survived the latest raid," it said. And Anna thought, *and I sit here, safe on our farm, and feel guilty.*

Her friend Miechen, who held down the fort in Freiburg with her three hungry sons while her husband was a prisoner of war, wrote: "Life is now reduced to a naked fight for survival." After a disastrous bombing of the city, where Miechen and Anna had attended university, she wrote:

> Freiburg is gone. Aside from the cathedral which was mostly spared, the whole old town is in ruins and the grave of countless people. For me part of my life ends with this and I find it hard to continue.

Anna thought of all the places she had loved there as a student. She simply could not imagine it all was no more.

The destruction of Dresden happened in mid-February: "Eighty percent of this beautiful city in rubble, 30,000 or more civilians dead, many of them refugees! This is not war, this is criminal," Anna wrote into the journal, which she had continued after Michael's death, although writing only sporadically. "This was not a target that needed to be hit for military reasons. The Allies are punishing us all."

One of the most nightmarish letters came from Friedel. Her son Dieter had apprenticed at a farm east of Berlin, but had recently left for fear of the Russian army, which was fast approaching:

> All members of Dieter's farm family were killed the day after he left and all farms in the area were burnt down. He was the only survivor. Please, send me the address of the doctor you know in Berlin. I intend to get sleeping pills, just in case. I understand, if you take twenty at a time, you won't wake up.

It seemed Friedel was nearing the end of her ability to endure.

Anna too was beginning to feel numb and worn down, without hope and very alone. *No one laughs anymore,* she noticed. *I wonder whether we will ever laugh again.* Enemy planes flew overhead. They had to black out their windows at night, and kerosene was scarce. What would happen? she wondered. Would the Russians come here, too? Hilde had urged her to leave, should that occur. Manfred's father thought she should stay. In early April Anna made her decision. She would not leave, come what may. Preparing for a Russian occupation, she buried valuables, photographs, and the journal. Before she put the book into the earth for safekeeping she made one last entry:

> If only this war would end, one way or the other. This waiting while destruction and chaos increase is unbearable. Every night that I can still put my child safely into bed, I am grateful. How long? Kathi and Vicek are still here. We continue to work and do only what is necessary. We don't have energy for more. It is an early spring, the meadows are already green, and next week we can drive the cattle out for grazing. The Russians are said to be close and we hear shooting. Nonetheless, I am calm.

Several of Anna's friends with children had asked to take refuge on the farm. Even though she had had no idea how to feed everyone, Anna had written back: "Come!" None of them had made it out before the official ban on civilian travel. The mail stopped in early April and Anna still had no news of her mother, or what had happened to her sister. *What will happen to us all?* she asked herself.

THE END
*May 5, 1945*

Anna looked out from behind the farm, at the greening meadows and spring flowers and dreaded the anniversary. Almost a year had passed, since she had learned of Michael's death, almost a year! Thank God the war was finally drawing to a close. Finally, after all these years!

Hitler was dead. He had killed himself, she had heard, less than a week ago, when everything seemed inevitably lost. American and Russian troops were now very close. Looking at this idyllic landscape was so deceiving. How peaceful it seemed here, and yet, there was unimaginable chaos not far away.

The next morning Anna woke to swarms of soldiers, who, she later learned, had come over the nearby pass from the Enns valley. She opened the front door to see about the unusual noise, when a rotund, limping officer approached her. "*Grüss Gott, gnädige Frau,*" he said politely. "Greetings, Madam," not "*Heil Hitler,*" Anna noted, reassured. "My name is Poguntke. You know as well as I that for all practical purposes this war is over. But we have orders to make a last stand further up the valley. Now, I think losing one more life at this point would be senseless, if not criminal. I can't put that on my conscience, and I wonder whether we might be allowed to hide out here until the official word of the end comes?"

It seemed a reasonable proposition to Anna, and she could not help but admire Poguntke's courage to defy his order. Even at this point it could cost him his life if the wrong people got wind of this. And of course it could endanger those who abetted him as well. "Well, I don't think this is only up to me," she finally said, mulling over his proposal. "Since our farms are so close to each other, I can't give permission unless the neighbors agree to participate. We would all be equally endangered. Let me talk to them."

In the end, the neighbors consented and the soldiers were divided among the three farms. It was decided Poguntke would stay at Anna's place. Anna thought, that besides wanting to "protect" her, he might also be looking forward to her company, to conversation with a woman, for a change, and she herself was starved for a good talk about other matters than the weather and farm work. There had been no visitors for months.

The soldiers were given strict orders to lay low and to behave. There was plenty of room to sleep in the haylofts. They had some provisions, and Anna supplied them with sacks of potatoes. They set up her large wash kettle in the courtyard to boil the potatoes and then dumped them into the tin bathtub for cooling. Erdmuthe mingled among the soldiers and the potatoes, amused by the unusual use of these familiar utensils. It had never occurred to her they could serve for anything but washing laundry or bodies. The uniforms reminded her of her father and that he was not coming back.

The next morning Poguntke, wearing civilian clothing donated by the neighbor, made his way to the village to investigate. Maybe he would hear news of the latest troop movements, or whether there were rumors about soldiers hiding out in the hills. Anna was in the kitchen washing dishes, a bit disoriented with all the commotion around her, when Vicek burst in: "*Bäurin*," he yelled. "There is big shooting machine behind the house!" Anna flew out the kitchen door, ran through the courtyard and out back. "Stop playing war and put that thing away immediately," she shouted angrily. The four soldiers clustered around the machine gun were not amused. "Anyone who comes within a hundred meters will be shot," one of them declared. Anna could tell from his voice he was not joking. "Who gave permission for this nonsense?" Anna demanded to know.

It was useless to argue with these fanatics, she finally realized, and raced to the neighbors to find someone up the ladder of command. She stormed into the *Stube* without knocking. Smoke enveloped the soldiers sitting around the table, the *Nachbar* among them. A soldier was just lifting a glass of cider declaring the death of his Führer was more painful for him than the death of his brother. "There is a machine gun behind my house and I want it removed immediately," Anna screamed. Suddenly everyone was silent. "Help me, neighbor," she pleaded. "Your farm is as much in danger as mine!" More silence. "Shut up, woman," the soldier who mourned Hitler's death finally said. "You have no idea what's really going on. You haven't experienced war up here!" "Wait a minute," the neighbor interjected. "This woman has lost her husband in the war and has stood her ground here on the farm." *He is not willing to defend his own farm,* Anna thought, surprised, *but he is willing to plead for me.*

A knock at the door broke the tension. In walked Poguntke, proclaiming *"Heil Österreich!"* Officially, no Austria existed yet, but this greeting, "Hail Austria!" was exactly the right word at this moment. "Who is responsible for this insanity?" he bellowed and ordered one of the men sitting at the table to follow him. Anna thanked the neighbor and left abruptly. This was no time for a social visit. She ran home, through the kitchen and into the pantry. There, amidst smoked meat, heads of cabbage and canned jars, she broke into tears. Through the window she could hear Poguntke dressing down the young lieutenant.

The next day the lieutenant was missing. So were the troop's cigarettes. The Americans reached the village two days later and Germany surrendered unconditionally on May 8th. The farmers gathered all the civilian clothing they could spare, and Poguntke sent the soldiers from nearby areas off to find their own way home through the hills and woods. Those from further away were to surrender to the Americans. Anna wrote a letter in English to the American military, saying a military officer at her farm could not come down to the village due to a leg injury. Their answer: "If he could get up there, he can come down." Thus Poguntke took his farewell and limped down the mountain as he had the day before.

The fields around the farm were littered with weaponry of all kinds and orders had been given to deliver such items to the village. Thus Vicek and Anna gathered them up, loaded them onto an oxen cart and hauled everything down the steep, bumpy gravel road. Anna expected the load to explode with every jolt, but they managed to deliver their bounty, unharmed.

A year after the news of Michael's death the war had finally ended! They had survived, physically unscathed. Their task now would be to heal their inner wounds, to find a new way in a Europe in ruins. Anna still knew nothing of her mother. For her there was no jubilation in this moment. She was simply relieved the war was over and she found solace in the thought that nature carried on, and that her task of running the farm would continue unabated.

## BREAD, THE STAFF OF LIFE
### Summer 1945

Klara Klausriegler of the *Oberhias* farm buried her wiry arms deep in the big wooden trough, filled with dough. The trough in which pigs were scalded during slaughter was set up in the *Stube* near the tile stove, hot from the fire in the adjacent kitchen. Klara was kneading enough dough for thirty big loaves of rye bread, enough for a month. It was strenuous work!

The dough needed to sit and rise and be kneaded repeatedly. Finally it was smooth and elastic enough to be rolled into log-sized pieces, which were then cut small enough to fill the round straw baskets. The baskets sat on the warm platform near the tile stove for further rising. Maridl helped and that speeded the work. Her mother was waiting for Maridl to get strong enough to help with the kneading as well. Thank God Maridl was out of school now and could pitch in with housework and help outside. She was not as handicapped as they had feared initially and though she was not tall, she was quite pretty with her black hair and thick braids, her mother decided.

Early in the morning Klara had made a big fire in the brick baking oven built into the kitchen wall, and a huge pile of embers was now heating the vaulted bricks. Soon she'd take out the embers and sweep the smooth baking surface clean. Then she'd place the loaves into the oven, using a wooden paddle attached to a long pole, so she could set them way back. It was hot work, especially now in summer. But you had to eat bread in summer, too, so there was no way to get around this chore. Klara was glad the war was over and hoped the requisitions would soon be reduced. She was thankful she did, at least, not have to worry whether or not they'd have enough flour. The rye field looked good. Hopefully there would be no big storm to destroy the harvest!

Even though the work was the same as always, everything seemed easier now that the war had ended. Klara did feel sorry for the *Nachbarin*, though. She had such trouble getting helpers, now even more so than during the war years when she had foreign workers assigned. Though that was not always easy either. She had been so lucky with Vicek. It seemed to her that leaving was hard for him, too. The *Nachbarin* kept mentioning how much she missed him. And of course she must miss the *Nachbar*, Klara thought. It was already a year and a half since the news of his death had come. They had so hoped he would be spared. Klara could never understand why he volunteered to go to Russia, although he might have been sent there anyway. So many from this valley had died there, so many!

And now there were rumors that all Germans were supposed to be deported from Austria. That meant the *Nachbarin* would have to leave too. It was a crying shame! After all, what Hitler had done was not the *Nachbarin's* fault! She had never been a Nazi and she had run the farm by herself for more than two years and done a good job, And now this! Maybe Konrad could put in a good word for her with the local authorities. Klara certainly could not think of a more helpful neighbor. Sometimes the *Nachbarin* helped them with health problems. Klara knew by now she was not really a medical doctor, but she did have books to figure out what the problem was and often gave good advice.

For Klari it would be a blow too, if she lost Erdmuthe. Both girls looked forward to going to school together and they had so much fun playing and doing chores. Erdmuthe, it seemed, liked to do chores here more than at home. And now, since the *Nachbarin* had to run around so much to various offices all over the district, Erdmuthe sometimes stayed overnight and the two slept together in the upper *Stube*. Erdmuthe was a bit much for Grandmother these days, and so Klara tried to keep the girls out of her hair. Her mother-in-law thought Erdmuthe too forward and outspoken. She still held the old fashioned view that children were meant to be seen, not heard, and did not realize times had changed. Grandmother was now eighty-seven and not ill, but she had little energy and mainly sat around. Klara was grateful nonetheless that she was still alive.

How long had she sat there, thinking, Klara wondered. The fragrance of baking bread wafted through the house. She had to take out the loaves and wet them, so the crust would turn hard! She was sure the *Nachbarin* would come over later and get a freshly baked loaf, still warm. She said there was no better bread on this earth and Erdmuthe loved to eat the heel of a freshly cut loaf. Klara could not remember a time when they had not baked this bread — Konrad's mother before her, and soon her daughters would take over when she got too old. If all failed, this bread could keep them alive. Bread had kept soldiers alive and at least some of the prisoners in those horrid camps the *Nachbarin* had told them about.

# FLIGHT
## *June 26, 1945*

Anna's mother, Margarethe Dahle, considered herself lucky. She was perched on Lesovsky's wagon, amidst cages of honking geese, quacking ducks and clucking chicken. But, at least she did not have to walk, like most of the others who were younger, or did not have wagons, or cows to pull them. For once, her age was an advantage.

They had expected the evacuation order, ever since the Russians had liberated Niebusch. *Liberated?* Margarethe thought. *It feels more like an invasion and occupation!* Although, she had to admit, Hitler had asked for this. Yes, they had expected the evacuation order, but not that they would only have half an hour to leave the place where most residents had lived all their lives. She herself had been there more than twenty years. But still, it had become home. She had lost her first home when her husband died, and now she was losing her second.

Watching the chaos of departure from her perch, Margarethe was glad she was settled. Cows were being hitched to wagons, mattresses uploaded, food supplies stored, suitcases heaved into vehicles. Maybe it was a blessing she had lost her possessions in the fire. She did not have to decide what to take. She had her documents, a bit of jewelry, a change of underwear, and a sweater. Her packed suitcase had been ready for this occasion for the past four months.

After much shouting, jostling and running, the trek was finally underway. The majority of the Niebuschers walked, among them Margarethe's brother Paul Steckmann, at seventy-five only two years younger than she. The fact that he was the pastor made no difference. Thanks to him, the trekkers had at least a goal they would try to reach.

The parishioners would stay together and make their way to Lärz in Mecklenburg, where Paul knew the pastor. They hoped to get help from parsonages along the way. Margarethe and Paul would separate from the throng and make their way to their sister in Berlin.

As they left the village, Margarethe looked back. She had already said goodbye to her house, but still, it hurt to leave, especially to leave behind her garden which had given her so much joy. Now they were on their way, part of the endless stream of refugees moving westward. Pomerania was Polish now, and so was Silesia. Poles, newly displaced from their former homes in Russia, would now settle here. As Germans they were now unwanted outcasts, Margarethe knew. This was home no more. It was as well that they had to leave. But would they find a new home where they were going?

Margarethe had little idea what would await her on the trek. She did not yet know she would be drenched in heavy downpours, that she'd sleep sitting up on chairs, or lie on beds of straw, that they'd catch fleas and body lice and bed bugs. She did not yet know that the cows and wagons and their meager possessions would be confiscated at the border by Polish authorities. She did not yet know that she too would soon have to walk.

Despite the hardship of the journey Margarethe was grateful for every bit of kindness she encountered along the way. Once she was able to stretch out on a mattress. Someone gave her a nourishing bowl of soup. A pastor's wife gave her dry clothing. The daily challenges of travel did take their toll on Margarethe, but she held on. Her great hope was Berlin, where their sister lived. *We need to last till we get to Martha's,* she admonished herself.

After two weeks of trekking, they neared the city of Berlin. In the outskirts they found space in a dilapidated cattle car, then walked through the ruins of the bombed-out capital. Margarethe and Paul had difficulty finding their way — it all looked so different and utterly desolate. But in the end they arrived at Gustav Adolph Street, where Martha's building stood, amidst the rubble, miraculously undamaged.

Trembling, Margarethe knocked on the door. This was where her daughters had boarded during their studies. This was where she had visited over the years, although not lately. True, Martha had often been unpleasant and self-centered, and she had declined to share an inheritance which belonged to the three of them. But these were different times. A family had to stick together. *We all need each other*, thought Margarethe, *especially now*.

She heard rustling inside, a slow shuffle to the door, the click of the peep hole. "Oh, no!" Martha said and slowly opened the door a slit. "I was afraid this might happen one day, that you would show up here. There is no way you can come in." All blood drained from Margarethe's face. She had trouble staying on her feet and Paul took her arm. "I can't feed you," Martha said. "There is not enough room for two more people. Maybe Frau Lietz — that was the cleaning lady — can give you shelter."

"Let's go," Paul said. They turned around and heard the door shut and the lock click. Margarethe did not know how she could go on after this. But what choice did they have? After two days' rest at Frau Lietz's they continued their journey, trying to catch up with the others and make their way to Lärz.


## BEGINNINGS AND ENDINGS
### *October 1, 1945*

Six months since the end of the war, Anna thought, and a semblance of normalcy was returning, at least for most. Schools had reopened and today was Erdmuthe's first day as a first-grader in the village school. Another milestone in both their lives, Anna realized. From now on she would not be able to protect her at all times and watch over her daughter's every move. From now on Erdmuthe would conquer part of the world on her own. Anna felt sorry for the fragile child, having to walk down the mountain in the rain, in boots that were not waterproof and too large. Who knew how long her daughter would attend this school? Germans were being evicted from the new Austria, and Anna was sure their turn would come soon, no matter how much she would want to preserve this home for her child.

Erdmuthe loved this place! She knew every tree, where the first primroses grew, where to find chanterelle mushrooms, or wild strawberries. And her friend Klari was like a sister to her! It would be very painful to have to leave the place that had been her home since birth and the place with memories of her father. But there seemed no way around it. All efforts Anna had undertaken so far to be allowed to stay had been fruitless. The local farmers had tried to intercede on her behalf, but the authorities seemed unmoved. *After all, I am a German and the Germans are the enemy, no matter why they came to Austria, and what they did here,* Anna thought, full of anguish. She felt bitter about it.

For her, the thought of leaving was not as painful as Anna had at first assumed. True, she had put down roots here, too, but for the past half-year she had been entirely cut off from all her beloved friends and relatives in Germany. She knew nothing of them! She still had no idea whether her mother was alive, whether her sister had gotten out of Berlin and where she might be, what had happened to Friedel or Felizitas. No mail had slipped through the closed borders and Anna felt entirely abandoned and alone in this world. Even the sympathy of the neighbors helped little. She could not see how they could possibly understand her pain.

Anna wrote many letters into the blue — letters to her mother, to her sister, to her friends — using old addresses and contacts with people who might know of their whereabouts. "Mother, where are you?" she asked. "Do you have food and shelter? How I long to hear from you!" She gave letters to couriers for hand delivery, to people allowed to cross the border. But all was for naught. No one responded and Anna wondered how much longer she could bear this isolation. Vicek had offered to write the first letter he was allowed to send home to Poland to Anna's mother. "Silesia is Polish now," he had said. "Maybe she is still there." Vicek's gesture had moved Anna. But nothing had come of it. Anna's despair grew daily.

Yes, Silesia was Polish now, Anna reiterated to herself, and so was Pomerania, where she had grown up, where her relatives had lived until recently. When would she learn what might have become of them? Although she accepted that Germany had to pay a debt for starting and losing this war, she mourned the loss of the Eastern territories. "I just can't wrap my mind around the fact that all that is now Polish!" she wrote into the journal that she had dug up again after it was clear that the war was over for good and that her entries provided no danger anymore.

Anna also mourned the damage to German culture through Nazi acts and German war crimes. Will our children still learn of the great intellectual tradition of German literature and philosophy? she wondered. Everything German was now sullied. Anna had been horrified to hear about the concentration camps. It was unfathomable what had happened there. And Mauthausen, less than fifty kilometers away, had already existed since 1938, since Hitler's takeover of Austria! How was it possible that no one knew? No one? Anna wondered. Certainly the people living right there had to have known! Did nothing trickle through to her because they were so isolated? Or was she too pre-occupied with her own troubles to keep her eyes and ears open enough? *Could I have known more, had I tried?* she asked herself.

She did know now and was shaken by the crimes her people, as well as the Austrians, had committed. Deported Jews, gypsies and political prisoners gassed, beaten, drowned in barrels, electrocuted, shot, starved and worked to death. In the millions! Near the end of the war people living near Mauthausen had helped to re-capture escapees from the concentration camp, hunting them down like rabbits. After liberating the camps, the American occupation forces had made residents of the town of Mauthausen dig trenches and bury the dead that were stacked like cord wood. They had put together a photo exhibit in the provincial capital of Linz, for people to see what had been going on, with or without their knowledge. Nazi leaders who were alive would soon be tried and hopefully hanged. Being German had become a terrible burden for Anna. She felt a great sense of guilt, while at the same time she deeply resented being ostracized and "marked." And she resented that Austrians claimed innocence. As though they had no hand in this, as though they had not participated!

And yet, despite such unsettling thoughts, Anna knew that for now, while she was still here, she had to focus on the practical task of keeping the farm going, even though it was more of a struggle than ever. At least this effort kept her somewhat centered. Her foreign workers had left soon after the end of the war. She missed Vicek, and even Kathi, despite her often irritating behavior. Now Anna contended with local help. The two displaced and hungry Viennese workers who had come to the farm to seek employment proved lazy and untrustworthy. They stole whenever they could. Sometimes Anna just wanted to give up! But the pigs, chickens and cows needed to be fed, and the milking had to be done. That was good and gave her at least some sense of immediate purpose.

Although the visitors' rooms were empty, Anna was not alone in the house. Refugees from the city sought shelter in the countryside and she had been assigned to take in a family of four from Vienna. Anna housed the Urbaneks in two small rooms upstairs and supplied them with bedding, furniture, and kitchenware. True, they were crowded, but it was preferable to being homeless. If her mother was a refugee, Anna hoped someone would care for her too. And the two Urbanek children, although younger than Erdmuthe, were good company for her daughter, especially since she herself was so preoccupied with preparing for their departure, which might happen any time.

Anna was sorting her possessions, deciding what to take, what to sell, what to leave, how to get her belongings transported to Germany, should she be evicted. The big, open question was where to go. She had an invitation from Manfred's father, and there was an organization that helped with house exchanges. If only she knew where her loved ones were! Then she could try to move close to them. She was hesitant to move near Michael's immediate family, since, she assumed, for them she was still the unwanted Prussian daughter-in-law. It was possible the war had softened their attitudes, but who knew? Everything was up in the air.

## NEWS
### *November 29, 1945*

Fog hung over the hills. It was another grey, dreary November day, when the mailman brought a letter. Anna did not know the sender, and puzzled, opened it. Inside was a letter from Felizitas, sent through an Austrian contact person, since no letters could be mailed from Germany directly. Anna nearly fainted. The first letter from Germany!

From Germany! From Mars would have sounded equally unlikely to her. Tears ran down her face when she saw Felizitas' strong and steady handwriting. Anna took the letter, went inside the *Stube*, and sat down on the sofa. She had to compose herself before she could read it. Who knew what news it would hold? A letter from Germany after all these months! Anna could hardly believe it.

It was dated November 20th, nine days earlier. Anna glanced through the letter and stopped when she saw Hilde's name. Hilde! She was alive! She had gotten out of Berlin, on the last train, with nothing but hand luggage. Miraculously, she had found her way to the trek of her Pomeranian relatives and she was now in a small town in the British zone, teaching mathematics. And there was an address! It all seemed so incredible! Hilde had written to Felizitas, hoping that she would get news to Anna, and that in return, she might find out her sister's fate through her. She said she was relieved the farm was in the American occupation zone and she hoped Anna had stayed.

Anna gasped. It was all too much. She still had a sister, her only sister in this world! But Hilde, too, had no news of their mother. *Our sweet little Mumm*, Anna thought. *Is she still out there, somewhere, or is she dead? Will I ever learn what has happened to her?* It was now almost ten months since Mumm had written her last postcard. Anna had heard terrible stories of the hardships Germans had endured fleeing from the Russians. Who knew what traumas her mother had experienced, if she had survived at all.

Anna was shaken for days after this letter arrived. She was exhausted and barely able to work. It seemed like a fairy tale to Anna that Felizitas knew about the fate of mutual friends and of Michael's sister in Munich from whom Anna had heard nothing. She had even seen some of their friends, with whom Anna had lost touch. That Anna could try to write back to Felizitas, through the given contact address, seemed miraculous to her.

But Felizitas' letter was a rare occurrence. There were no more letters after that. Without direct mail service, and with failed attempts to get letters carried across the border, there was no news from loved ones and limited information about their well-being and whereabouts. Anna's state of isolation continued to grow. She wrote to Felizitas:

> I experience life as through a veil. Nothing reaches me and life has taken on a sense of unreality. I am so homesick, so hungry for contact with people close to me. I don't know how much longer I can bear being so cut off.

## EVICTION
### Christmas 1945

Although not unexpected, the eviction notice, which came shortly before Christmas, hit Anna like a bombshell. *Now I have to tell Erdmuthe that we will have to leave,* she thought. But she was determined they would have a merry last Christmas here! She was not going to spoil the child's joy and anticipation. And she was going to try to postpone their departure which was scheduled for January 1st. How ridiculous! A few weeks' notice was simply not enough time. What were those bureaucrats thinking! Should she leave the cattle to starve in her stable? These people had no idea what it meant to dissolve a farm. They just sent out their notices without concern for man or beast! And at Christmas! For the first time, she felt the plight of Mary and Joseph during their flight to Egypt as though it was happening to her personally. She had, over the years, collected images of the flight, but now she knew in her body what it was like to be stranded, without shelter, homeless.

Anna ran to the neighbors to tell them, to ask them to take in Erdmuthe while she made her rounds to the authorities. How could this happen just before Christmas, when she had hoped to bake cookies, to wrap the few gifts she had collected for Erdmuthe, to get her tree from the woods. Anna hoped she'd be able to pull it all together in the end. For now she'd have to try to get temporary permission to stay, at least, till she could settle things at the farm and finish packing her belongings. She did not relish tromping through the snow, waiting for buses and trains, confronting hard-nosed men in the offices in the district town Kirchdorf and the provincial capital Linz. Travel was cumbersome when everything was in a state of transition. It was a monumental undertaking, but what else could she do? She had nothing to lose!

Up to now Anna had tried to protect Erdmuthe from her anxiety that they might be evicted, but now she had to know. While her mother ran around to work things out so they could stay, Erdmuthe worried. What would happen to all her toys, her doll house, and the sled Vicek had made for her birthday. And their dachshund? What about Klari and every place she loved at the farm? She just could not imagine living anywhere else! And where would they go? And how would *Grossmutti*, as she called Anna's mother, ever find them if they left here? Why were they supposed to leave at all? She just could not understand that being German was such a bad thing that they were to be sent away from here. It just could not be! This would be a horrible Christmas, Erdmuthe was sure!

In the end, when the time came, Erdmuthe forgot all her worries and threw herself into the excitement of Christmas Eve. *Christkind* flew down from the Kruckenbrettl and brought a beautiful tree. Her dolls got new dresses — Anna had made them, unbeknownst to her daughter, late at night, from fabric scraps. There were cookies and apples and walnuts. And Anna was happy about the drawing

Erdmuthe had made for her as a surprise, a drawing of spring flowers. *Oh, where will we be, come spring?* Anna wondered.

Anna tried hard not to let her daughter see how difficult this Christmas was for her. In the past she had sent packages and received letters. Now there was no mail, she was all alone on her farm, considered the enemy, and this would be their last Christmas here. Yet, she knew she had reason to be grateful. They were not in the Russian zone. She had good neighbors. Her sister was alive. She had a sweet daughter, her greatest gift. She had no idea what would happen, but on this special night she would relish her daughter's happiness.

## IN LIMBO
### *January - May, 1946*

Anna still knew nothing of Mumm and none of the letters Hilde and Anna had attempted to send to each other arrived at their destinations. Where were the millions of lost letters going? Anna waited and hoped, but she could not worry too much about lost mail. She was busy organizing her belongings, packing, and trying to find someone to take over the farm after her departure. At the same time she was applying for a reprieve. Preparing to leave and to stay simultaneously was a disconcerting experience.

In the first week of January, the Sattler family appeared, assigned by the district farmers' organization to take over as official tenants of the farm. The farm had been confiscated as "German Property" and put under trusteeship of an organization responsible for such holdings. A week later was Anna's deadline for departure. Anna was frantic. She was furious that the candidates she had finally found to take on the farm had been ignored. She was beyond belief that all her efforts to keep the farm and gain further extensions to stay, as well as the neighbors' pleas to the village government, had borne no fruit.

*Well, they don't want me here. So be it,* Anna fumed. She had enough of this back and forth, she was ready to leave it all behind and start over. She was glad she was allowed to take as many of her possessions as she wished, provided she could prove she had brought them with her. Fortunately she had kept the shipping receipts for all these years. At least it would be easier to connect to her friends and relatives, once she was in Germany. Although she did not relish the thought, she would go to Bavaria, where Michael's relatives were. It was the only place she could go under the circumstances.

Then Erdmuthe intervened by becoming seriously ill. She came down with pyelitis — a bacterial infection causing an acute inflammation of the renal pelvis — the doctor had explained. Her condition was grave and Anna felt torn between worry about her daughter's health — the child was fragile enough, after all — and relief that this medical emergency granted another reprieve. Maybe this illness had been brought on by all the stress? The child was very sensitive and did not want to leave. It seemed a crazy thought, after all this was an infection, but Anna still wondered: had the child unconsciously willed this health crisis?

Erdmuthe was in bed for weeks and out of school for two months. The new deadline for departure was May 15th, the day after Anna's birthday. *Fine present,* Anna sneered. But at least there would be enough time to leave in a more orderly fashion, to think things through more carefully, not to make rash decisions.

Since the Sattlers were now living downstairs, Anna needed to set up temporary living quarters on the second floor. She had to unpack again, at least bedding and essential household items. *Where have I packed Erdmuthe's spring clothing? And where are the cooking pots? I am sick of these boxes!* Anna was exasperated.

They set up house in the small former nursery and slept in the room above the *Stube*—Erdmuthe on the couch, Anna on a mattress. Their new "living room" contained some of their fancier furniture: a sofa, a small table, Anna's comfortable chair, a desk, a washstand, and a small woodstove for heat. That was all there was room for. Actually, Anna thought, it was quite pretty and comfortable! Even if it was temporary, the aesthetics of the place were important to her. It reminded her of the rooms she had set up as a student—small, but cozy and with a sense of beauty. Despite all the turmoil of the past months, Anna realized she still needed to shape the environment she lived in and to create a place she and Erdmuthe would be able to enjoy.

That was especially important now that she had to contend with the nastiness of the Sattlers. They treated Anna like an unwanted enemy. Unfortunately Anna had to share the cooking stove and pantry and the cold water faucet in the downstairs kitchen. Thus daily contact was unavoidable. She could feel they hated her sight and could not wait for her to leave. Well, thought Anna, they would have to wait and she was going to do her part to try to get rid of them, while she had the chance. She could see they would run the farm into the ground in short order. Their appointment was unconscionable and only due to political connections, Anna was sure.

It seemed strange to Anna that she was relieved of farm work now. *Vacation on the farm,* she thought. *Who could have imagined!* At least she had been allowed to keep part of the garden! She had more free time now and as soon as weather permitted she threw herself into gardening, but she could not really enjoy it. The moment Erdmuthe was better, she started visiting the authorities with renewed vigor. She had trouble figuring out which of the various local, district and provincial organizations were responsible for matters relating to her farm, and what influence the German trustee association, the German Delegation, and the American occupation forces had. They all seemed to be involved and working against each other. Even though nearly a year had passed since the end of the war, governmental entities were still poorly organized. Would she ever be able to sort all of this out? At this point, Anna decided, she had to deal with everybody who might have a stake.

Thus Anna was often on the road. Although it was tiring and she had to neglect Erdmuthe and leave her with the neighbors, roaming the countryside as she had to, often on foot, wasn't all bad. She realized she had been to more places in the past few months than in the seven years before! She was getting to know the region in new ways, the hills and valleys, the little villages with their onion-towered churches, the nearby towns with their squares and baroque buildings, the handsome four-corner farms strewn on the hillsides. The landscape was so pastoral and bucolic in spring! She discovered wildflowers she had not seen before and she came upon magnificent views of the mountains.

The beauty of this land touched her deeply. All this had become home to her. Nonetheless, she still mourned the loss of her childhood home in Pomerania, the sand beaches on the Baltic Sea, the pine forests, the birch-lined roads, the wide open sky. And now she might lose this place, too. She could not imagine finding a new home, putting down new roots again, somewhere else. If only this state of suspension would end, one way or another! And still she knew nothing about her mother.

# RECONNECTED
## *May 5, 1946*

Anna felt torn between happy and sad memories during springtime, when the trees were in blossom and the warm air made her feel alive again after the cold winter months. Two years ago, she had learned of Michael's death. Last year the war had ended. What would these May days, so portentous in the past, bring this time around?

After Felizitas' letter six months earlier no mail had gotten through the border. The waiting grew more and more intolerable. Severe penalties for smuggling mail stopped people from taking risks. Re-establishment of official mail service between Austria and Germany seemed to take forever! Anna could not understand what the difficulties were to achieve this. It was bad enough people could not see each other. Why could they not at least have the pleasure of communicating in writing?

Then, on a shining day in early May the miracle occurred. Anna had just admired her tulips, wondering where Manfred was, when the mailman brought a letter, a letter with German stamps and Anna's address written in Hilde's handwriting! Anna had been waiting for this moment for so long that now she was not sure whether or not she was dreaming. But it was true! Hilde wrote: "Mumm and Uncle Paul are alive! I found them, through the Red Cross, in Mecklenburg and here is their address!"

Oh, it was all too much! Anna was shaken to the core. Hilde said she had been in correspondence with Mumm since Christmas. How Anna envied her! And since then her sister had known the terrible story of Mumm's and Paul's trek from Silesia. Anna was overwhelmed and could only take in part of what she was reading. *Our poor little Mumm, how much she has had to endure!*

Anna called in Erdmuthe: "*Grossmutti* is alive!" she said, still crying. "And you can write to your grandmother! Can you imagine!" Even though earlier letters by Hilde relating all that had happened had never arrived, even though Mumm herself had written to no avail, Anna felt consoled by the thought that at least Mumm had known for some time that Anna and Erdmuthe were still at the farm — at least for the time being — and that they had come through the war! *Everyone knew of each other, only I knew nothing for all this time, for a year and a half,* Anna thought with some anger. But soon her resentment gave way to pure joy.

Erdmuthe was overcome too. How often had she prayed for her grandmother: that she would be alive, that they would learn where she lived, that she would have enough to eat, that she would be healthy, that they would see each other again. And now God had answered the most important of her prayers. *Grossmutti* was alive and she and her mother did not have to wait any longer for news!

Erdmuthe sat down immediately and wrote: "My dear, dear Grandmother, now we finally know you are alive. We are so happy! Many kisses from your granddaughter, Erdmuthe" She was almost finished with first grade and although she had missed much school due to her illness, she needed no help with this letter. It came straight from her heart. Anna, on the other hand, did not know where to start:

> My dearest mother, I can't tell you what I am experiencing, just writing your address! I am very much shaken. I only hope that since God let you survive such horrors and pains, he'll grant us all a few peaceful years together. I don't know yet what the circumstances of your life there are and I long for a letter from you.

Her mind started racing: How much she had to tell Mumm, how much she wanted to know! Could she arrange to visit her? How could she send things her mother might need? It was all so overwhelming. She had to talk to someone. She would go over to the neighbors and tell them everything, tell them how Mumm had suffered.

"I just got a letter from Hilde. She says my mother is alive," Anna shouted, running into the *Stube*. "I still can't believe it! And I now know what happened to her at the end of the war!" Talking about her mother's ordeal was even more overwhelming than reading Hilde's account. "The Russians arrived there on February 14th, on Erdmuthe's sixth birthday, of all days, and we celebrated and knew nothing," Anna said, full of dismay. She took out Hilde's letter, which related the trials of the flight. "Poor Mumm, and she was seventy-seven years old!"

When Anna told of her mother's tribulations and Martha's shocking behavior, denying her siblings lodging, she was enraged anew! Unbelievable! Such selfishness was unimaginable! "I hope Martha will roast in hell, or better yet, I hope God will punish her here on earth." Anna rarely wished evil on others. But this was too much. Turn away your own flesh and blood! At least she now knew where her mother and Paul were. "I wonder what their life is like there, but at least they are alive. Yes," said Anna, again overcome with tears. "They are alive!"

## A GOOD DEATH
### *May 16, 1946*

*I can't believe Konrad's mother is dead,* Klara Klausriegler thought, as she made her way over to Anna's place. They had thought she would not make it through this spring, but then it happened so suddenly that Klara was not quite prepared. Anyway, they had to be grateful she had lived to eighty-eight! That was a long life indeed and she had been ready, Klara knew. How fortunate she had been in bed for only a day and a half!

Klara remembered just in time not to knock on the *Stube* door downstairs. Anna lived upstairs now, she reminded herself. She had wondered about her new living quarters, but she would have liked to see them under more pleasant circumstances. Anna was surprised to see Klara in front of her door. It was unusual that she came over, unless there was an emergency. Or maybe she wanted to wish her a belated happy birthday? "Please, come in. Sit down," Anna said.

"Konrad's mother died last night," Klara said, not waiting to make small talk. "She could not get out of bed the day before and last night, sometime after three she died, peacefully. Actually, Klari was in her bed when she died." Anna frowned. "Sometimes Klari liked to sleep with her grandmother," Klara explained. "In the evening her grandmother had encouraged her: 'Come Klari, don't you want to sleep with me?' she had asked. And Klari jumped at the occasion. Maybe she did not feel well and did not want to be alone," Klara surmised. "We checked on her during the night and it seemed to us she was getting ready to pass. I wanted to take the child out of her bed, but she said: 'Why don't you leave her here?' So we did. And when we checked again, she had stopped breathing and Klari was sleeping quietly next to her dead grandmother. Maybe it gave her comfort to have the child close by."

"I am so sorry you lost her," Anna said. She would have liked to hug Klara, but she knew such expressions of affection were not customary. "You know how much I liked her and how grateful I am she watched over Erdmuthe for all these years. I know the child was getting a bit much for her lately. What can I do to help?"

"Oh, I just wanted you to know." Klara said. "We'll let you know about the funeral when everything is fixed. You can come over any time to say goodbye to her."

When Erdmuthe came home from school Anna said: "The *Nachbar* grandmother died. Let's go and see her." Anna picked a bunch of fragrant lilacs from her garden, made sure Erdmuthe's dress was clean, and then they went over to the neighbors'.

Grandmother lay in repose on her bed, dressed in her formal black gown, her head resting on a lace pillow. Candles burned and flowers sat on the nightstand. Erdmuthe looked at her with great curiosity. She looked like she was made from wax. Erdmuthe touched her hands folded over her belly. They felt cold. "Is she in heaven now?" Erdmuthe asked. She did not feel this was Klari's grandmother. She felt this was someone else. She was glad she had not seen her father dead. Like this. She remembered him alive and now he was dancing with Orion's stars. And her grandfather? She did not quite know where he was now.

For three nights the neighbors and relatives assembled and prayed. Then the priest came to give a blessing and a long procession of people walked down the mountain. The closest neighbors carried the coffin. After the funeral mass Theresia Klausriegler was buried in the family grave and everyone assembled in the village *Gasthaus* for a meal in her honor, the traditional meal of beef with horseradish sauce and a special white roll, served only at funerals.

Anna was there with everyone else. She was grateful to know her own mother was alive. When would she see her again? *God, don't let her die before then,* she prayed.

# WAR STORIES
## *Summer 1946*

Weeks after the first news about Mumm, and Anna's first letter to her mother, the return letter came, written by Mumm herself! Her handwriting looked a bit shaky, Anna thought, but it was her orderly, elegant handwriting — so different from Anna's scrawl. Not that Anna had doubted Mumm was indeed alive. But seeing her handwriting again, after all this time, gave her such certainty and joy she was downright giddy, even though it pained her to hear in what deprived circumstances her mother now lived. It was so typical, Anna thought, that she did not complain and was only grateful they had finally reconnected. "After all, we don't have much else left in this world except the connection to our loved ones," Mumm wrote. "Now my greatest wish is that God may grant us one more meeting on this earth."

Slowly letters arrived telling stories of the end of the war: reports of treks westward, as the whole German population in the Eastern regions, now Polish or Russian, was expelled. *How lucky we did not end up there as Neubauern,* Anna thought. *I doubt we would have gotten out alive.*

Hilde had joined a trek of fifty-three people from the Pomeranian estate of her cousin. They moved on back roads, as the main routes were reserved for military, and traveled in every available vehicle: tractors, a trailer, cars. A steamroller carried luggage, food and livestock. Hilde described unimaginable chaos: soldiers, prisoners of war, refugees, all together on the roads. Burned cities, broken-down vehicles, dead animals along the way. She told of people committing suicide, dying of exhaustion or illness, being raped, shot to death, abducted. Once they were among the only Germans interned in a camp of 12,000 Russians, Poles, Frenchmen and Dutch. And yet, after one month on the road, they reached the West. A good portion of luck, humor, gumption, and inventiveness had helped carry them through, and no one had died.

Other stories did not end so well. Cousin Werner, who had stayed back at the Karwen estate, was shot on the spot when a Russian soldier discovered a revolver in his backpack. Old Uncle Georg was forced to do hard labor on his own estate for the Polish occupiers, and his health was crumbling. Payback time, Anna concluded, remembering what had happened to Vicek's parents. Werner's in-laws, abducted from their estate, were never heard from again. *And we sat here on our farm in relative peace, knowing nothing,* Anna thought. Most painful of all was the news from Anna's friend Lo, whose mother, sister, and brother-in-law committed suicide as the Russians entered Berlin. "They feared my brother-in-law would be sent to Siberia and decided they would not be separated," Lo wrote. "They told the children, two and four years old, they would go to heaven to polish the stars and all five took the poison saved for this eventuality. We only heard a year later."

Anna knew there was nothing unusual about these stories. They happened thousands of times. They were what happened at the end of wars, wherever, whenever. They were the punishment for Hitler's lunacy and his blinded followers. But these tales were not abstractions. Anna knew these people. She had spent time on these Pomeranian estates. She had gone to university with Lo and eaten at her mother's table. All her friends, it seemed, were starving and homeless, starting over amidst rubble.

And she sat here in Austria, unable to help. Her isolation continued. Sometimes Anna almost despaired. She still did not know whether she would have to leave, but at least for now she and her daughter had shelter and enough food. Sometimes she worked in the neighbors' fields in exchange for eggs, butter or bread. She was grateful she had this option and did not have to make arduous trips, like her friends, scrounging for a few potatoes. The thought that soon she might be displaced, too, become a refugee among millions, terrified her. Thus she continued her efforts to secure permission to stay in Austria. In mid-October they bore fruit: Anna and Erdmuthe received permanent permission to stay. *Now I must try to get rid of Sattler,* she swore, *and find a better solution for the farm.* But she was tired, very tired indeed, and only in retrospect she realized what a toll all the uncertainty had taken. She would take a break, put her garden to rest and prepare for Christmas.


## TWO CHRISTMAS CELEBRATIONS
### *December 24, 1946*

Mumm celebrated her Christmas by writing to her daughters. What a gift to know about each other! She would not tell Anna what her present life was truly like. She had no tree, not even a candle to light; she only had a torn dress and no shoes, only slippers; she and Paul slept in beds without sheets; their food supply was barely enough for survival; Paul had to scrounge for wood and the people in this godforsaken place in Mecklenburg, in the Russian zone, let them feel they were unwanted refugees. Knowing the minister had not helped. He had left before they had arrived. No, she would not write about any of this to Anna. Instead, she wrote that she was grateful they had survived the horrors of their flight, that they were alive, and that now she could at least write to her daughters. "It is so lonely without you, so empty of love, so ordinary," Mumm wrote, in pencil, since she had no pen, on paper she had had difficulty in securing. "And yet, it could be so much sadder if we did not know of each other."

Unfortunately she could not bake anything, Mumm wrote, but Mrs. Theiss, their landlady, had given them a piece of cake and she was grateful for that. She did not say what a miser her landlady usually was. No, she would not tell in what destitute circumstances they now lived. There was no sense to worry her daughters unnecessarily! But she could not help mentioning her sorrow about being unable to go to church on this special day:

> The church is still shot up and I can't stand the draft. The substitute minister lives far away and made no appearance Christmas Eve or on Christmas Day. The Mecklenburg people don't seem to be churchgoers in general But the rectories I have seen so far look like estates!

It was a good thing Paul was a minister, although he was not allowed to fill in. At least the two of them could make their own service, alone. After all, Jesus had said, "When two or three meet in my name, I will be in their midst." Margarethe trusted God would hear their prayers, especially the most fervent wish for a reunion with her daughters, while she was still on this earth. If only Hilde and Anna could come to visit! It was next to impossible to travel from one zone to the other, let alone from Austria. *What times we live in,* Mumm thought. She could so identify with Mary, finding no place in the inn and giving birth to her child in a stable, away from home, in poverty and deprivation.

This was the second Christmas they had spent apart. Two years earlier Hilde had still come to Silesia from war-torn Berlin, despite the danger and difficulty of travel. Last year she had reconnected with Hilde and learned she was alive and had gotten out of Berlin. But they knew nothing of Anna then, and of her granddaughter. Over four years now, since she had seen them! At least now she knew that Anna had been able to stay in Austria and was spared having to start over. Maybe God would grant them a reunion next Christmas, if she lived to see it.

Anna remembered how sad Christmas had been the past two years: In 1944 after Michael's death, and in 1945, after they had received their eviction notice and knew nothing of Hilde and Mumm. This Christmas would be different. They would celebrate joyfully, now that they knew they could stay at the farm. Anna would do everything to create a festive celebration for herself and Erdmuthe!

She had saved up a bit of butter and sugar, so she could bake a few cookies. She asked neighbor Konrad for a tree, since her woods were not her own anymore. He picked out a particularly pretty one and even put it into a handsome stand for her. Anna and Erdmuthe made their own candles from wax remnants they had collected over the past year. "This is fun," said Erdmuthe, as she dipped the wick into the molten wax again and again, watching the candle thicken. Anna thought of the first Christmas on the farm, when she and Michael had dipped their candles and of their first crooked little tree from their own woods, when Erdmuthe was not yet born and the future lay before them, wide open. And she remembered the perfect small tree Michael had cut in the woods for their last Christmas together, three years ago.

Anna had made Erdmuthe's favorite dishes: applesauce and potato salad — not exactly Christmas fare, she thought. How fortunate that her daughter loved these two dishes that she could make from farm staples. The potatoes came from the required food payment by the tenants and the neighbors had given her apples, since the Sattlers had decided not to let them have anything they were not forced to give. But Anna was determined not to let such unpleasantness spoil their Christmas.

For years now Erdmuthe had fervently wished for a doll with "real" hair and eyes that opened, and Anna had hoped she would be able to get it across the border from Bavaria for this Christmas. There were tears when Erdmuthe found a letter under the tree saying her angel had made a mistake and brought her doll to another child who would otherwise have had no presents at all. Erdmuthe would have to be patient still until a doll for her would arrive at a later date. "How can an angel make such a mistake?" she cried. "I have been so patient for so long." Anna's heart almost broke, but what could she do, when packages still could not cross the border and she had found no one to smuggle the doll from Bavaria to Austria.

Erdmuthe cheered quickly when she saw the new coat for her teddy bear, the beautiful lace gown for her old, somewhat battered baby doll. "What glorious childhood memories these dresses brought back, when I refurbished them for Erdmuthe!" Anna wrote to her mother. "You are very much part of this Christmas! If only my packages to you would arrive, so you will have something special to eat." She had packed smoked meat she had received from the neighbors and cookies and given the package to a personal carrier, hoping he would mail it in Germany, in exchange for a good-sized piece of bacon. But you never knew. Sometimes the temptation to keep food packages for oneself was just too great.

## WINTER DEPRESSION
### February 1947

It was still dark and snow fell heavily when Anna sent Erdmuthe out into the winter cold in her leaky boots. Poor child, she thought, worrying about her fragile health. At eight, she weighed only forty pounds and looked thin and very pale. Since she had started school, she had had the mumps and measles, whooping cough and nasty worms, boils and a sty in her eye, not to mention numerous colds and, of course, her serious illness that had saved them from deportation. No wonder the child could not put on weight with these constant setbacks! No matter how hard Anna tried to keep her out of school in weather like this, Erdmuthe refused to stay home. No way would she miss school; she objected and usually she prevailed against Anna's better judgment.

The fire in the small stove crackled and gave off warmth, despite the green wood the tenant supplied. Tea water simmered and the dog lay in front of the stove and grunted. This was a cozy and pleasant room. How many refugees would consider such living conditions palatial, Anna thought. And yet, she felt miserable. She felt, she could not fight any longer. She was disheartened. She wondered how much longer she could hold on. All the struggles of the past year had exhausted her.

There was the strife with the tenants, their constant efforts to make her life as unpleasant as they could. When she arranged to take a bath in the kitchen — unfortunately she had no other choice — she found the windows wide open and the room freezing. When she came to cook one day, her pot was smashed. They stole from her supplies in the pantry. Herr Sattler, who drank heavily, abused her verbally and called her "stupid bitch" and worse. Anna had tried to distance herself from such insults and let them roll off her back. But, she realized, she was afraid to go downstairs and face these people. *I feel like I am going into battle every time I enter their kitchen,* Anna thought. Yes, it was their kitchen, and she had to share it against their will. She needed her own, but how? There was hardly space for a cooking stove in her little room and she had no way to secure such a stove anyway.

She had tried everything she could think of to get rid of these people who were ruining the farm. She had run from one office to the next, trying to get the authorities to hear her out, to investigate — to no avail. Several times it had looked like she was getting somewhere, only to be disappointed again. She knew Sattler had his means — a bottle of homemade plum brandy was a treasure those days and he had made barrels of the stuff from the unusually bountiful harvest of plums last fall. And he had his allies. Plus, he was Austrian and she a mere German! She felt like she was running in circles, starting over and over again and getting nowhere, like a hamster spinning endlessly on his wheel. It was so infuriating, especially since she had found good local candidates who were ready to take over the farm. The local farmers, in particular the neighbors who knew her best and could vouch for her past, had tried to advocate on her behalf. But that had not made any difference either. She was banging her head against a wall and it was beginning to crack.

Worse than these personal annoyances was Anna's worry about her mother, her inability to help. *I feel so defeated, so helpless in this situation,* she thought. She had things her mother would need — woolen socks, a sweater, shoes for Uncle Paul. And yet, she was unable to send packages from here. She had mobilized her network in Germany, tried to get goods over the border through personal contacts, to be sent from there. And Michael's relatives were willing to send supplies of their own. But, it seemed, the majority of packages never arrived, or the best items inside were missing. Some people just kept for themselves what they were supposed to send on. She had learned tricks, like sending one shoe at a time. But what good was that if one of the packages got lost! Sometimes Anna just wanted to scream with frustration!

The very worst was that she got nowhere with her efforts to secure travel permits to see her mother. She could not get permission to cross the border, and even if she succeeded in crossing, how was she going to get from the American zone into the Russian? She was stuck here on her mountain, unable to see her poor old mother! Even her sister who lived in the British zone had not succeeded so far! These regulations were brutal and inhumane! What else was there left in this world but human contact! Anna wavered between tears and fury when she thought of it all. She knew the Allies were punishing the Germans and Austrians for the war — and she could not even blame them — but her poor mother who could not hurt a fly did not deserve this!

And all her friends were in Germany. True, she should be grateful she knew where they were, that they were alive. She should be grateful for the occasional letter she received. But she longed to hold them in her arms, to sit through the night talking about what they all had endured during the war, to cry together over their losses. Letters were a lifeline, but they were no substitute for physical contact, for embracing her mother, for hearing Friedel's laughter, for sitting across from Felizitas, drinking a cup of tea with her, as in old times.

Anna had to admit she was slowly making new friends here. Erdmuthe's first-grade teacher Gertrude had become a friend with whom she could share her sorrows. She felt close to Christl, a fellow Pomeranian, who worked at the German Delegation. But she lived too far away for regular contact. There were a few others she was beginning to get to know better. But that was no substitute for life-long relationships and years of mutual sharing. *If only I could go to Germany to visit,* Anna dreamed.

Another worry was money. Anna was running out. They simply could not subsist on the meager sum Sattler was paying. She needed to find a way to make a living. Maybe she could teach at the local school. In spring she would start listening in to see what it was like and whether that was something she would be capable of doing. Better yet, maybe she could take up writing again. Shortly after the war ended, the Americans had helped start up a new newspaper in Salzburg. Maybe she'd have a chance to work for them. But so far she had not found anyone who had contacts there and nothing worked here without personal connections. Where to begin? It took so much energy to start something new and Anna had no initiative.

The more she thought about it, the more Anna realized that she was depressed. A great apathy was overtaking her, she was losing her determination and persistence. She was more and more discouraged. *How ironic,* she thought. *I have been fighting so hard to get permission to stay here in Austria, and now that I have achieved it, I don't give a damn. I am not interested in it anymore. I just want to get away. I can't stand this isolation any longer. I feel so lonely and homesick for Germany.*

She could not sit all morning and brood, Anna finally decided. She would write a letter to her mother. And she had to cook something for Erdmuthe: Potatoes and salt, with carrots, sometimes cabbage were their staple foods in winter. In summer their diet was more varied, thanks to Anna's garden. It provided not only work and food, but also joy. Especially the flowers boosted her spirits. But it would be months till planting time. *The Nachbarin* had given Erdmuthe two apples and two eggs for her birthday in February. But such luxury was rare.

And yet, she had to be grateful they could fill their stomachs and were not suffering hunger, like so many refugees and city dwellers. Friedel, for instance, had to travel long distances on crowded trains and then walk for twenty-four kilometers with her hand wagon, just to buy potatoes from a farmer for whom her son worked. Or Miechen, who did not know how to stuff the hungry stomachs of her three growing sons! Luckily Miechen had diamonds to sell to supplement their income. At least she and Erdmuthe had small appetites, so their supplies lasted longer. Anna knew she should be utterly grateful for all they had. But she was getting so sick of all the struggles. She wanted to lean on somebody's shoulder. She just wanted to leave, go to Germany, even if the food situation was better here. She lacked food for the soul, and for Anna that sometimes was more important than feeding the body.

She heard Erdmuthe stomp up the steep wooden stairs. Erdmuthe opened the door and shook the snow off her wet pants. "Mutti," she laughed, "the snow is so beautiful! We made snow angels and later Klari and I will build a snowman! Winter is so much fun!"


## SPRING AWAKENING
### May 14, 1947

Anna was touched. Erdmuthe had gotten up early and set up her birthday table before she'd had to leave for school at seven. She had gone to the garden and picked a big bunch of the traditional *Tausendschönchen*, the special large-size garden daisies which had been Anna's birthday bouquet from childhood on. Erdmuthe had made a colorful drawing of herself picking flowers, her very favorite thing to do. And she had learned a little celebratory poem by heart and had recited it when Anna came out of her bedroom. Sometimes it was almost scary how solicitous the child was, how anxious to please her. Her daughter was almost a companion and friend and even though she sometimes wondered whether this was healthy for the child, Anna relished Erdmuthe's attention and caring.

The day before Anna had received a birthday letter from her mother, remembering the Pomeranian birthdays of her childhood:

> I am so grateful I have my two children, that I know where they are, that we can write to each other and look forward to a reunion. There is no king in this world that I'd wish to trade with!

Dear little Mumm, Anna thought. Since there was nothing more she could do for Mumm, maybe she should just take care of herself, to gather strength for whatever lay ahead.

Anna relished the quiet time she had for herself. She sat on the bench in front of the house and admired her garden. The tulips burst with lushness, like every year; the peonies budded and would open soon. Radish greens peeked out, lettuce flourished, and peas stretched their feelers. Bright green cress was ready to cut and would add vitamins to their diet. Anna could not wait for all the vegetables to grow big enough for harvest. Erdmuthe had her own little garden bed this year and was proud her carrots sprouted and beans showed their green tips.

Christ Ascension, a church holiday in Austria and the day of Erdmuthe's First Communion, was rapidly approaching. Although she was Lutheran, Anna made an effort not to hinder Erdmuthe's participation. She wanted her to be part of the life here in every respect, and First Communion was the biggest event for second graders. But it was a bittersweet occasion for Anna. She felt pained that this was not her tradition, that she could not fully share Erdmuthe's joy.

Getting ready had been a big worry. Where to find a white dress, a candle, all the supplies needed. Thank heaven the Wasserburg relatives had come through and that their package had arrived already. What excitement for Erdmuthe to unpack the white silken dress, made from an old curtain *Tante* Ilse had sacrificed. The candle, although broken in two, was the very one Erdmuthe's father had held at his own First Communion. They had also included Michael's prayer book and a little rosary from her grandmother, and white stockings. Unfortunately the shoes were too big, but no one else would have white shoes either. "Now I'll be as pretty as the other girls," Erdmuthe had said, relieved she'd be able to keep up with Klari, who was all set and would wear her sister's dress.

Spring, glorious spring! Anna breathed in the lilac-scented air. The white blossoms had opened just in time for her birthday! The fruit trees had finished blooming. This year the *Nachbar* grandmother had not been alive to enjoy the bounty and they all had thought of her. She was now truly in the Garden of Paradise, like Michael, Anna thought. Now that Anna had only one tree of each kind — cherry, apple, plum, and walnut — she watched their progress carefully. It looked like the cherries were going to do well, but her apple tree had some spider disease and there might be no apples! Where would she get apples for Erdmuthe? She'd probably end up stealing a few here and there from the Sattlers' trees, when they were not home. But why worry? Somehow God, or nature, or friends would provide. There was no use worrying about everything that was out of her control. Anna was beginning to learn to enjoy the moment. Who knew what tomorrow would bring? She would enjoy this bright morning. She would sit in the sun and be lazy!

Suddenly, Anna realized, that she was over her winter depression and that she was happy right here, at least at this moment. True, letters from Germany still provided her with her most intense emotional experiences. She still wanted to visit her friends there and, especially, see her mother again. But she was not so sure anymore she needed to live there. Maybe this feeling would not last, but for now there were things that made her happy right here. Hiking with Gertrude lifted her spirit. How beautiful this country was! How energizing to climb a mountain, breathe the clear air, and look far across the landscape.

*Sometimes I am simply happy*, Anna noticed. *Happy for many reasons: Because the sun shines, because my child is healthy, because I love Gertrude and spend time with her. And I feel such a deep gratitude that we are allowed to live at the farm, safely. How lucky we are and how insignificant is the unpleasantness of the Sattlers if*

*I think of the misery of refugees, all the people displaced through the war, of poor Mumm!*

But somehow, it occurred to her now, it was more than gratefulness. She felt some of the happiness she used to feel in spring when she was young, a feeling of pure joy! She felt new energy pulsing through her body, like the juices rising in a tree in spring! She felt as though she was waking from a long sleep and a deep numbness. She felt a kind of bliss she thought she'd never feel again. Spring happiness for no other reason than that she existed, here and now, at this very moment.

## REFUGEE LIFE
### *July 12, 1947*

The rucksack full of food for Mumm and *Onkel* Paul felt heavy, as Hilde made her way from the train station in Lärz to the Theiss house. How long she had waited for this day! How many times she had envisioned her arrival at Mumm's, their embrace, their joy at seeing each other after all this time! It seemed like a fairy tale that she had finally reached her goal, that she was here, climbing the stairs to the room where Mumm and her brother had lived for almost two years. As she knocked, Hilde dreaded opening the door. She braced herself for what she might find, but, as she looked in, she realized quickly, her imagination had been entirely inadequate.

The tiny room was stuffed with furniture. A bed, a couch, a table with two chairs, an armoire and a stove filled the room, so that there was hardly space to turn around. At the table sat an old woman in a tattered dress, peeling potatoes with trembling hands. Her body was swollen, her face unrecognizable. Hilde knew it had to be Mumm, but there was no sign of recognition at first. Then, finally, a smile: "Hilde, thank God you are here! I feared I would not see you again in this life," Mumm said. "How I have been waiting for this moment! My dear, dear child, how are you? Tell me everything."

Hilde was so shocked she could not speak or embrace her mother. All she could do was sit on the second chair and hold her hand. "Oh my God, Mumm, this is how you have been living for two years! Why did you not tell us what it was like!" "Look, Hilde, there was nothing you could have done. Why worry you?" Mumm said. By and by Hilde found out everything. How they had had only potatoes to eat for weeks, and, in the end, only bread, that Mumm's body could not tolerate. No wonder she had these swollen legs, this edema, a result of hunger. Mumm told Hilde that a few days earlier they had finally fetched a doctor who had given medication that would eliminate excess water in her body and encourage her heart to pump better.

They sat there, for hours, and since *Onkel* Paul was out searching for food Mumm could talk freely. "In the summer, when we cook, the room heats to temperatures of fifty degrees Celsius and more," Mumm said. "It's like being inside a furnace, but Paul is so worried about drafts, he keeps the windows closed! I fear I'll faint every time we heat the stove." After a while Hilde realized Mumm did not get up because she could not. Her legs were so swollen that standing up and walking a few steps required Herculean effort and caused great pain. You could not tell where her knees were. Her belly was huge. It seemed the doctor had come just in time. A few more days like this, Hilde was sure, and Mumm would have died. Thankfully, the medication worked and her face and arms normalized in the three days Hilde was there. Getting to the bathroom in the hall required all the strength Mumm had. She was bathed in sweat each time. She eliminated buckets of water.

As she took inventory, Hilde fell from one shock into the next. Aside from the pillow cases she had sent, there were no sheets or bed covers, only bare down-filled bedding. "Why did you tell me not to send any linen?" Hilde asked. "I just did not want to burden myself with anything here, I wanted to be able to leave at any time," was her mother's explanation. She did not want to feel trapped. Rather, she preferred to do without linens for two years! Hilde was aghast. Mumm had nothing. Her dress was in shreds. She had no shoes, just wooden clogs, in which her swollen feet hurt excruciatingly. Her sweater was full of holes. Mumm had only asked for things for her brother while she herself was wanting.

The armoire housed all their belongings, few as they were: clothing, food and a few books. Hilde decided they could not continue living in this place. She was going to make every conceivable effort to help them leave, but first Mumm needed to get well and be transportable. "Heart-rending misery," was Hilde's summary in her letter to Anna. "I have to get them out of there!"

Reading the news, Anna was heartbroken. Why did her kind and gentle seventy-nine-year-old mother have to suffer so much? If only she had stayed at the farm during the war! Now Anna was not going to rest until she secured her travel permit. *I have to go and see Mumm as soon as possible. All else is immaterial.*

Meanwhile Mumm's health was improving. Hilde made every possible effort to get travel permits and accommodation for Mumm and Paul to bring them to her area in the British zone. Finally she found a place that was suitable and would accept them both.

# THE GREEN POSTCARD
## *September 10, 1947*

Anna was getting closer to reaching her goal. She would go to see her mother, with or without travel papers. In a few days, she would bring Erdmuthe to Munich, then go to Lärz and bring Mumm and *Onkel* Paul to Hilde! Maybe she could then go and get Erdmuthe, so the child could see her grandmother and aunt also. They would finally be united! Anna could hardly contain herself at the thought! If she could not get permission in time, she would take the risk and cross the border illegally, she had decided. There were ways to get across: one could cross streams at hidden locations, walk through forests at out-of-the-way places, climb up and down mountain sides. Anna had gathered the necessary information from people who had done it. It was risky, but she simply had to go and see her mother. She could wait no longer.

When Anna stopped at the village post office on her way to do an errand at the town hall, a bright green postcard from Wasserburg awaited her. Mail from Bavaria arrived more regularly than from other places. Thus Hilde sometimes took this route to get news to Anna faster. Maybe this was about Mumm? The postcard was mailed ten days earlier. "Just received the news your mother died peacefully last night. I am so sorry! Your sister-in-law Ilse." It took Anna time to comprehend what she was reading. "No, it can't be!" she cried out. "Why now? Now that I was ready to go and see her! How can life be so cruel? No, it can't be!"

Anna continued to do what she had set out to do, as in a trance. Back home she dug out her mother's last letters and pictures from long ago. *How can life be so cruel?* she wondered again. If anyone deserved better, it was her mother. That lovely photograph of her as a young girl, how much promise was in that face! She looked so shy and pure, and yet there was a certain boldness in the expression of her mouth, Anna thought, an indication of the great fearlessness of her heart. What possibilities might this young girl have had, had she grown up in more peaceful times. As it was, she had lived through two world wars, barely survived the Spanish flu that had killed millions, had lost her home not once, but twice, and had now starved to death as a refugee, in utter poverty. "Unfathomable, such suffering," Anna moaned. "Why? Oh why?"

Anna thought of her mother as a young woman. Margarethe Steckman had worked as a companion to a well-to-do older lady, had traveled Europe with her employer, and only at age thirty-five had become the second wife of Max Dahle, a well-off merchant in the Pomeranian town of Pollnow. There she had supervised a prosperous household with maids and a cook and given birth to her first daughter Anna at thirty-eight and to Hilde three years later. When the Great War began, in 1914, everyone had to tighten their belts. The maids had to go and Mumm did the housework herself. Food was rationed and luxuries vanished, but somehow Mumm had managed to find ways that at least her children did not suffer hunger.

When Anna was sixteen, her father became ill and Anna left for Berlin to make her own living. Anna reread the first letter her mother had written to her then. It was filled with so much love and anguish over this early separation and, not surprisingly, advice for a young girl leaving home. "If you encounter temptations, think of your mother. Always act in such a way that you can look her freely in the eye," Mumm had admonished. And although there was much about her years in Berlin that Anna could not have told her, she hoped in essential matters her mother would have approved of her life there.

Widowed, Mumm was booted out of the house by her stepsons, who also tried to cheat her out of her inheritance. And she, who found it difficult to ask for anything for herself, fought like a lioness for her daughters, battling bankers and lawyers. How much that must have cost Mumm who hated conflict! Finally Mumm moved to the small Silesian village, Niebusch, where she kept house for her brother Paul, the Lutheran minister there. Her letters provided a small inkling of how hard it had been for Mumm to give up her home and her friends, to live in such rural isolation. Mostly though she wrote about the joys of her garden — blooming forsythias, the first snowdrops, the last asters, the magnificent dahlias! Anna remembered that she had still wondered what was blooming in her Silesian garden when she was a refugee in Mecklenburg. Her greatest joy, though, she always said, were the visits from her daughters. How heart-warming those visits had been, how warm their Christmas celebrations, even in times of war when Mumm had little.

And then the horror of her flight in 1945 and life as a refugee in Mecklenburg. Even there she cared more about her brother than herself. At least she was able to sleep in sheets for the last few days of her life! How good Hilde had sent them, even though she thought it would be for only a brief time. "I had forgotten how comfortable it is to sleep in linen," Mumm had written in her last message. And, how happy she was Anna would come. Anna burst into tears again, thinking about it.

She had finally decided to go, and now it was too late! She would never see her mother again. She would now have to do without the letters that felt like her mother's warm embrace, the letters that had brought her so much hope and joy. Anna had so longed to be able to bring her mother comfort, and now she would not be able to do that. Why did she have to die so suddenly, after her health had improved?

Why now? Anna could still not grasp it. And she had not even been able to attend the funeral. It took ten days to learn of her mother's death! She assumed Hilde had been able to get to Laerz to bury her. How she envied Hilde, that she had been able to see Mumm before she died. Life was so unfair!

The next day, a letter from Hilde arrived, telling her of Mumm's last days and the funeral. Her health had greatly improved. She had been able to walk in the garden, unaided. She happily looked forward to leaving any day. Then, one morning Paul found her in bed, unconscious. She died the next day. According to the doctor, her heart had given out. "I went though her possessions," Hilde wrote. "They fit into one cardboard box. I found the coffee I had sent to her to help raise her blood pressure. She had not drunk it, but put a note on the bag. It said "For Anna's visit." "Oh Mumm," Anna moaned. It was all too painful, too overwhelming.

In the weeks to come Anna's pain softened and she came to accept that Mumm had had a good death after all. She died knowing of her impending departure, sleeping in fresh sheets and awaiting her daughter's visit. At least her last days on earth were filled with hope, Anna thought.

THE JOURNEY
*November 1947*

All autumn Anna mourned her mother and all her other loved ones who had died so far away. Their graves were scattered throughout Europe: her father's grave in Pomerania, now Poland; her mother's grave in the Russian zone in Eastern Germany; Michael's grave in the Ukraine.

Eventually her sadness lifted and nature's irrepressible abundance buoyed her spirit. Although her apple harvest had been diminished by the spider attack this past spring, bright blue plums bent the branches of Anna's little tree. Her garden repaid many times over the labor she had put into it all summer.

Even though Anna was not sure whether she would remain on the farm and eat this bounty of nature, she could not help but preserve what the harvest had provided. If for no other reason, she could not see nature's gifts and the fruits of her labor go to waste. She harvested and stored carrots, onions and cabbage. She canned green beans and red beets. She hung up herbs to dry and saved leaves of black currants and mint for tea.

She brought bunches of flowers into the house and feasted her eyes on them. She filled vases with blue asters and rust-colored chrysanthemums, but most of all she loved her mother's dahlias: their robust boldness, their rich purples and yellows, their manifold variations, some shaped like small pompon balls, others like large spiky sun wheels. They would bloom for years to come and bring back the memory of her mother again and again! Her garden with its flowers, it seemed to Anna, replaced her mother's grave. She felt closer to Mumm there than she could have in any cemetery.

After Anna had put her garden to rest, she turned her thoughts to her long delayed trip. *I must seize the day and go to Germany,* she decided. True, it was too late to see her mother, but there were her friends to visit, her sister to see, Erdmuthe to bring to Michael's relatives.

She still did not know what to do, whether to stay in Austria or move to Germany. How could she decide without seeing for herself! She knew she had to go, that she simply could not wait any longer even though she had no permit to enter the American zone in Bavaria.

She was tired of waiting and battling bureaucratic obstacles. She'd sneak across the border secretly. If only she had done this while her mother was alive! But she'd go now and not let any more time pass. Christmas would be a good occasion to visit.

Erdmuthe was excited, especially when she heard they might cross the border illegally and that they might get caught and be put into jail. What an adventure that would be! They would be in Wasserburg for Christmas, she would see her grandmother and her aunts, and there would be gifts, she was sure. Maybe she'd finally get her long awaited doll with real hair and eyes that could close.

In the end, Anna found a safer way to get across the border. They traveled at night in a railway car filled with furniture and Erdmuthe slept, fully dressed, on a table top. When the train jerked to a stop she awoke instantly. She spurred her mother on to hurry, knowing they had to get off and vanish into the darkness of the station before the patrols came. But Anna was still struggling with her shoe laces when a border guard appeared in the doorway. Erdmuthe was already out, but Anna was stopped. "Where are you going?" the man demanded gruffly. "Oh, back to wagon two," Anna said, trying to cover her nervousness. "You visited in the middle of the night?" the controller said, sarcastically, and looked Anna up and down. "Well, then get back there," he finally said, "but quickly!" and Anna slipped out and into the shadowy recesses of the station, where other illegal travelers had hidden. *He knew I had no papers,* Anna was sure. *Thank God he let me go.*

Erdmuthe was in a state of high excitement. It was her job to check and make sure the coast was clear for everyone without papers to return to their wagons. She stealthily made her way back to those who had hidden. "You can come out now," she whispered, feeling like a spy who had completed a dangerous mission. Anna was a wreck. Erdmuthe returned to her makeshift resting place and slept until morning when the train arrived in Munich. "I can't believe we are finally in Germany," Anna said. It seemed to her as though they had been traveling for an eternity and to another planet.

## GERMANY
### November 1947

*Finally I am here in Germany!* Anna was full of expectation. The connections of Michael's relatives eased handling all the formalities. Anna quickly received her residency permit and ration cards. She made contact with her friends and set up her travel route. She was impatient and anxious to see her old friends after all these years!

Yet, despite the unexpected ease in making her arrangements and her happiness at being near loved ones, Anna felt troubled. Wasserburg was full of refugees — visibly outsiders. She could feel the resentment of the locals against these newcomers who disturbed the long-established order of this close-knit conservative Bavarian town. She was shocked by Michael's relatives' selfishness, how they seemed to live just for themselves, how unsympathetic they seemed towards others who had lost everything. She realized, if she settled here she would be an outsider too, her in-laws notwithstanding.

Relieved to get out of town and leaving Erdmuthe behind with her grandmother, Anna reunited with her sister whom she had not seen for over three years, ever since Michael's death. The sisters shared the grief over their mother's death and their war time tribulations. Anna finally learned all the details how Hilde had gotten out of Berlin on the last train, how she had miraculously joined the trek West of her Pomeranian relatives, how she had made a new life for herself in the British zone, slowly replacing needed items she had lost in Silesia and Berlin, and how she had started from scratch and landed on her feet, working as a math teacher. Her mode of transport was a bicycle and food was often hard to come by — but she had a roof over her head and a job. Everything else would follow eventually.

*Hilde has mellowed,* Anna thought. But it did not take long for the old tensions between them to re-emerge. Anna realized that despite their sisterly bond they would never get along. She knew her attitude toward her "little" sister had been overbearing in the past. Hilde probably suffered more on her account than Anna did in reverse, she had to admit. But that did not diminish the irritation the sisters felt about each other. Nonetheless, they decided to spend Christmas together in Wasserburg. Hilde wanted to see Erdmuthe after all these years, see how she had changed and grown.

Anna's reunions with her friends in different parts of the American zone were entirely reassuring. No one had changed for the worse, Anna felt, despite the miserable situation in Germany which she had not been able to imagine while living on her mountain farm in Austria. Despite all the pains and losses Anna and her friends had suffered, she experienced nothing but the old love and friendship she remembered. She was distressed that she could not see Friedel, who lived in the Russian zone near Berlin. But her visit with Felizitas was heart-warming. All the resentments expressed in her wartime letters had vanished. These long-standing bonds were irreplaceable, Anna knew. Still, she was unsure this need for old friends could outweigh the increasing ambivalence she felt about the new Germany.

Germany still lay in ruins. New residents struggled to make a new life. Those not displaced seemed mainly concerned with re-establishing their material welfare. Few seemed to care about spiritual values. Anna was beginning to see she'd have difficulty living in Bavaria. She felt so torn, and delayed making a decision. First, she would return to Wasserburg to celebrate Christmas with Erdmuthe and Michael's relatives.

## SIMPLICITY AND WEALTH
### *Christmas 1947*

Klara knelt on the floor and poured soapy water on the dirty boards, scrubbed with a hard brush and soaked up the excess water with an old rag. She hadn't scrubbed the floor for some time. Today, on the afternoon before Christmas Eve, it was a must. She was almost done and pleased how white and clean the wide boards came out. Konrad and Maridl had gone to cut a tree and soon Klari who had known for some time the *Christkind* did not really exist would hang the ornaments. Konrad would bless the house and the fragrance of incense would fill every room.

Still, this Christmas would be quieter than earlier ones. The *Nachbarin* and Erdmuthe were in Germany, and who knew whether they would come back to stay. Klara hoped they would, especially for her daughter's sake who would otherwise lose her best friend. Konrad's mother and Resl were missing for the second year, one having died and the other having left home.

Klara still missed Resl. She had only seen her a few times since she had moved to her aunt's farm in the flatland. Klara could not tell how her daughter felt about living there, whether she still missed her parents and sisters and the farm where she had grown up. She could imagine it was not easy for the girl, her father's favorite. But it had to be done and her reward would come later, when she would find a good farmer husband who would hopefully not just marry her for the farm she'd inherit. Maridl, she was sure, missed her sister, since she now had no one to talk to about her worries and problems. Klari was too little for that and Maridl was more like a second mother to her.

Klara wondered how Anna was faring in Germany. It seemed to her she was caught between two chairs. Here she had to contend with Sattler's nastiness, and who knew whether she'd ever get her farm back. It was such an injustice! In Bavaria she might be better off and have a chance to start over. But from what Anna had told her, those relatives would never accept her, a Prussian. And she could not see how Erdmuthe, who was so attached to the farm, to Klari, to her life here, could be happy anywhere else. Although children were adaptable. Many, whether refugees or evacuees, had to adjust. It was hard to know what would be the best solution. She was glad she was not faced with such choices. She'd live here, on this farm, till she died.

Well, the *Nachbarin* was smart and she'd find her way through this problem, she was sure. Klara was not happy that the Sattlers were still here. Too bad that so far Anna's efforts to get rid of them had led nowhere. Somehow this man seemed to have connections in the right places. But she was sure the *Nachbarin's* persistence would succeed eventually. When Anna put her mind to something she usually achieved what she wanted, sooner or later. *Well, today is Christmas Eve,* Klara thought. *I'll wish the Sattler family a happy holiday, if I find time between all the chores I have left to do. Walking to Midnight Mass will be hard going with all the snow coming down.*

For Erdmuthe Christmas Eve in Wasserburg was more splendid than she could ever have imagined. The house had been cleaned from top to bottom. The parquet floors shone and the Biedermeier furniture gleamed. The fragrance of cookies wafted through the rooms and now duck was roasting in the oven. Duck! Erdmuthe had never eaten duck. She was excited, although she felt less tension than in other years. When the bell rang, the door opened and revealed an enormous tree, hung with silver stars and bells and birds. It was prettier than Klari's and much much bigger. It was lit with, it seemed, hundreds of candles, and under it lay many packages.

A long table with a white damask table cloth and delicate china was set in the parlor for a feast for the many relatives: Grandmother, *Tante* Ilse and *Onkel* Lutz, *Tante* Lily and *Onkel* Gusti, *Tante* Hilde and Anna and at the very bottom end Erdmuthe, the only child in the whole clan. It seemed like a big crowd to her who was used to celebrating alone with her mother. And everyone's attention was focused on her!

After the meal, which seemed to take forever, Erdmuthe was finally allowed to open her presents. She did not mind that no one bothered to read the story of the birth of Christ or to sing "*Stille Nacht*," as they did at home. She was tired of waiting! What incredible treasures were wrapped in these packages!

First there was the doll, the porcelain doll, which had real hair and could open and close her blue eyes and bend her elbows and knees. She had black hair and real eyelashes and wore a lace dress, fancier than any Erdmuthe had ever owned. For so many years she had waited for the *Christkind* to bring this doll and now her grandmother had produced it! Klari had told her before she left that there was no such thing as the *Christkind* and Erdmuthe found this news very upsetting. But her mother had said Christmas was the birthday of the Christchild, and people gave each other presents to celebrate this very special occasion. And since the *Christkind* did not bring the presents, as Erdmuthe had formerly believed, she had seen the packages in advance and could guess at their contents. The long skinny package held skis, as Erdmuthe had assumed, and in the heavy box, which Erdmuthe had repeatedly shaken to intuit its content, were ski boots. Boots to ski and walk to school in — this would be the end of wet feet! Then there was a book and beads and games, and a warm winter coat with hat, scarf, mittens and more! Erdmuthe, overwhelmed by all these riches, gave a round of thank-you kisses to each of the aunts and uncles who looked on with pleasure and approval.

Eventually she fell into her feather bed, exhausted. Alone, she thought of Klari and the farm and the Christmas Eve fragrance of incense in Klari's house, and how much she missed playing in the snow, sitting by the tile stove, or reading by the kerosene lamp. Despite all the attention here she felt bored amidst all these adults and uncomfortable in these fancy rooms where one always had to be careful not to create a mess.

Erdmuthe was ready to go home and was relieved when her mother told her they would leave after New Year's. During her stay in Wasserburg it had become clearer and clearer to Anna that she would not be able to live permanently in Germany. She was distraught, even shaken by her experience. She realized how rich her life at the farm was and how much easier daily existence would be there.


# HOMECOMING
## *Epiphany, 1948*

Fatigued, yet full if happy anticipation, Anna and Erdmuthe jumped off the train. It had been an arduous journey. Crossing into Austria at a secret, unguarded spot, they had walked for miles to reach the main road. At first they tried to be unobtrusive, for the skis Anna was carrying and the doll sticking out of Erdmuthe's pack made it obvious they had come from the more prosperous "other side." But as the distance from the border lengthened, they became more daring and eventually they marched on the country road, singing loudly. Until an unexpected border guard, standing high up on a hill, stopped them. They were driven to Salzburg, locked up over night and interrogated the next morning. For Erdmuthe it was all an exhilarating adventure, but Anna was nervous. "I tried to find my mother's grave," she explained and told the story of her mother's flight and death. In the end the authorities let them off with a warning.

Now they had finally arrived at the small Haunoldmühle station. Soft snowflakes fell. *Hard to believe I arrived here for the first time over nine years ago,* Anna thought. Although she had only worn them for trips away from home, Anna's boots were now battered and scuffed. One could hardly tell they had once been green. "Ach, Michael," Anna sighed.

She remembered how she and Michael had walked up the mountain that first time and how oppressive the dark kitchen had seemed to her, the kitchen which had been a place of terror during the past two years of Sattler's reign. *I am going to set up my own cooking stove,* Anna decided now. She had given the neighbors her laundry mangle when she thought she'd have to leave. Maybe Klara would consider it a swap for the small old cooking stove that sat in the corner of their courtyard. Yes, she'd make her own kitchen corner in their little room. She would turn their current bedroom into a proper *Stube* eventually and reclaim another room to sleep in. And she would make her living by writing! Her thoughts seemed to clarify more and more as she climbed up to the farm. These plans excited Anna. She felt a new sense of belonging here, a slow recognition that this place was home after all, despite everything. Still, could she justify depriving Erdmuthe of the material advantage she'd have in Wasserburg? How would the child feel about coming back to carrying buckets of water up the steep wooden stairs, to lugging the kerosene can on her way home from school, to eating potatoes and carrots.

Erdmuthe had run ahead, carrying her rucksack with her Christmas doll peeking out. Anna finally caught up with her as she reached the woods at the border of their farm. Erdmuthe stood there, quietly, her face glowing with joy. The red tile roof of the farm above stood out clearly against the white snow. The dark lacework of pear trees surrounded the square building. The hills glittered in the late afternoon sun. "Mutti," she said, in broad Upper Austrian dialect, her eyes large and moist. "*Dahoam is dahoam!*" "Yes," said Anna. "This is our home. We belong, both of us." She hugged her daughter and they hurried up the hill in the slanting afternoon light. "We missed the three kings," Erdmuthe remembered. "But there will be next year," Anna consoled her daughter.

THE END

# NOTES

1 (p. 16) *Oberdonau*
Upper Danube region. Under Hitler Austria was dissolved after the
1938 invasion and integrated into the Great German Reich.

2 (p. 21) *Kristallnacht*
November 9-10, 1938, the Night of Broken Glass, wholesale nationwide destruction of Jewish homes, shops and synagogues.

3 (p. 27) *Mein Kampf*
Hitler's autobiographical book *My Struggle*, published in two volumes
in 1925/26, in which he discussed his political ideology.

4 (p. 35) *Ahnenpass*
Official ancestral record book, documenting Aryan lineage of citizens
in Nazi Germany.

5 (p. 112) *Blut und Boden*
"Blood and Soil" — Nazi phrase celebrating the relationship of the
German people to the land they cultivated. The Nazis placed a high
value on rural living and issued a law according to which only people
of Aryan descent were allowed to be farmers.

6 (p. 113) *Neubauernschein*
An official document granting permission to become a new farmer in
German-occupied areas, especially in the East. This was an effort at
colonialization and creating additional living space (Lebensraum) for
people of German descent.

# ABOUT THE AUTHOR

Christine Saari grew up on an Austrian mountain farm during World War II and the postwar years and emigrated to the United States in 1964, at age 25. She is a visual artist and writer who lives in Michigan's Upper Peninsula and spends part of her life each year with her American husband on the farm in Austria, now owned by their two sons.